AN UNEXPECTED KIND OF LOVE

AN UNEXPECTED KIND OF LOVE

HAYDEN STONE

Entangled Publishing, LLC
10940 S Parker Rd
Suite 327
Parker, CO 80134
rights@entangledpublishing.com

Embrace is an imprint of Entangled Publishing, LLC.

Edited by Heather Howland
Cover design by LJ Anderson/Mayhem Cover Creations
Cover photography by SketchMaster, Sky-Designs, and irstone/Deposit Photost

Manufactured in the United States of America

First Edition August 2021

embrace

At Entangled, we want our readers to be well-informed. If you would like to know if this book contains any elements that might be of concern for you, please check the book's webpage for details.

https://entangledpublishing.com/books/an-unexpected-kind-of-love

For the poets.

Chapter One

There are two kinds of people in the world: people who put things away as they should, and arseholes who shelve books with no respect for the alphabet.

I hold the two—yes, two—misfiled copies of *Pride and Prejudice*. What sort of heathen would put Jane Austen's *Pride and Prejudice* all the way across the shop with the thrillers? The other copy had been over in Comedy.

I'm a tolerant man, but only some sort of twisted individual would go that far. Like I don't have enough to do to keep my Soho bookshop afloat without some rogue bookshelving action to muck up my inventory.

The other day I found Oscar Wilde's *The Picture of Dorian Gray* shelved with Mil Millington's *Things My Girlfriend and I Have Argued About*. Before that, Brontë's *Wuthering Heights* was caught canoodling with Gabaldon's *Outlander* in the G section.

Vandalism, pure and simple.

The last customer for the evening left five minutes ago. The radio's on, playing the Arctic Monkeys as I put the shop to bed for the night. I head over to Romance, Jane Austen in tow. Along the way, I neaten up a stray stack of bestsellers on the front table.

Each book has a place, and that place follows the rules of the alphabet. Most people have some passing familiarity with the alphabet before they start school. And *A* is the first letter they should learn if they paid any attention at all as a four-year-old.

As I shelve the wayward books, I spot Madeline Miller's *The Song of Achilles* in Romance when it ought to be in General Fiction.

Oh, for the love of–

"Getting worked up again? Or still?" My only employee, Gemma, leans across the counter, amused, rubbernecking shamelessly at the scene of the crime. She's curvy, something decadent. She's in a lightweight silver blouse over her skirt, the hot day having shifted into evening. She's ready to go out once we close. Something I won't be doing tonight.

There was a time not that long ago when my Friday nights were spent out. Now, that time's better spent working and not thinking about the past. Or the future, for that matter. As in, there'll be no future if my shop goes belly-up.

Behind Gemma, built-in oak bookcases with classics and collectible editions reach nearly to the tall ceiling. Light spills into the front of the shop from the streetlamps.

She snaps her gum, because she knows that will drive me mad. One day, I think she's expecting my brain to literally melt out of my ears. One day, it might actually happen.

"What did I say about snapping gum? It's seriously annoying."

She waves a hand. "Loosen up, Aubs. You're the youngest grumpy old man I've ever met. You might look cool with the piercings and band T-shirts, but to be honest, sometimes I worry about you."

I stand to my full height, which can be imposing I'm told for someone not quite hitting six feet. "It's Aubrey. Not Aubs. How many times have I told you?"

She laughs, unrepentant as she peers at me from beneath a blunt-cut dark fringe. "That's brilliant on your dating profile. Or Grindr. Mr. Aubrey 'How Many Times Have I Told You' Barnes."

We look at each other across the shop. Or, more accurately, I glare at her. Thankfully, there're no customers present to witness my daily mortifications by a uni student barely younger than me who loves to mop the floor with my pride.

The truth is we met in a book club a couple of years back, and we became fast friends. She gave hilarious reviews, which turned out to be handy for the shop. She thought I was delightfully quirky. It would have been the perfect spring romance, except that I'm attracted to men, and I was together with my ex. At any rate, we've got the banter down, especially now that I rely on her help in the shop. Customers love her too.

She pretends to reconsider. "Or how about 'Aubrey Barnes, Fierce Defender of Books'? That's got a superhero thing going on. More sympathetic, I think. Am I right or am I right?" Gemma gives an impish smile.

Once upon a time, I was just Aubrey Barnes, ready to go for pints or a gig or the occasional big night out. Back before life became too real. Now, I'm twenty-three going on forty-three.

I sigh, noting the untied lace on one of my Docs. I bend to fix it. "You're here as the weekend help, remember?"

"And to give solid dating advice too. Value-added. You really ought to pay me extra for that." She grins.

Gemma dates like it's an unofficial Olympic sport. She also has a habit of telling me all the gruesome details, no matter how much I protest that I'm her boss and don't need to know those things. She says it's for my own good.

"Heckling is a bonus feature, I take it?" Resigned, I cross the shop to file *The Song of Achilles* in the right section.

"You can thank me another time." Gemma at last straightens, adjusting her messy bun. "So am I done for the day yet? I'm going dancing after work."

I check my watch amid my stack of black and brown leather bracelets. The watch is proper vintage, aviator style, with a black dial and white numbers, complete with a rich brown leather strap. Beautiful—and a glum reminder. Not just of the passage of time, which at twenty-three years old I'm still getting used to. No, even worse, it's a reminder of Eli and last year's birthday gift. To be honest, I should put it away or give it away, but he knows my taste so well. Besides, it really is a brilliant watch. It's not the watch's fault that he gave it to me.

"Aubs?"

"Yeah, sorry. Right. Go on, then. I'll flip the sign in a minute."

Studying me for a moment, she nods. "Cheers."

Gemma heads off into the back to gather her things. I go to the shop front and switch the sign over to CLOSED and lock the door. It's late enough that even the Friday evening book browsers have moved on to other things. The beauty of owning a shop is that I set the hours. And the rules, though the truth is that I'm no enforcer and Gemma and everyone else in London knows it.

I head to the back into the small kitchen to put the kettle on. The kettle sits on the old pine sideboard, which has been there since approximately forever. There's no dancing for me, not my usual scene these days. I'd much rather stay in and enjoy some of the classic introverted activities. Like hiding. And reading. Classical literature? Art books? Tawdry smut?

I'm game for anything to stop my relentless brain doing time trial relays inside my skull. Maybe I'll start one of the trade-ins that were brought in today.

While I wait for the tea to steep, Gemma pokes her head into the pocket-sized kitchen. She's wearing the most mini of spray-on miniskirts and some vague suggestion of a blouse, a sheer black number over a halter top. She's put on makeup for the night out, including an enviable shade of lipstick.

And I thought she'd been dressed up to go out *before.* My eyebrows lift.

"What, you're telling me you were never part of the mesh shirt and thong set, dancing on a speaker?" Gemma asks archly.

I open my mouth and blush something furious. What a horrifying vision. "Oh no. God, no. *Please*, no."

She giggles, obviously pleased with my reaction. "You sure you don't want to come out with us tonight?"

"Never."

The idea of a dance floor with too-close writhing bodies, strangers, sweat, and too much brash sexuality in my face is something I'm definitely not up for. Not even with Gemma. Probably not even in my first year of uni.

I once went to clubs, to their dazzle and bright, sticky floors and even stickier booths for overpriced drinks. Although never in a mesh shirt, thank God. Even Eli's influence couldn't lure me that far. Not his, or anyone else's.

Gemma gives me a wry smile. "Maybe the pub another night? We haven't done that in a while."

"Maybe," I concede, pouring the tea. "Have fun. Remember, I need you in at noon tomorrow."

"I'll be here. Sober, even."

"Thank heavens for small mercies."

She grins, something dazzling that would doubtless work on most people. Probably anyone other than me. Blowing a kiss, she heads out, and I lock the door after her.

Taking my tea, I head up the stairs at the back to the bedsit over the shop. It's crammed with books, usually serving as an extra stockroom and office. Now it's home. The walls are painted midnight blue, or at least what can be seen of them where they're not covered by bookcases or prints left by the three generations of Barneses before me that worked here.

I once had a proper home, a flat. Well, Eli and I had a flat together. Now, it's Eli's flat with his live-in boyfriend. I better not start the dreary cycle of thoughts on what they could be doing on a Friday night together in our old home. These days, I literally live and breathe books by living in the shop. The good thing about this new arrangement is that there's no shortage of things to read.

I flop down on the leather sofa jammed between two bookcases under the window. Floor-to-ceiling shelving wraps around the room, heaving with books. Since there's no more room on the shelves, books are stacked in neat piles in front of them. The low coffee table is full of books too. A small desk in the corner has my old laptop with the shop files, and a wooden crate beneath it is filled with notebooks of half-written poems, a couple of sketchbooks, and art supplies. My cat sleeps on the desk chair on top of the accounts book. In the corner, another sofa lies converted into my bed. As far as sofa beds go, it's moderately comfortable.

Mum's been too ill the last couple of years to work. She signed over the shop to me last year. Now, it's just down to me to run everything. I should catch up on the bookkeeping tonight, but I don't have the willpower to go through things. The result is always the same: never enough income. Our family business is fading. People want Waterstones or independent mega shop Foyles just down the street. Or even the actual Barnes and Noble, over in America.

If only I'd taken business classes instead of literature. If I had, I might be in better shape or know what to do to turn things around. Instead, I muddle on and hope for the best, for some miracle that I can tell Mum without it being a lie that everything's fine, that we'll be all right.

That *I'll* be all right.

• • •

Before noon, the shop is full of Saturday morning browsers. The bell on the back of the door chimes as it swings open again. This time, it's not another wave of tourists coming through, but Eli himself looking all too fresh from a morning run, with windswept golden hair like something out of a health and fitness magazine. Muscular. Tanned. He's in a white T-shirt and black shorts that leave little to the imagination. Eli's grin is dazzling and he holds a takeaway tray full of coffees.

I really don't need this today.

"I come in peace. Here's proof: coffee from down the street. Charlie says hi." Eli's unfazed by my looming grump. I haven't even said anything yet and he already knows my mood.

"You should warn people ahead of time before you show up looking all…" I wave a hand at him. "You'll distract the customers."

Even after everything, I still have eyes. Unfortunately.

Eli beams, clearly loving the idea as he sets the tray down next to the till. "I can only hope."

"Attention whore. Dare I ask what brings you here?"

"Other than the pleasure of seeing you after my run? Just want to say hi. Is that fine? Did you know there's filming up the street?" He chuckles, pulling a coffee from the tray and sliding it over to me. "Here. You need this. Clearly. You never used to be such a crank."

"I wonder why," I say drily, sipping my coffee.

Eli gazes around the store, looking impressed at the sight of the crowd of customers. "This is a good sign."

"Maybe."

It's too much to hope for good signs or anything else. Hope hasn't done me much good, to be honest.

When Gemma arrives a couple of minutes later, she practically swoons as Eli passes over a coffee. To her credit, she's on time, but there are shadows under her eyes. Who knows what time she went to sleep.

"You're an angel." She raises her cup to him.

A customer comes to the till, and I focus on her. She's taking stock of everything. She's middle-aged, dressed head to toe in linen, with a long floral scarf in dilute pinks the only color she wears. She peers at me behind the counter with Gemma, then Eli. She picks up a business card, reading it carefully: *Barnes Books—New, Used, and Collectibles.*

"Is this like Barnes and Noble?" she asks, frowning. "Owner: Aubrey Barnes."

"That's me," I say.

"You look young to own a shop." She looks at Eli, brightening. "Are you Mr. Noble, then?"

"No. This is definitely not like Barnes and Noble," I assure her. My balance sheet guarantees that. "And that's just Eli. He's fake news."

He unleashes a devastating grin that no reasonable person can resist and she blushes. "You'll have to forgive Aubs. He hasn't had enough coffee. Plus I broke his heart, so."

"Oh," she manages, startled.

I frown at him. It's old news now, but hardly fodder to fling at innocent bystanders out of nowhere. "Don't scandalize the customers. Behave yourself." I focus on her. "How can I help?"

"I'm looking for green books," she says crisply, down to business. "Preferably forest green, leather-bound, or with gilt lettering or some such."

I purse my lips. Gemma's already pretending to look busy and hiding a smile.

"Is there…an actual subject you're interested in? Like, say…horticulture?" I ask.

"Oh no, subject's irrelevant. I'm looking for something purely decorative. Something that will look striking on the mantle, you know. Eye-catching."

Out of the corner of my eye, Gemma's smile is unmistakable. Eli is blatantly intrigued.

Taking a deep breath, I gesture vaguely at the shelves, pained. "If you just want…green books…you will see them out there on the shelves with their…green covers."

It practically kills me to say the blindingly obvious.

"Well, I just want green books *today*," she clarifies. "I'm decorating with books by color. Last week was oxblood. Next week could be blue. It's all about the look, you know? Who actually has time to read these days?"

A strangled sound escapes me.

Eli gives her a sympathetic look. "Let me help you."

He takes her arm and she blushes brilliantly, all too happy to have Eli's devoted attention. Of course the arsehole would help her pick books by color.

Traitor.

When I look at Gemma, her eyes are bright with suppressed tears of laughter. "That was fucking hilarious," she manages, dabbing the corners of her eyes with a tissue. "Your face. Brilliant. Makes up for the hangover."

I gulp down some coffee, trying to refocus. Eli's right that it's good that there are plenty of people in the shop this morning. So far, however, there are a lot of morning browsers but not buyers. Probably shoppers seeking refuge from

Oxford Street.

She winks. Soon, she's flagged down to help a customer. I focus on my coffee. I'm probably not winning at sparkling customer service. Eli's new friend is engrossed as he shows her books. It's only a matter of time before they circle back to the Classics and Collectibles section behind me.

Before I can escape the front desk, another customer approaches. A young man. He's gorgeous—but never mind that. More important, he has a book in hand. I'm hopeful. A paying customer, thank God.

He's dark-haired, about my age. Stunning, actually. There's something very appealing about him, and he's attractive in a styled sort of way. Even his hair cooperates, medium length in controlled waves. Clearly, he's a man who knows about grooming. Meanwhile, I'm in a rumpled blue shirt and jeans as usual. To my credit, I did drag a comb through my mop of hair this morning, even if I gave shaving a miss.

"How can I help?" I ask.

"I bought this book last week." American accent. Southern, maybe. A leather messenger bag is slung over his shoulder. The way he's holding the book, I can't see the title. The cover's hidden against his trim chest, his hand cradling the spine, receipt poking out.

"All right." A sinking feeling hits my stomach. Not a paying customer, then.

"I want a refund."

"A refund?" I frown.

He nods, gazing at me in an entirely disconcerting way. It's not helping my mood, even if he is attractive.

"The author's an asshole," he says, matter-of-fact. "I don't want to support him."

"A lot of authors are arseholes." It tumbles out before I can stop myself. "Actually, it's not just writers. Loads of people are arseholes. In most economies, the arseholes are doing quite well for themselves."

Oh God.

He lifts an eyebrow. "I want a cash refund. That asshole doesn't need more of my money, especially if the assholes are doing all right, as you say."

I sigh. "How about store credit instead? I don't do cash refunds."

Eli's going to give me a dressing down later if he can hear this. At least the shop's full enough, the bell signaling the comings and goings of customers. At last glimpse, he carried several green books from the classics section.

"Shop credit's not gonna do me any good back home when I go back in a couple of weeks. I think your policy is…" He smirks and his eyes dance. "Bollocks. That's what you Brits say, right?"

I start to count to ten. Therapy's taught me the value of taking a minute. "What's wrong with the author?" I ask reluctantly, already regretting the question.

He waves a hand. Elegant fingers, I can't help but notice. Long and lean, something that would be brilliant for a musician.

"I told you. Asshole. He did something on Twitter…" He shrugs.

Wearily, I rub my face with my hand. I do not like this man, even if he's gorgeous. That's merely a distraction, and I won't be swayed. "Let me see the book. And social media's best avoided, for the record."

"You should know I'm a hit on Instagram," he says cheerfully.

Of course he is.

He hands over the book. A poetry book. Second-hand.

"The author didn't get any royalties from this sale. At least you can take heart in that." It'll be me that takes the hit, but I don't want to share this information with a stranger.

I look at the receipt. Eight quid. Gritting my teeth, I open the till and retrieve a tenner and slide it to him across the counter. Our fingers touch. I snatch mine away as though seared by the sun.

"I recommend that you stay away from poetry," I say. "The ratio of poets to arseholes is high. Alarmingly high. Rabble-rousers, the lot of them. In fact, it's probably best to skip anything related to that entire form of literature, just to be safe. That includes prose poems and poetic prose."

I stare him down. Not only am I a bookseller, but I want to ensure the protection of would-be readers from the ravages of poets. Best keep him away from Bukowski and Baudelaire.

"This is more than I paid..." he says, startled as he looks at the cash in his hand. "Are you sure?"

I nod once. "What's that saying Americans have? The customer is always right?"

He chews his lip before flashing a grin to rival Eli's. It doesn't help my dark mood.

He takes a shop card, glances at it. "Is this like the British Barnes and Noble?"

"No. Certainly not. Out."

The grin returns, a searing dazzle of bright through the dark of the shop. Quickly, I turn away as my face burns. Never mind him.

"See you next time!" And with that, the door jangles shut behind him.

Chapter Two

On my best behavior, I ring through a shocking number of green books. It turns out The-Woman-Who-Wanted-Green-Books is a most serious connoisseur, with at least a couple dozen selected from the Classics and Collectibles section. There's no rhyme or reason to the subjects, ranging from textbooks on botany to world cultures to Victorian literature. All hardcovers, all vintage, with a strong preference for gilt lettering. Eli's in cahoots with her that it's better to catch the light. He says bling books sell. We make arrangements for someone who will come by to pick the books up for her later in the afternoon. They sit in a pile on the back counter, along with the parcel I need to take to the post office.

I take a drink of the dregs of my coffee. It's more like I'm drinking the memory of coffee, but in a caffeine emergency one does what one must. I feel like the one who's been dancing all night, and not Gemma. Maybe the sofa bed is catching up with me after all.

Eli joins me.

"Remember those heady days of yore, when people used

to read books?" I ask.

"Such cheek. You just sold thirty books." Eli's grin is unrepentant. "It's not even one o'clock and you can close shop for the day."

"Very funny. So far today I've sold books based only on their looks, processed one return due to a misbehaving poet, and sold two bestsellers that were ghostwritten."

"It's fine," says Eli. "Look at how busy it is in here."

The shop is still impressively busy for a Saturday. There may even be more legitimate book buyers in the lot.

"I just don't want books to become ornamental fetishes for decorators."

"Who knows what sort of fetishes decorators have?" Eli shrugs. "Besides, she wasn't a decorator. Not quite."

I glance at Eli as I shuffle some of the collectibles on the shelf to fill the gaps left by the Green Book Debacle, as I will now think of it. "What was she, then?"

"A designer. A set designer, actually."

I frown. "A set designer?"

Eli nods. "That's what she said."

"Isn't that an ungodly sum of money to spend on books that will never be read?"

He claps my shoulder. "Clearly, they have some sort of budget. Now, darling, I must be off. Ryan will be wondering what happened to me."

"Thanks for your help." It's true: I am grateful. If only I didn't feel so raw inside.

As though Eli's reading my thoughts, he gives me a hug and kiss on the cheek.

"Cheer up, Aubs. One day it'll all be old news. You'll see."

I sigh. "Say hi to Ryan."

"I will. Stay out of trouble. Or find the right kind of trouble. Saturday night in Soho and all that." Eli winks. The bells on the door ring behind him as he leaves.

Before long, my dark mood starts to lift as several paying customers come through after all. A couple of hours pass in the blink of an eye before Gemma and I get a break.

"I need to run a parcel up the street to the post office," I say.

Gemma hops up to sit on the front counter, her legs dangling in polka dot Mary Janes. "Go. I've got this."

I hesitate. She just laughs. "Take your phone. I'll text if there's a mob. Does that make you feel better?"

"Marginally."

She waves me off. Taking the parcel, I head into a sparkling afternoon. The sudden brightness hurts my eyes as I put on my sunglasses, the parcel tucked under my arm. Heat rises from the tarmac. The pavements are full of people coming and going. There're also quite a few parked lorries and trailers jamming everything up. A queue of traffic is at a standstill, backed up the lane.

The end of the street is blocked off. Which is where I need to go to get to the post office.

Frowning, I look around. On the other side of the barricade stand people in the occasional cluster in every spot of shade to be had. One group has people with lists and headsets, engrossed in serious conversation. Another group has people holding...plates of food?

Someone walking past the first group calls out cheerfully to them. "Better get over to catering before I eat it all."

Catering? What is this, an impromptu street festival?

Craning my neck and doing my best to glimpse between two trailers from where I stand at the barricade, I can almost see the post office. Or where the post office ordinarily is, and the yarn shop beside it. Instead, the post office and several of the usual shops along the street front have changed into an entirely different streetscape. The post office is no longer recognizable as such. It's been transformed into a grocer's.

Westminster City Council or the event organizer should have sent out notices about whatever's going on, because this is bloody inconvenient when a man needs to get to the post office on a Saturday afternoon.

Or the wool shop, for that matter, even in July.

When a man walks by with a boom mic over his shoulder, I finally clue in.

A groan escapes me. Filming. Eli mentioned it when he arrived at the bookshop earlier. I should've remembered. The day's chaos has already worn me down.

Resigned, I shift the parcel under my arm. It doesn't need to go out till Monday, and I hardly want to spend my lunch break wandering London for a post office that hasn't turned into something else.

Instead, I come up with a new plan for a takeaway coffee and sandwich to bring back to Barnes Books. After a couple of false starts, thwarted by more trailers and filming-related inconveniences around the neighborhood, I reach the coffee shop. Mercifully, the café hasn't fallen victim to the chaos.

I round the corner to the café's entrance. "Oh!"

"Holy fuck!"

I nearly crash into a man hurrying on his way out of the coffee shop, who stumbles. Veering to the side, I barely keep upright.

He does an awkward juggle with the coffee, but his leap back is easy and athletic. For a long, terrible moment we both see the coffee flip up, then careen to the pavement, exploding in a hot mess. In the chaos, I drop my parcel, which now sits in a puddle of coffee.

"Oh my God, I'm so terribly sorry—" I blurt.

"No, it's my fault—"

"Are you all right?"

"Fuck, your package—" he says.

Even in this terribly embarrassing moment I gulp and flush scarlet about unintended package innuendos, and packages suitable for fucking, and oh fuck, it's that infuriating man—that very beautiful man, I may add—from earlier.

I swallow.

"I hope you've been avoiding poets." Desperate, I rummage in my pockets for napkins. Did he get burned?

He bends in a swoop and fishes my parcel out of its coffee bath before passing it to me. We nearly knock heads.

"Shit—"

"Are you sure you're all right?" I ask.

We're in an awkward sort of crouch, staring at each other. Coffee drips from the parcel.

My face burns, rivaling the scorching afternoon. With my complexion, it's plain for the world to see. And especially by this man, who has a front row seat.

On the edge of my vision, a young hipster couple stops. They murmur to each other, something on the edge of my reality.

What's more pressing, aside from an immediate stiffening in my jeans, is that it's impossible to draw in a breath. When I manage, hot air fills my lungs. His gaze is very intent on mine, his eyes the color of storms and seas.

So much for oxygen. It's a casualty too, like his coffee.

"I'm fine," he says at last.

Finally, we rise, breaking the moment, me holding a dripping package and him looking mercifully unburnt and unharmed. Though, there goes an opportunity for some restorative mouth-to-mouth.

Where did that thought come from?

"C-can I get you another coffee?" I ask. "I should've paid more attention to where I was going. Off in my own world as usual."

"It's okay. Plus you gave me a tip earlier, remember?"

He checks a very swish watch that probably rivals my shop's stock valuation. "Fuck, I'm late. They'll notice I left when I shouldn't have—I'll just grab something from catering. I probably should have done that in the first place, but then I wouldn't have gotten the chance to crash into you, would I?"

The grin he gives before he sprints off leaves me reeling, left standing alone on the pavement, blood pounding a heartbeat in my ears and somewhere considerably lower.

When I return to the cool sanctuary of the shop, flustered and holding a sodden package, there's no way of avoiding Gemma. I remove my sunglasses. She's still sitting on the wood counter with the fan, engrossed as she reads…the book I'm currently reading. *Maurice*. Apparently, I've left the book somewhere where she would come across it.

She lowers the paperback to peer at me. Her eyebrows lift as she gazes at the bedraggled package in my hands. "It didn't go well, then?"

"I don't want to talk about it."

"Cool. Say, Aubs, I never figured you as the romantic type." She holds up the book. "Niche Victorian smut. Nice."

"Give me that." I try to pluck the book from her fingers as she laughs, holding it away from me. "It's not smut. Or Victorian. It's a gay fiction literary classic, and, for the record, Edwardian. Though potentially scandalous when it was written. There's nothing wrong with erotic works."

She inspects the page with the publication details, looking dead disappointed. "It was published in the 1970s. Doesn't sound Edwardian to me. The cover doesn't look that old-fashioned."

"You know that thing about not judging books by their covers? The author wrote the novel in secret. It was published long after it was written." I set the parcel down on the counter, unwrapping the book, praying that the cardboard sleeve has kept it from being ruined. "E.M. Forster."

"Really?" Intrigued, she flips through the pages.

"There might be a note about the author or an introduction to the history of the work."

"I skipped the introduction on purpose." She frowns. "It's got spoilers in it. At least they have the decency to warn people in the first paragraph."

"There's also a film..." I put the wet paper wrap into the bin. The cardboard sleeve is wet, too.

"A film!" She perks up. "Ooh, tell me."

"You ought to read the book." I work on freeing the book from the sleeve, soggy cardboard melting under my fingers.

"Aubrey, please tell me. I don't want to search it and use data on my phone. Why won't you set up wifi in the shop, anyway?"

"Because you'll spend your life Twittering or scrolling or whatever it is that you do." I crack open the unsoaked portion of the cardboard sleeve, fishing the book out. The invoice is a bit damp.

"Whatever. You're very unhip for a hipster." She snorts, then prods me. "The film?"

"It's cleverly also called *Maurice*." I flip through the book. It looks like it was spared a coffee indignity. Thankfully, it's not a stock loss. "And I'm *not* a hipster. Take that back."

"Ha. Never."

Time to save face.

"The film was made in the eighties. Not a John Hughes film, by the way. In case you're getting your hopes up."

"Look at you, Mr. Barnes. All film nerd, too cool for school."

"Hardly."

"Is anybody I know in it?"

"You might've heard of Hugh Grant."

"Shut up!" Gemma gawps. She sets *Maurice* down while I sniff the salvaged book to check that it doesn't smell of coffee.

"I'm so checking that out." At last, she hops off the counter. "What exactly are you doing? Did the heat get to you?"

"Sniff this." I present her the copy of *War and Peace.* "Does it smell like coffee to you?"

She sniffs and rubs her nose. "Nope. Just dust."

Relieved, I put the book on the back counter. It's where we put the day's holds or orders. I try to keep it clear for things needing immediate attention. There're a couple of official-looking pages lying on the otherwise bare surface. I pick them up. A filming notification, date-stamped from last week, plus another notification for a location request and to contact their location manager at my earliest convenience.

"When did this arrive?" I demand.

"Dunno. When you were out. I can't keep track of everything." She waves a hand airily.

"I wasn't gone that long."

Gemma shrugs. "Their location scout dropped it off. Alice something. She came with someone and they picked up all of the green books."

"Right." Belatedly, I realize the back counter is free of the palette of green hardcovers we put aside. "Did they say anything?"

Gemma reflects for a moment, leaning back against the counter beside the till. "That the shop is perfectly charming and with a few small changes it'll be perfect for their shoot. Which is true. It's very inviting, actually."

She gestures broadly at the shop with its oak bookcases and colorful displays neatly arranged. A couple of rugs have been placed on the floor, which adds to the effect.

I scowl.

She nods. Then, alarmingly, she reaches into the front of her black and white polka dot V-neck blouse and plucks a business card from the strap of her bra. "Yeah, I think that's it. Here. This is for you."

It's my turn to gawp. "I don't want that."

"I put it in a safe place. Don't be uptight. God. There's nothing wrong with breasts for safekeeping." She shakes her head and puts the card down on top of the notices. "She said you could ring her or just stop by the shoot and ask security for Alice. I gave her your card and said you'd love to talk about filming."

"Gemma! You didn't."

She looks entirely unconcerned. "Of course I did. You could use the cash. They pay for locations, you know."

God, has she been going through the shop accounts too while my back is turned?

"I cash out here, remember? I know what you take in." Gemma gives me a knowing look.

Weary, I rub my face. Why isn't today over yet?

"There's no shame in it. Booksellers are having a tough time. You need alternative revenue streams."

"How ghastly."

She cracks up. "You know, cross-marketing? Maybe sell gifts too? Or even dildos? I don't know. I mean, this is Soho, right? People expect that. The dildos could be all literary or something. Match books with sex toys. You won't be able to keep the crowds at bay."

It's all horrifying talk. I'm not a prude but it's quite something to be getting this kind of cross-marketing advice from my shop assistant.

"It's either that or *really* cool stationery. You know, like the stuff imported from places like Japan and Germany. You can even do something like have a credit for a film download with the book purchase or something like that. Or a book credit with a film purchase," she muses.

"It's usually the other way around." Weary, I sigh. It's not just the heat getting to me this afternoon.

Gemma's unfazed as she neatens up around the till, which is a magnet for book stacks. "If you like struggling, suit yourself."

"I'm making tea," I say curtly. "Then, I'm going to find this Alice person and put a stop to this filming nonsense before it goes any further."

Chapter Three

Instead of putting the kettle on as usual for tea, I stride down the lane flanked with glass-fronted shops toward the filming barricade. The afternoon swelters, close and sticky. Traffic remains at a standstill around the filming diversions. There's the occasional beep or shout. The sun, meanwhile, is relentless, doing its part to crisp what skin I have visible like a human toastie.

This will be quick. There's no time for filming shenanigans. Certainly not in my shop.

Whatever patience I usually possess has evaporated like any hint of moisture this July, shattering heat records for London, along with my nerves. Today's been a nonstop crush of one thing after another. After over a year, there shouldn't be a rip in me like an open wound, with Eli's visit the latest salt.

Tourists swarm Soho like a tide, spilling down main roads and side lanes. They tote maps. They take selfies. They're a curse and a blessing. If only they bought more books, but everyone reads on phones these days. They don't want to carry heavy books home in their luggage.

Winding through the crush of humans and the gawpers at the barricade, I stride up to the filming fortress with purpose. A security guard eyes me. He looms, a man of substance, and clearly no whimsy. He folds his arms across his vast chest like a wall. Behind him is another city of industry with a sea of trailers and people engrossed in filming and filming-adjacent activities.

"Yes?" he asks.

"I'm here to see Alice Rutherford." I show him her card and the notice with the film location request, and pass over my business card. "She said to stop by. I own the bookshop down the street, Barnes Books. I'm Aubrey Barnes."

"ID."

I show him a dreadful driver's license where I look rumple-haired, as usual.

He grunts in reluctant acknowledgment and keeps my business card, stepping back to let me through. "Third trailer. Go on in."

On the other side of the barricade, people come and go with kit. When I reach the third trailer, there's a dilemma. There're two identical white trailers, one to my left and one to my right. Closed doors. No signage. I look around. No one is near to ask which one is Alice's. Odds are even on which trailer is hers.

I knock on the door of the trailer to my left. After no response, I try the door handle. The door opens easily, and I step inside. Instantly, it's cooler, thanks to the air-con.

"Oh!" I say when the man from my bookstore and then the coffee incident spins around to face me, just as startled as I am. He's bare-chested. I try not to stare and fail miserably.

He's stunning. Especially shirtless.

I shiver, partly from the shock of the chill after the sun, and partly from the shock of the half-dressed man before me in the low light. Of course it's him, the man I can't seem to avoid today. He's lithe and toned. Dark hair curls around his ears. His face is all angles, caught between shadow and light, something timeless that would be a dream for a sculptor of any era. And he has that grin that's becoming familiar, last spotted over my ruined parcel.

And now, the ruin of me.

"You're not Alice," I blurt. "I don't think. I'm sorry to disturb you. I'll leave."

Whirling around to retreat as quickly as I arrived, my hand is on the door handle again when he speaks.

"Wait!" he says in that soft drawl. "Just wait."

Gulping hard, I freeze. I don't dare turn around. Mortified, my face burns at the intrusion. I should have waited for an answer and not barged in. Foolish.

"The security guard said to go on in…"

"You're right. I'm not Alice." He laughs. "I've got to say, one of the things I'm loving about London is blending in plain sight. It's refreshing. You don't know who I am, do you? What a relief."

I frown at the door, my back still to him. "You're a man with no time for poets who are arseholes. And I'm evidently an arsehole, so I'd best be off."

"Hang on a sec. Please."

Something in my stomach melts a little. Which is ridiculous.

"Would you look at me?" he asks.

Reluctantly, I turn around. He's still there, this strange man. Still beautiful. He runs a hand through his hair, just to torture me, holding a heather-gray T-shirt in his other hand. Slightly backlit by the filtered light from the window, with the main lights off, his skin has a soft golden glow.

There's something vaguely familiar about him. I'll be damned if I know why that is. "You're not Timothée

Chalamet, are you?"

Delighted, he laughs and the sound fills me. "I wish!"

"Sorry. I'm just making things worse. I'll stop talking. Every time I talk, I make it worse."

"That would be a shame, if you stopped talking. We keep bumping into each other today," he says in a soft drawl. "Third time's lucky, I think. The universe is telling us something. Like, to pay attention to each other."

My face still burns. Apparently my tongue's plastered to the roof of my mouth.

"Like fate, maybe," he says.

That brings an immediate scowl. "I don't believe in fate. Things just happen. For no reason."

He laughs, seemingly unfazed by my brusque response, and pulls on his T-shirt, which skims over a fine chest. It's a shame to cover up such a physique, but the shirt still leaves little to the imagination. By comparison, I'm still rumpled and probably liberally covered in cat fur after I dressed in the dark this morning.

"How about we try again?" He tilts his head. The light catches reddish hints in his hair. "Like, make proper introductions?"

"You took my card." There are goose bumps on my arms for no good reason. "Earlier. You must know my name."

"It's true, I did. I do. Aubrey Barnes."

The way he says my name is like honey rolling off his tongue. Like it's something to be savored.

Like my name is something special.

"And you really don't know mine?" He smiles. It's devastating, to be honest.

I shake my head.

"Usually everyone else is at an advantage. I've got to say it makes for a nice change."

"Are you famous?" I ask.

That grin again. Nothing held back. It's overwhelming to have that unleashed, like I'm the only other person in the universe.

"Not really. Not Timothée Chalamet famous, no way. I'm like a C-lister. But I'm a triple-threat, I'll have you know. Everyone on set knows who I am, anyway."

"I don't even know what that means…and I still don't know your name." My voice is a whisper.

He steps closer, an arm's reach away. So near I could touch him. And God help me, I want to touch him. Badly. His face, his lips, his hair.

Everywhere.

"I'm Blake Sinclair. I act and sing and dance."

Even in this light, his wintry eyes grip me.

"Aubrey Barnes." Somehow, I manage to say my name without stammering. It feels important to say my name in return, even if he knows it already. To retain my name as mine, a reclamation in our strange introduction where he has the upper hand. And, oh God help me, that's a thrilling prospect. Thank heavens for one small mercy. My mouth is dry. "Bookseller."

At last, he reaches out his hand. "It's good to meet you properly, Aubrey. I also know that you care very much about the sort of books that people buy, and why they buy them."

I gulp. "Oh…"

Probably he heard about that disaster with the set decorator, then.

I grip his hand in mine. At the touch of his warm skin, I can't help a shiver that runs the length of my spine. It's a firm grasp. Not too soft, not too hard.

Some tiny sound gets caught in my throat.

I die. I'm dead. Bury me in this trailer, here and now.

"I should confess something," Blake says.

"What's that?"

"I picked up your card the first time last week when I was in Barnes Books. It's a really nice store, by the way. I knew your name then."

I swallow. "Is that right?"

"You know what else I thought?"

"No…"

"That you're beautiful," he says simply. "It more than makes up for the prickly customer service situation."

I just gawp at him. Something in me feels reckless at the tease of this man before me.

"Oh no," I say instantly. "I'm not beautiful. Not at all. You've mistaken me for someone else, I'm afraid. Maybe it's the accent fooling you, that you evidently have an inherent weakness for the Queen's English. Or you're hallucinating with the heat. I'm real, though. And fuck, why am I still talking?"

"Aubrey?"

"Yes?"

Blake stands with enviable confidence, partly backlit by the sun, which outlines a trim physique. "I want to kiss you."

"Sorry?"

He's smiling. "I see the way you're looking at me."

My cock, which was already in full approval of this situation, stirs. I lick my lips. Caught out. Fair, I'm probably being less than subtle by a train's length.

We're close in the confines of the trailer. His hand is still in mine. This is bold. Bold to burst into his trailer, bold to talk to him like this, bold to face the smolder between us that's grown all day. Channeling up some long-forgotten Aubrey, a younger, wilder me, I give in to the tease of Blake.

In the end, I'm the one who leans in, unable to resist the torment of him any longer.

Blake brushes his lips against mine, light at first. It takes approximately two seconds for that to heat up like the blaze of the afternoon outside. Despite the air-con, I'm on fire.

It's not like I'm a stranger to men, to hookups, to tempestuous encounters. However, that all feels like a long time ago, like a life that belonged to someone else. Like there's life before Eli, and life after. Like a fictional Aubrey who's free of obligation. Of heartache.

Fuck Eli.

Blake groans softly too. Our kisses are hungry, seeking, clumsy. I run a hand along that fabulous chest, over that well-toned stomach, and south to the taut fabric at his groin.

"Do you…?" I ask.

His hand pressing on my shoulder is answer enough.

I go to my knees. My mouth follows the path of my hand, teasing him through his shirt. Till I press the outline of his cock through his jeans and the strain of him makes me feel alive, like I'm high, like I'm someone daring. His desire is intoxicating. To think he's responding like that because of me. I shiver at the very idea.

The last man was a Grindr offering, so brief and so quick that I can't remember what he looked like, never mind his name. He barely looked at me, seeking release while I wanted human contact again.

At least Blake's paying enough attention to know my name.

With unsteady fingers, I unfasten his belt, his jeans. I shove down his boxers and jeans to his knees. His cock is glorious, like the rest of him, already seeping pre-cum that glistens in the sunlight hitting us, bright together in an otherwise dark room.

He groans as I press my mouth around his hot stiffness, filling me.

And I give in to that hunger, that desperation, that seldom seen and long forgotten part of me. The part that says fuck caution—live dangerously.

Live now.

Then, I'm stroking him, working him, tasting him. Blake's fingers are a vise into my shoulders as I take him deep into my mouth.

Each shiver he gives, each groan, encourages me. My mouth is ruthless. Urgent, I show no mercy despite the ache in my jaw.

"Fuck, yeah. Like that." Blake gasps. "Oh God."

As he thrusts, fingers caught rough in my hair, the taste of him overwhelms me.

There's no yesterday, no tomorrow. Just today, just right now, and oh God, I want him. I want to see him undone, messy and hot, because of me.

I stop abruptly and look up at him. His cock is fierce with desire.

Blake opens his eyes, dazed. He's breathless. All he needs to say is one word.

And he does.

"Please." The way Blake says it is almost like a prayer. Reverent.

So I do.

I work his cock, a rhythm of my hand and mouth, to the quickening of his heartbeat, the rush of blood in my ears. His fingers still grip me in place by my hair, and God, I want him. I want this.

Together, we're brave. Together, we share this sear of a moment.

Blake shudders hard as he surges, flooding me, his taste spilling over my tongue like the essence of summer itself. And I take him, all of him, as deep as I can. Gripping his arse, I hold him tight. Hold him there within me till his muscles stop trembling with release, till at last his cock begins to soften, and I dare breathe again.

Oh God, I'm drowning in him. And I can't think then,

not of anything else, or anyone.

Instead, I dare savor the heat of a man who isn't Eli. An incredible, greedy moment. And I swallow, taking our desire to my core to keep. To remember that I was once brave and daring too. Someone a stranger would want to remember.

Even if it's just my accent working some kind of temporary magic. He'll come to his senses soon enough, but right now, I'll take this yielding, this brief connection.

Gasping, I sit back on my heels and gaze up at him. He's magnificent, even half dressed. Maybe that visible unraveling in our lust makes him even more attractive.

A man who wants me. Right now.

A very beautiful man.

Eventually, Blake helps me up, catches my jaw and gives me a kiss best described as devastating.

"Do you want me to…?" Blake asks, his hand in the small of my back. A gesture that is my undoing, holding me against his body. Is that my heart thudding or his? Or does it even matter? His other hand works progressively lower.

"No." I shake my head, unsteady on my legs as though I'm the one who just came, light-headed.

Reality rushes in like a violent tide. The air smothers.

Blake brushes my lips lightly, still holding my jaw. His taste lingers on my tongue.

His gaze is intent. I die again. And again.

What does he see, taking me in like that? Like he's committing me to memory. Even though I'm fully clothed, I'm naked before him, every secret and past hurt and want marked bare on my skin like a text to be read.

And, oh fuck, what is he reading?

"I need to go," I blurt, as heat rises in my face.

Everything's too hot, too near, too much.

Definitely too much.

From negative ten to a hundred—Jesus, something's

wrong with me. Sucking off a stranger like that. Like something feral had taken hold of me, and just as violently as that desire had appeared, it's replaced with panic.

Darkness seeps around the corners of my vision, a rising tide. God, I can't faint. Not now. Not here.

What have I done, so recklessly? With a man I know nothing about? Once, I could do those things, but not anymore.

As quickly as I've arrived, I bolt.

This time, I don't turn or stop when Blake calls out for me to wait. I disappear into the sweltering afternoon, the one left undone, heading anywhere but here.

Chapter Four

Adrenaline courses through me. I walk blindly through Soho for who knows how long despite the sweltering heat. Everything's too near, the searing day clinging to my skin. Meanwhile, my brain careens inside my skull. No matter how far I walk, I can't make sense of what I've just done.

Who I've just done, actually.

One Blake Sinclair.

Stopping in the shade of a building, I drag my forearm across my brow in an effort to wipe away my perspiration. If the gesture could take away my thoughts too, so much the better.

Around me, the din of Soho continues. Tourists knot on pavements. Traffic stands mostly at a standstill. Heat rises in waves from the street.

Jesus. What just happened?

If I was religious, which I'm not, I would pray to a higher power for an intervention. For strength. Possibly even for absolution. But there's none to be had today.

When I'm tired enough and resigned enough that I can't

escape my brain, even with a heatwave, I make my way back to the shop.

Pausing just before the entry, stalling, I rake a hand through my hair, pushing it out of my eyes. God, what must I look like? Not that I particularly care under ordinary circumstances what I look like. I have strawberry blond hair like my mum, which resists combing at the best of times.

That was terrible. Impulsive. Risky. Check, check, check. All of those things.

I mean, I know I'm clean after my last Grindr hookup on a lonely night's fit of desperation a couple of months back. I regularly get tested at the clinic. Everything's fine on my end.

But is Blake careful? I mean, being famous, even as a triple-threat, C-list celebrity, he's guaranteed to see a lot more filth and debauchery than any London bookseller. Even in Soho. Particularly when the bookseller is me.

I look at my reflection in the glass-paneled door of the shop, at the green painted trim needing a fresh coat. The carefully hand-lettered sign says OPEN and the other sign reads 10–5 DAILY, CLOSED SUNDAYS.

Definitely stalling.

The problem is that Gemma's inside. Even though I'm the shop owner and she's my employee, she would doubtless start in on questions about why I was gone so long, why I'm acting weirder than usual, and all of that.

Good points, to be fair.

I definitely don't have the presence of mind to come up with any kind of convincing cover story. There's no way I'm going to reveal a hint of the truth. Not to her. Not ever. Because, well, that's beyond the usual realm of employer-employee relations. Even if I'm only a few years older than her at most, and everything else about our working relationship has questionable boundaries on her end. Cue our odd friendship. I may grumble, but we have each other's backs. Still, I don't want her to know. This is too private.

I fish my keys out of my pocket to unlock the nondescript green door next to the shop's entry. It's the alternative entrance to upstairs, which is the usual stockroom access, and now the entry to my makeshift bedsit. It's had a checkered history, my bedsit. Supposedly my parents lived up there before I was born, running the shop. And the room was old even back then. Doubtless it's full of original lead piping from when piping was first invented at the dawn of time, eventually followed by the invention of electricity a few minutes past that. Likely the building has wiring which should have been replaced decades ago. I ought to look into that for the insurance, and general safety.

Pushing the wooden door open with its usual creak, I flip on the light in the cramped entry at the bottom of the too narrow, too steep stairway and make my way up through the sweltering dead air trapped there, walking through the gruesome tickle of spiderwebs. Hopefully, no adventurous spiders have seized the opportunity to crawl over me.

At the top of the landing, I unlock the second door into the stockroom and lock it once more after me. I push the laundry basket out of my way with a toe, then carry on through the corridor. My clothing clings to me, and I strip down as I beeline to the equally cramped shower room, separate from the toilet room beside it. It's so small I can put a hand on each wall. Wedging myself into the shower stall, I turn on the water, letting the pipes shriek for a moment before a spray of cool water splatters feebly. I douse myself in cold water, or as cold as it can manage today.

Come back to reality, Aubrey.

No film star would want you anyway. Even if you wanted a film star. Safest to forget about his all-American looks, the ease in his own skin. The way he looked at you with a ready smile when you showed up like a buffoon in his trailer, catching him half dressed. Almost as if he'd been expecting you to stop by, like you were a friend or someone who mattered to him.

Not as though we kept having unfortunate encounters all day.

And then—

No. Not going there.

Every time my mind went there, which was often, I scrubbed myself all the more vigorously. As though a shower could wash away the memory, even if it could wash away the sweat from the day, from—

Right. Toweling off, I struggle as I stand staring at the heap of clothes on the floor of my stockroom home. If I go downstairs in another set of clothes, Gemma will be suspicious. She'll be suspicious why I showered. I mean, does she notice if I've showered? I don't doubt I'll get some commentary if I go back into the shop sopping wet.

I mean, it's damned hot out there. Even for London. So I needed a shower in the middle of the day. Maybe she'll buy it?

Probably not. She has a sixth sense.

So I dress in my slightly damp clothes and hope for the best when I go back downstairs. I'll simply have to avoid her for the rest of the day.

• • •

It would be a lie that I walk in through the front door of Barnes Books with my head held high, and with Eli's—or Blake Sinclair's—confidence, like I own the joint. I do, but that gives me no strength today.

Instead, in my effort to avoid Gemma, I embrace hiding. I slink into the shop from the back stairs down to the pocket-sized kitchen. It's generous to call it that, a nook fashioned into a makeshift kitchen, with a tiny sink and microwave and hotplate. Adjacent is my tiny office and overflow stockroom, partitioned off with a paisley green curtain. Even that looks wilted in the heat of the day.

I flip on the fan and park myself in front of it, both for the airflow and also in the hopes it will dry my hair enough just in case Gemma pays attention to me. Sitting down at my desk, I turn on the computer. Work in the office might also help me put some distance between me and what just happened this afternoon. There are a few emails: a special-order request, another email asking if there's a certain book in stock. I get through them all too quickly.

I check my calendar and sigh. There's yet another problem. In two weeks' time, it's my friend Ryan's birthday. Which means a party. Which means a gift. If only there was an occasion gift for your ex's new lover.

I mean, it's not Ryan's fault. Ryan's lovely. Eli didn't cheat on me. I didn't cheat on him. Everyone's perfectly agreeable. They look to be very well suited to each other. If only I could take the high road and move on, but I'm evidently not cut out for that.

I screw up my face. Ryan was my friend first. We met one day a few years back, when I blew a tire cycling home one night, going back to my old flat that I had with Eli. Ryan was also cycling home, living not far from me. At least he happened to be a prepared cyclist. He helped me with my bike and we ended up going for a pint, Eli joining us. That was before the accident.

Chewing my lip, I idly browse online for gifts. Getting a book would be a cop-out. I need to get something that's artfully casual, not like I'm still obsessing over Eli.

I need something personal for Ryan, but not too personal. Something that Ryan would like. Something not stupid. A gift card is another cop-out. A card seems both too sincere and not enough. Like I forgot the gift.

The best I can do with my online searches is find advice on what not to buy your exes. Apparently, jewelry is out. Luckily, I'm not wanting a ring for Ryan. Or for Eli. No flowers. A T-shirt? Clothes are hard.

At least I still have two weeks to figure this out.

While I look for both appropriate and inappropriate gifts for Ryan, a new email chimes.

My inbox has a fresh message from one of the major chains about their July sale. The problem is I haven't signed up to any mailing lists, so someone has done this on my behalf. Probably somebody's sick corporate joke from one of the mega shops down the street.

Scowling, I hit delete.

Like I can afford to have a sale to compete. Shit. Another thing to stress about. If they're having one, customers will expect it from me too.

Instead of a brilliant retail comeback, I do something even more daft. I search for Blake Sinclair. Worse, it's an image search. And I gawp at the screen full of Blake Sinclairs beaming into the camera lens. Maybe he's obscure, but there's definitely proof of life out there.

Against my better judgment, I click on one of the top results: Instagram.

The top picture is of a shirtless Blake taking a selfie on a sunny balcony. The man's fit. In the American sense. And the British sense too, I suppose: he's well-toned and gorgeous and fuck, there went my resolve not to look.

Apparently, I'm doomed. If only I could give Ryan my brain as a gift. He might make better use of it. Oh well.

My phone buzzes in my pocket. I pull it out, along with the filming notice. I crumple the paper, dropping it on the desk. It's a text from Mum, but I can't face her quite yet.

Not when I can still taste Blake on my lips. Even post-shower.

I pop into the front of the shop where Gemma's holding things down without any signs of the horsemen of the apocalypse having arrived for sales bargains—yet. She looks at me from the front display table where she's neatening up stacks of books.

Before she has a quip about why I'm freshly showered in the middle of the afternoon, I approach, keys in hand. "I'm taking the rest of the day off," I manage, handing her the keys. "I'm not feeling well."

Which is a fair and true point. I have a serious case of Blake Sinclair to shake.

"'Kay," she says easily, patting my arm reassuringly. "I'll close the shop tonight."

With a nod, I disappear back inside. Definitely not with another furtive trawl of Blake's Instagram, or wondering about what might have happened next if I'd stayed longer in his trailer.

• • •

Sunday promises to be more offensively hot than Saturday. Because I live alone and there's no one to judge me, I decide to get ice cream for breakfast. I venture to the nearby corner shop, safely away from the location of the filming. All of my Blake-related lusting and angsting last night kept me up late, and even with the smother of the day, I slept in.

Now, chocolate ice cream melts on my tongue.

I go to the coffee shop for a flat white to bring back. My friend Lily's gotten me addicted to them, with all of her trips to America and savvy to the latest things, right down to coffee fashion.

Even though Barnes Books is closed today to the public, it doesn't mean I get the day off work. It's just a different sort of work. Ice cream down and some coffee in me, I'm as ready as it gets to face the day. I turn on the radio and there's a countdown of the top songs of the week. They're up to number seventeen, a track from London's Halfpenny Rise, a friend's band, a great showing from Soho.

There's far too much hoovering of area rugs with my vacuum that spits more than sucks. Dusting brings a barrage of sneezes after a thorough once-over of everything with my wool duster, a splurge in the cleaning product department. The duster's from a foray into a zero-waste shop that Ryan took me into once. I didn't have the heart to come away empty-handed with all of their environmental initiatives and earnest looks.

Once the work out in the heat of the afternoon finally wraps up, and another cold shower and a takeaway sandwich later, I sit down for the bookkeeping. Which amounts to me tracking things in a written ledger like my mum taught me, and her dad taught her. It's straightforward enough, since I don't exactly have high volume sales in the bookshop. Not like Foyles or Waterstones or the actual Barnes and Noble.

I go to the kitchen for water, only to find out that the wobbly faucet has only become wobblier and is now leaky. Fuck. I dig around under the sink for my toolbox.

Scowling, I fish out a wrench and try to tighten the fastener around the neck of the faucet. I'm no builder, but by God, I'll fix this.

With a final turn of the wrench and a metallic wallop on the side for good measure, I turn on the tap. Water squirts out the side in an alarming manner, from a place water has no business to be spouting.

"Motherfucker."

After shutting the faucet off, I loft the wrench with more force than needed into the toolbox. There's a satisfying clatter of metal.

Seizing on the duct tape, I tear off a length and start

winding it viciously around the faucet.

Standing back, I look at my haphazard taping job and try the tap again. Water pours as and when it should. Triumphant, I sit down at the kitchen table with a fresh glass of water. Successful repair completed. Take that, shit plumbing.

I trace condensation on my glass with a fingertip, leaning the back of my head against the wall beneath a framed poster of the Sex Pistols, bought by my dad for my mum a few lifetimes back. Supposedly it was some private joke between them that I didn't want to know. But it's still there. And even after he passed, it's left up because neither one of us has the heart to take it down.

When I go back to the office to shut everything down properly for the afternoon, I can't help another quick peek at Blake Sinclair's Instagram, quickly becoming a new reward for every task I finish this weekend. Today, he's shirtless in Hyde Park, all gleaming teeth and impressive chest. Behind him, the sky is a stunning blue with a filter that brings out his eyes.

Gulping, I shut down the app quickly. Even so, I can still see his incredible body, his defined muscles—and still taste our urgent kiss.

Chapter Five

Monday's sticky. The heatwave shows no sign of letting up. A fan moves the air around in an illusion of coolness. The front door's propped open in case a breeze shows up. A sunbeam spills in on the red area rug, highlighting my main table with a colorful display showing books of note.

A win for adulting the right way, I skip the ice cream this morning in favor of pastries from the café.

We're onto day five of the heatwave. I'm starting to crack.

I've given up on trousers and their full-leg coverage, perfect for disguising my stick legs that would look far better on a sapling. The heat's made me nauseous. Fewer clothes are necessary. Now, I'm down to a rumpled pair of sage-green cargo shorts, found in the depths of my chest of drawers, and a short-sleeved linen shirt. Far too exposed for my liking, I'm compensating by hiding behind the safety of the front counter with my laptop while Gemma stocks the bookshelves.

Ordinarily, Monday morning would be fairly quiet, but it's bustling like Saturday. Is it because of tourists? Filming? Summer students? Who can say, but I won't question it. Today, no one claims to buy books based on aesthetics. Everything goes surprisingly smoothly, which should have been my first clue to not let my guard down.

Then, a courier arrives.

They usually wheel in stacks of boxes filled with bestsellers listed on the book charts, but not today. Instead, the delivery man walks in with something bright in his arm—a stunning, intimidatingly large arrangement of flowers: pale pink peonies, blue cornflowers, a smattering of reddish something-or-others from the daisy family. Straw flowers? I have no idea. It's wrapped in tissue and kraft paper, a satin ribbon around the middle, set in a beautiful stoneware vase. It looks terribly expensive and posh. Somewhere, a bride's been robbed, I'm sure of it.

He looks around curiously before making a beeline to the front desk. And me.

"I've got a delivery." He peers through his bifocals at the slip of paper in his other hand, gleaming faintly with perspiration. "For Barnes Books. I'm looking for Aubrey."

How a luxury bouquet has ended up in Barnes Books defies all sense of reason. I give the man a wary look. "I'm Aubrey Barnes."

"Excellent news, that makes my job a bit easier. Sign here." He gingerly sets the flowers down on the front desk and shoves his clipboard at me. Beyond him, a couple of customers curiously watch on.

Gemma appears in the periphery of my vision, peeking out from behind bookshelves. She creeps closer, like the proverbial moth to the inevitable flame, not one to miss an opportunity to witness me embarrassing myself again. She gawps. "Wow, Aubs."

"Clearly, there has to be some sort of mix-up," I say to the courier, ignoring Gemma. "This isn't a florist shop. It's a bookshop. And I'm expecting a stock delivery today—books only. There's not a single flower in my order. I didn't even order any gardening books."

The man runs a finger down the page, reading the delivery details. "It's not for the shop. It's a personal delivery. For you."

"A personal delivery?" I ask, frowning. "From whom?"

He shrugs. "Guess you'll need to read the card, mate. Now, I've got another dozen deliveries to make before all the flowers wilt from heat. The air-con's just gone in my van."

Hesitating, I look from the clipboard to the truly magnificent flowers. I pluck the card from the wrapping and open it. It's written in a hand I don't recognize.

A thanks for Saturday. You're incredible. Sorry for making you uncomfortable.

Oh, shit.

These can't be from Blake Sinclair.

My face burns hotter than the sun. Immediately, I stuff that card away into my chest pocket, away from anyone's eyes. Especially Gemma's, who creeps closer to the flowers. Never mind customers. Or—God—what if Eli saw them? It's more difficult to evade him. And, it's stupid, but I feel guilty.

I snatch the clipboard, scribble a signature, and return it to the courier just as quickly. The man does a double take at my sudden move into action.

"Must be a good card." He looks amused. "Right. I'm off."

So he goes and Gemma approaches, clearly awed by the flowers.

"These are beautiful." She gently touches a peony, then leans in to sniff, her dark ponytail hanging over her shoulder as she does. Today, she's in a blue dress slightly darker than the cornflowers. She turns to me, hands on her hips, and gives me a broad grin. "Now you gotta spill everything."

My glower is intimidatingly ferocious, I'm sure of it.

"They're not from Eli, are they?"

I give her a wry look before doing my best to go back to looking fierce. Which, unfortunately for me, is about as convincing as being a vicious golden retriever. I'm also the furthest thing from an actor that there could possibly be, and I wear everything on my face, whether I like it or not. "I'm not answering that."

I don't know if it's a good thing or a bad thing that she thinks they would be from Eli rather than someone new. I mean, I'm nothing if not predictable in my newfound curmudgeon lifestyle. But still.

"Well, someone obviously likes you. A lot. God, how romantic. I wish someone would send me flowers like that." Gemma sighs dreamily, gazing at the arrangement.

"I'm fairly certain there's some books in urgent need of stocking—"

And then comes the second unwelcome interruption of the morning. A woman wearing a baseball cap enters, accompanied by a man who carries a camera and measuring tape. They both wear black lanyards with some sort of identification hanging down. There's a determined air about them.

Of course my scowl returns instantly and whatever this is, I don't like it already. They don't pause to look at any books. Rather, they're making sweeping looks, sizing up the shop in a way I don't care for.

"Hi," says Gemma brightly, straightening from another sniff of the arrangement. "How can I help?"

"We're here to start work," says the woman, checking her clipboard. Already, the man starts taking measurements of the doorframe. "Sorry we're late. We were held up on set. Hope you don't mind."

Gemma smiles. "Not at all. Aubrey would be happy to help you out."

And then she disappears into the depths of the shop.

I miss the flower courier already. Whatever this is, it already promises to be highly irritating. "You people already bought all of my green books. I'm fresh out."

The woman chuckles. "I'm Alice Rutherford. Sorry to miss you the other day." She extends a hand.

I grit my teeth. The location scout. Right. "I didn't agree to anything."

She blinks, going back to her form and showing me. "There's a signed consent form to use Barnes Books as a location. It's perfect. Absolutely charming. We'll need to make a few changes for filming, of course, and compensate you for the inconvenience—"

"What signed consent form?"

"This consent form? The one you signed?" She shows me a piece of paper that looks worse for wear and taps on a signature.

"I've signed nothing. I'm the owner."

"Aubrey Barnes?"

"That's me. I didn't agree to this."

"It looks like you have. This was delivered to me this morning."

We both consider the form in awkward silence. It's the crumpled paper from my study. It's been smoothed out, but the creases are still there. And that scrawl could only be Gemma's signature. The first and only legible letter is a *G*.

A headache creeps around my skull, pressing like a vise. I rub my eyes wearily. The signature's still there when I look again. "It's a mistake. That's not my signature." I fish my wallet out of my pocket, pulling out my ID. I drop it onto the clipboard and point to the signature. "Look. Does that look the same? I'm the owner. No one else signs for me."

She makes an unhappy sound. "I'm willing to have you sign a fresh contract—"

"I didn't agree to this in the first place!"

"Mr. Barnes, we're offering a generous fee. We've all fallen in love with the charm of this bookshop. The corporate shops don't have the same feel. It's so perfectly old-fashioned in here."

She likes my shop? Against my better judgment, curiosity is winning. I struggle. "What...are you filming?"

Alice Rutherford's face lights up, like she had been waiting hopefully for this moment for a long time, and I've finally done her the courtesy of asking. "A rom-com."

"Oh God. Couldn't it be a thriller or space film or something?"

"It's very clearly and unmistakably a romantic comedy. Please, consider our offer. I'll give you twenty-four hours to read over the contract. If you don't mind, could we take some photographs and measurements today?"

"I don't like romantic comedies," I blurt, my face warm. Talk about triggering. The flowers must be some sort of setup, then. To secure the location. That must be it. It makes more sense than Blake Sinclair actually liking me—or my blowjob—enough to send flowers.

Mortified, I wilt.

"We'll compensate you. How does five thousand a day sound? It's more than fair." She hands me an unsigned contract. "It'll be brilliant publicity for you," she assures me. "Please think about it. Give me your answer tomorrow morning."

"Fine," I say grudgingly. That *is* a lot of money.

If only I could disappear upstairs and delete Monday morning. And Saturday, for the record. Obviously no good comes from chance encounters with film stars, no matter how C-list.

My phone chimes then.

"Excuse me." I turn and head into the kitchen, grateful for the excuse to get away from everything.

I turn on the kettle for tea, gripping the edge of the counter for a moment while I force myself to take a deep breath. Then, I take a look at my phone.

It's Lily.

Back home again in the Big Smoke after my Grand Tour. Drinks tonight? Lxx

I text back immediately.

Are you free now? Crisis. Axx

In short order, we assemble at our usual, a pub that could legitimately be described as charming, about a ten-minute walk from the shop. Mercifully, it's in the opposite direction of the filming nonsense. Despite the melt of the afternoon, the pub is pleasingly dark and cave-like. Unlike the Victorian building and its traditional decor, the pub itself has very modern air-con that packs a wallop. It's one of those places that fancies itself as a gastropub, meaning a decent food menu and a tendency toward craft beer—and, unfortunately, the occasional unironic hipster. The location's ideal for us, and the pints are well priced, so here we are.

I sag with relief to be away from all of it. No film trailers, no flowers, no books. No Blake Sinclair and no Gemma.

And there already in a corner perched on a barstool with a drink is Lily, all chic elegance in her cream summer dress with black geometric designs, platform sandals, long blond hair, and cobalt-blue glasses. We met three years ago when she came into Barnes Books looking for art books to help her with background research for an exhibition and very quickly became friends.

I go over immediately, pre-pint, to give her a hug and a kiss on the cheek.

"God, it's good to see you." I sag into the hug for a moment longer than usual. She wears a soft floral perfume.

"You're worrying me. Is it your mum?" Lily frowns, squeezing my arm.

Trust Lily for some much-needed perspective.

"No, thank God." I give her a wry smile. "It's not Mum."

""Is she okay with the heat?"

"She's fine. Everyone's fine," I say.

"You said there's a crisis."

"Well, there is. Maybe it's a middling sort of crisis, but I will need alcohol to face it. Very unhealthy, I know. But you also know I'm maladapted to life by now."

She waves me off, sipping her cocktail. "Go on, you misanthrope."

Despite everything, I laugh.

Before long, I return to Lily with two packets of crisps in my hand and a pint of ale in the other. I sit down with a sigh of relief. "I figure I could at least order appetizers. For your trouble."

Lily grins. "Trust you to provide. I'm starting to think this is a made-up crisis."

I shrug a shoulder, words caught in my throat. Even with Lily, it's taking me a little while to work up the courage to put the last few days into words. "How was Europe?"

She waves a hand airily. "Oh, you know. The usual ruins and crush of humanity. Old world charm. Bedlam in the airports."

Smiling, I already feel cheered for her company. "I've lost track of you lately. I knew about the conference in Rome..."

"Mm, Rome." She bobs her head. "Then Prague, Spain,

and home again today. I just went to my flat long enough to make sure it was still standing and to drop my bags before texting you."

"Sorry. You must be exhausted. I should have let you rest..."

Lily shakes her head. "When was the last time you texted me with a crisis? Work can wait. I've been on the road for ages. The rest will still be there later."

"How was the art?"

"Lovely."

"How were the artists?"

"Even lovelier. Shame the ones I met were either married or straight or seventy-five years old." Lily gives me a rueful smile, stirring the ice in her glass with one of those eco-friendly metal straws.

"Lil, even seniors need love."

"Not that sort of love. Not from me at twenty-five from someone old enough to be one of my grandparents."

"So, no luck, then."

"Not entirely. There was a woman in Spain..." She grins broadly. "She made the work week in Andalusia all the better. Good thing I have another exhibition-planning trip in few weeks' time." She raps the dark-stained oak bar with her knuckles. "Now you have to quit stalling and tell me about the crisis. Or no more intel about my Spanish lover. You're cut off."

Groaning, I rub my face with my hands. "It's going to sound terribly daft. Which is fair, because it *is* terribly daft."

She perks up, leaning in. "It's not about Eli, is it?"

"It's not about Eli," I acknowledge while opening up the packet of crisps for us to snack on. "Yay personal growth?"

"Start at the beginning," she prompts, intrigue across her face.

Frowning, I try to think back to the beginning and realize

only three days have passed, but it feels like an eternity that's aged me. "I guess it was Saturday. Just passed."

"Right." Lily waits patiently.

"First clue something was off was that the shop was very busy."

"That's brilliant, Aubrey." She hears my worries about the shop on a regular basis.

"Really not. Lately, some wanker keeps misfiling books throughout the shop and I was busy sorting that mess. Then, someone bought a stack of books—as props." I can't help a shudder. "After that, another customer insisted on a cash refund on a poetry book because the author was an arse on social media." I sigh with the memory of it all. And, admittedly, the memory of Blake's very blue eyes intent on mine as he handed over the poetry book, full of enviable easy confidence. And then I think of his social media, and the shirtless photo of him on display like a peacock on Instagram. And that grin that's probably been the ruin of a thousand men, with me his latest victim. Shameless. Flushing, I gulp down a mouthful of ale.

Lily leans in as she studies me. "And?"

"What?"

"We haven't got to the crisis part yet. I know disrespecting books gets under your skin but even you wouldn't go so far to call it a crisis."

I bite into a crisp. The crunch is very satisfying. "Mm, maybe. You've got a higher opinion of my limits than I do."

"Cute. Go on."

I study the crisps, then fidget with my beer mat. "You asked for this." I groan. "Right, so. I ran into the poetry wanker again on Saturday. Nearly collided outside the café by the bookshop." I spill everything: the filming chaos, the request to use Barnes Books as a location. "And—and, well, long story short…I go to their set to tell them to stuff it with their film location and instead run into this poetry wanker *again* in what turns out to be his film trailer, because apparently he's some sort of actor..."

"Who?" she demands, eyes lighting up with unreserved glee.

I glance around. We've our own corner of the pub in the quiet of the day. No one's nearby. A couple of people sit at the bar. We have the section at the back to ourselves. I lower my voice to a conspiratorial whisper, not that I'm booming at the best of times.

"Blake Sinclair, actually. And then... I can't explain it."

"Try," Lily encourages.

"Well...then I gave him a blow job." I cough in a last-ditch desperate effort to save face, because obviously my mouth can't be trusted with either words or proximity to Blake Sinclair. "As one does."

My face is on fire as Lily stares, abruptly lowering her drink with a *thump* and a dangerous slosh.

There's a long silence.

At last, she lets out a long whistle.

"Say something. Anything." I beg before I hide my face in my hands. "It sounds like a pack of lies, doesn't it?"

"If it was anyone else, I'd say they were full of shit, but it's *you*."

Flustered, I might die now, literally die, of embarrassment in the cool pub. That would be good because it would put an end to this story. A sinking feeling strikes. I've overshared. "That's not what you meant, is it?"

"Not...exactly." Lily continues to stare, brown eyes wide. "Shit. Blake Sinclair's hot. And...not gay, I thought? I've only seen a couple of photos of him online, but he's usually with a woman?"

"I haven't the faintest clue who he is, to be honest. Apparently, he's not famous like Timothée Chalamet or

Hugh Grant, who are probably the only two actors that I know of."

"Blake Sinclair's up and coming in Hollywood. Don't you ever pay attention to films? Or tabloids?"

"No. I run a bookshop, remember? I'm a film-free zone."

"I walked into that one."

"It gets worse, don't worry."

"Oh?" Lily gives me a wary look. "How does it get worse?"

"I, er, ran away. After we… I bolted. I've obviously lost it, Lil. Shit like this doesn't happen to me. I mean…" Shrugging helplessly, I don't even know what I'm trying to articulate. "Then—*then* a bouquet of flowers arrived for me, immediately followed by the arrival of an uninvited film crew ready to start ripping my shop apart, because Gemma signed the filming consent form without permission. You texted right about the time I was ready to run screaming murder down the street. You know that saying about mad dogs and Englishmen in the midday sun and all of that. Oh God, what is even happening with my life anymore?" I moan into my hands. "Hide me in your museum. Somewhere in the back. With the old, dusty things."

"I need a moment to process all of this. I'm getting the next round," Lily declares, neatly sliding off her stool and going up to the bar.

Meanwhile, I try to rally, compulsively eating crisps.

What if Blake Sinclair actually sent those flowers? Not as a trick. What if he actually meant what he said in the card?

Impossible.

Things like that don't happen to me. I mean, I don't sleep with actors, strange or familiar ones. Not that I know of any familiar ones. Perhaps this is all a prolonged state of heat exhaustion, which is definitely a risk this week in London. Maybe I should seek refuge in a cooling center. Or Antarctica.

When Lily returns, I've attempted to talk myself down from the ledge, with mixed results. She places a fresh pint in front of me and sets down her cocktail before resuming her seat. She contemplates me, bemused. "I've ordered some food, because I have serious doubts you've eaten anything all day with the way you've gone after those crisps."

Blinking, I look down at the flayed foil packets, where I was trying to pick up the crumbs. "Sorry for the brain dump and overshare. And thanks for listening. And sorry again."

"There's nothing to apologize for. Though, for the record, I would believe you at this point if there *had* been a murder in the shop. Are they filming one?"

"No. It's a romantic comedy, they say. And there's to be *no* filming in my shop. The finale is that the location scout's given me twenty-four hours to reconsider their offer."

"Offer?" Lily looks at me, curious. She tucks a long lock behind her ear, red earrings dangling.

I sigh. "They think the shop is perfectly charming and they want to offer five thousand pounds per day for the location."

Her eyebrows shoot up. "How many days?"

"Haven't the faintest idea. It's impossible. And—if there's filming, that means I'd have to see him again. Blake Sinclair." My mouth goes dry at the thought. As if there's another him we're talking about right now.

If the man sent me flowers today, does that mean he's thinking of me? *Me.* A nobody. Just one of eight million people living a perfectly ordinary life in London as perfectly ordinary Aubrey Barnes.

Except for last Saturday, where I quite literally lost the plot.

"Say yes," says Lily immediately.

"What?"

"You heard me." She tilts her head. "Say yes to the filming

offer. Purely from a business sense, even one day is more than you take in a week."

I make an unhappy sound and gulp more ale.

"And then you can also find out more about Blake Sinclair. Wouldn't that be a good thing?"

"Oh no. He's an illusion and I'm just me. We haven't the faintest clue about each other. What on earth would he see in me?"

"Even a no-strings fling would be brilliant, don't you think?" Lily considers me, tapping her finger against her lips. "But do you want to know what I think?"

"What's that?"

"It's more than a one-time fling if he's sending you flowers. Which is, by the way, lovely." She beams at me. "See, there's life after Eli. I promised it's an actual thing, didn't I?"

I groan, shaking my head. "By the way, it's Ryan's birthday soon. I need to get a gift. So do you."

"I already have one. Found a lovely wall hanging in Spain, actually."

Another groan escapes me. "Of course you did."

It'll be perfect and it's just so Lily. It's part of her rather charmed existence. Finding the perfect gift is something she can do in her sleep. Things like that just work out for her. She can even make parking appear out of nowhere in central London.

"Sorry," I say.

"Aubrey?"

"Yes?"

"Say yes. For me. For—for the shop. To help your mum. Do it for her, if nothing else. Wouldn't that be brilliant, not to have a financial noose so close around your neck for once? There's nothing to think about, as far as I'm concerned. And, importantly, it's a chance to see Blake Sinclair again." She winks.

Flushing, I shake my head. "I…well, I'll think about it. The location. Not Blake Sinclair."

"Promise?" Lily looks so hopeful that I don't have the heart to say no and let her down. Even though someone like Blake is a fantasy far removed from my daily life. But…he's a bit more tangible than a fantasy if he's coming into my shop, I suppose. Though how to explain what happened in the trailer?

"I promise."

I do mean it, because Lily is my closest friend, and I wouldn't lie to her. And she's got me on the finances side. Even one day of filming would be an incredible boon for the shop. I can't imagine what it would be like to have money in the bank for the shop, an actual savings reserve. Money to do the repairs that need doing. But, most of all, money to make sure Mum's all right.

"And promise me you'll give this new man a chance, even if it's a fling? I mean, at the very least, you ought to thank him for the flowers."

"I'll think about that, too. I mean, yes. I'll do that. Of course." I surprise myself, swallowing hard. "Let's try not to be overly sincere, though. I've got a surly reputation to maintain, Lil. Truly offensive, in fact."

"Go on with you." She waves me off, not buying it for half a second.

However, the flowers were spectacular, and thoughtful. Obviously, he must have thought of me to send them at all. Acknowledging the flowers would be a start, wouldn't it? No harm done. Then, there's the question of the appropriate way to do that.

Mercifully, our sarnies arrive then, all fresh bread and colorful salads and grilled meat and vegetables. Relieved, I tear into the meal.

After we part ways with our ritual of air kisses, once I'm

safely away, I pause in the shadow of a building. Admittedly, there's some secret part of me that's tempted to know what Blake's up to on Instagram. Before returning to the shop, I give in to temptation by downloading Instagram on my phone for a convenient way to get another selfish peek at Blake Sinclair. Why didn't I pay attention before to film people?

Then, I get sucked into a social media downward spiral in the street. Instagram leads to YouTube and a recent interview with Blake Sinclair, sitting relaxed on a talk show with his glorious tan and ready grin that warms me from my core out. "Yeah, I'm excited to film *Hollywood Ending* between L.A. and London. I've always wanted to visit the UK. Can't wait to go and see what happens once I'm there."

Chapter Six

When I return to Barnes Books after drinks, Gemma's locked everything up for the night. Down the street, there's still activity around the trailers. Commuters grumble their way home through public transport and pavements in Soho. The street's alive with the evening theatergoing crowd. One intrepid cyclist maneuvers through traffic in bright yellow for visibility.

Once inside the shop, the air is still and hot. Flipping on a fan and parking myself in front of it, I gaze over at the small selection of cards that I have in a display by the entry. I've made a point to stock cards from London-based designers. There must be something in there I can use for Blake.

Going to the rack, there's an assortment of the usual themes: happy birthday cards and sympathy cards, good luck cards and thank you cards. Plus, there's a selection of blank cards. There's no occasion card for a spontaneous blow job or to thank someone for the flowers that follow.

The obvious choice is a thank you card. Sign my name and it's done. Except…that's a cop-out. My gut twists at the thought. I hesitate over a thank you card before returning to the blank cards. I'll make it personal. But which one?

I pluck one out, a pen and ink illustration of Soho. At least that's appropriate. Cheerful-looking and bright. People like cheerful. The more conventional choice would be one of the cards with flowers on the front, but it doesn't feel right.

Retreating to the fan by the front counter, I retrieve a fountain pen from the drawer. Now comes the hardest part: what to say.

There's the simple and direct: *Thanks for the flowers.* Neutral. Nobody could take fault with that acknowledgment. Except…it has no soul.

Another take could be: *Thanks for the flowers, they're beautiful like you.* I flush. Not a chance. Far, far too earnest.

Or maybe: *Thanks for the beautiful arrangement. I'm sorry I left so quickly.*

Which… I think that might be the way forward. Because all of that is true. And even though that apology makes me feel vulnerable, I imagine how he must have felt after I fled. Probably a bit shit, to be honest. Which makes me feel shit, because honestly? That's the last thing I want him to feel.

Gulping, I write that last message into the card. At least my penmanship is decent. Which leads me smack into another problem. How to sign? First initial only? Before I can think too much about it, I add my phone number at the bottom.

Just in case he actually wanted to talk to me again.

I mean, if he had wanted, he could have put his own number on the card. Though, that's probably risky for a celebrity. Even a third-string celebrity as he claims to be. Who knows who wrote the card? Did he write it himself? Or did someone write it for him? Privacy must be a thing.

Well, the good news about me being a nobody is that it doesn't matter so much if my number's out there.

But a card feels woefully inadequate after the flowers he

sent. Obviously, the flowers are spendy, and by comparison, I don't have any sort of budget for a grand gesture. Or even a medium gesture. However, I do like to make things.

And so I go upstairs to my tiny flat and retrieve a felt flower I made as an experiment. A smaller one will fit inside the envelope if I squash it, so I do and it fits. Before I can think about it any longer, I seal the card. On the envelope, I carefully write Blake's name. When I do, a thrill runs up my spine, leaving me in goose bumps. Like he doesn't even need to be present for my body to respond.

Shaking my head, I put the card aside and find the blank contract. With a deep breath, I sign the papers and stuff them into an envelope. God, I hope I don't regret this. But the idea of helping save the shop, helping Mum, and the promise of seeing Blake again is too much to pass up.

• • •

At seven the next morning, I'm full of second thoughts when I'm startled awake by a sharp rapping on the front door. After throwing on clothes in record time, I hurry downstairs.

Sun streams through the shop's paned glass door. I meet Alice Rutherford, flanked by her crew, at the entry to the shop. Bleary-eyed, this is no sort of hour for any normal human. I haven't even put on the kettle and had my first cup of tea yet to make the day civil.

I unlock the glass door and push it open with its usual *squeak* and ringing of bells.

They all hustle in past me. A woman with green hair eyes the bells critically, reaching up to silence them.

Yesterday evening after the catch-up with Lily, I dropped off the contract and card with the film's security people. The guard recognized me from before and only grumbled a small amount about being asked to drop the envelopes off for me, which he seemed to like better than me going in to hand-deliver the pair of envelopes without an invitation.

Privately, I must confess I—or some small part of me—was hoping he would bin everything. Then I would have tried and failed and life would move on.

However, when I sent the note to Alice stating she could come by anytime to talk about logistics, I didn't expect her to turn up at the crack of dawn, raring to go. So much for writing daft things because apparently people take them quite literally when I was just being polite.

Does that mean Blake got his card? Oh God. What have I done?

"Good morning, Aubrey," Alice says brightly, handing me a coffee as soon as I've opened the door to her. Behind her, the city awakens with the hum of traffic snaking past. "I've brought you a vanilla latte. Extra hot. And also my backup. Right on schedule."

She glances at her watch with approval.

I flip on the overhead lights with a wince. "I take it that you received the updated contract, then." I stand back as a crew of five take over, all purpose and clipboards and tape measures, already snapping photos on phones and having animated discussions. They gesture and wave hands and take notes. They even pause to take a photo of me, where I doubtless look wide-eyed and startled, perfect for a murder wall on some crime show.

"Yes, I did. Thank you. Did you get my text about the seven a.m. start? This place is so perfect." Alice beams, gazing around. At the moment, everything's still in order as it should be. "We're delighted."

I blink, my mind still muddled. Text? I sip the coffee in a desperate attempt to wake up enough to process the conversation. "There's no bookshop murder, is there? In the film?"

"I've told you, it's a rom-com." Alice pats my arm reassuringly. Her ponytail swings. "And it will be good. You'll see. The actors are excellent and we have a fantastic crew. We have a few scenes to shoot in here."

"A *few*?"

"Oh yes. There's the meet-cute, for starters. And the romantic leads bumping into each other again."

I'm not entirely sure what she's on about, except this all feels a bit too close to home. Well, it's literally my home, I suppose. And far too close to what passes for my regular life.

"I see." Which I don't, but I don't want to confess that either.

"If you sign an NDA, I'll even let you have a peek at my script," Alice says generously.

"NDA?" It sounds like some kind of punk band, but I don't think that's what she means. Some lawyer thing, I think. Eli would be useful on this point.

If only I had my tea. I swallow a mouthful of coffee. Too hot as it sears on the way down. On the other hand, I'm definitely wide awake now.

Alice laughs with delight. "A non-disclosure agreement. Where you are sworn to secrecy about not revealing what's happening here. I mean, you'll need to sign one anyway today."

"Another contract?"

"Oh yes, we have plenty of them. But don't worry. We also have excellent insurance coverage. Any damages will be covered."

"You expect damages?" Oh no. "I didn't agree to damages."

"We don't plan on any. But it's always a risk. And we'll put everything back exactly as it is when it's done."

I gulp down more latte in the hopes it's an elixir of strength. Probably it would have been better if it had been a punk band after all. I'd at least know what to expect.

"I'm running a business—"

"That's why we're compensating you for the days you'll need to be closed." Alice gives me her best reassuring look. I set my coffee down to rub my temples, a foreboding ache creeping in. "There's not too much to do today. Painting and moving furniture around, and we'll load a lorry—that's what you call trucks, isn't it—"

"You must keep the books in order," I say desperately, watching two men nearby picking up books from the shelf and flipping through them. If I had any control in this situation, it's slipping away, fast. "It's terribly important. They need to be kept alphabetical—by section."

"And that's why we're taking so many photos. We'll spend the day getting the set ready and cleaning up. Then tomorrow morning they'll do a rehearsal and start filming later that day."

"How many days do you need?"

"It's hard to say. It depends on how smoothly the filming goes. Up to a week, I'd say. No more than that. I mean, we return to America in two weeks, so it wouldn't be longer than that. We have a tight schedule to keep."

"A week!" I stare at her. She can't be serious. How am I supposed to put up with this nonsense for a week? But...extra money. That would be a good thing, right? What if they tear the place apart, like what happened to my friend Murphy at his cycle shop a few streets over when there was filming two years ago? I struggle with myself.

In the meantime, she rifles through a stack of papers and hands over some to me. "Here's your NDA to review and sign."

Clutching the document, I watch as crates are shuffled in with painting supplies, and another set of empty crates where someone starts to box up the cookery section. Unable to bear it, I flee to the kitchen for tea and biscuits for distraction, a rising commotion behind me, and a wild thundering inside my skull.

The rest of the day passes in chaos.

I call Gemma in early to help supervise the filming carnage, her penance for her part in helping unleash this filming hell.

I'm on one side of the shop. She's on the other by the entry, looking authoritative with her arms folded across her chest like some kind of punk enforcer, a fountain ponytail spilling down over her shoulder. Opposite her is someone from the film's official security detail, evidently guarding the honor of the film crew. He's not any sort of defense against the havoc unfolding in my shop right now. Plus, in the unlikely event of a brawl to defend my—or my shop's—honor, my money's on Gemma.

Avoiding eye contact with her, he toys with his handheld radio, unleashing the occasional screech of feedback enough to set my teeth on edge.

Maybe in truth everyone needs to be protected from me.

Hour by hour, my shop's undone. Bookcases are carted out. Other bookcases are tarted up. Props are carted in. Walls are painted. Would my father have approved of aubergine? I chew my lip watching the mint green walls disappear. They're not allowed to paint the oak bookcases or trim on pain of death.

Warily, I sit sentinel at the front counter for as long as I can while people paint and polish, buff and sand. What would my relatives and the Barneses before me make of such a thing unfolding in the family shop?

They're closing in on the front counter. There, I defend

Blake's bouquet with the ferocity of a cornered animal like on some wildlife show. I let my guard down for half a moment and someone's hands are on the arrangement.

"Back off!" I snap as I shove myself protectively in front of the flowers as a human shield. The crew member recoils and slinks off. Pleased, I fold my arms over my chest and stand my ground. Flowers safe, I refuse to move to give them another go until a commotion at the entry catches my attention.

The door is propped open for airflow given the paint fumes, which waft most effectively into my flat and promise a headache later.

"Aubrey!" calls Eli. "Security won't let me in. I need a safe word. A password. Something!"

The cheek. Rolling my eyes, I get up. And freeze. Shit. The flowers. If he sees the flowers, he'll have questions, but it's impossible to hide them. They're rather large and showy and bright. In the chaos of everything, if I'm lucky he'll think it's part of the filming prep, even though the place otherwise resembles a building site at the moment.

"It's Noble." I make myself go toward the door. I glance at the actual security guard opposite Gemma. She's giving Eli stink-eye, something I'm privately very pleased about. "He's fine. He's with me—well, adjacent to me, anyway."

Eli looks stunned as I wave him in when the security guard steps back to let him pass. His mouth hangs open slightly as he takes in the spectacle, and a spectacle it is. There's people and crates and equipment everywhere. He's dressed in a suit, and judging by the angle of the sunlight spilling through the front window, he must be on his way home for the day. Which also means that this nonsense has been going on all day and should end soon. Maybe.

"What..." Eli manages, still casting looks around while the crew works industriously. Someone totes in lumber. I don't want to know.

"Filming. It's contagious, apparently. Green books are a gateway." My lips twitch.

He gives me a sharp look, startled. "I had no idea. Jesus. How long has this been going on?"

"Since approximately seven this morning. Give or take a few minutes."

"You...*you*...agreed to this? How did you manage this since Saturday?" Eli asks. At last he gazes at me, in disbelief. He loosens his tie, sliding it off and folding it neatly to tuck away into a pocket. He undoes the top button of his pink shirt. He must be sweltering in that lawyer gear.

I chew my lip. "Well, I didn't agree to this. Not the first time. Gemma did. Allegedly."

He lets out a low whistle. "I bet that went over well."

"I..."

In the midst of the chaos and drop cloths, sat on the front counter with my ledger and laptop, is Blake's magnificent bouquet. The blooms are dramatic, all pinks and purples and blues. It's impossible to miss the posh flowers.

Eli blinks. "What's...that?"

"Flowers," I say helpfully, gesturing at the bouquet. "You can tell by the petals. And the green bits."

My sarcasm is lost on him. What a shame.

"For the filming?" he asks, still staring at the extravagant bouquet, which really is out of place in the upside-down shop.

I hesitate a bit too long. My lips twitch, an unwanted tell. "Not...quite. Sort of. It's related?"

"You don't know?"

"It's complicated." Flushing, I look away. God, stupid complexion. If only I could keep a poker face.

Eli takes me in, perplexed. "You're all right?"

"Aside from the fact it's hotter than the fucking sun in here and I'm high on paint fumes and my family's shop is in bits? I'm perfect."

"I just saw the trailers and people outside the shop. There's a catering tent."

"So I hear."

We're quiet.

"They're very nice flowers," Eli admits, bemused. He shoves his hands in his pockets.

"They are," I agree. "I'm going to take them upstairs in a few minutes before they do whatever they're going to do to my front counter."

He fidgets with his tie in his pocket. I continue to chew my lip.

A crew member comes up to us, interrupting our prolonged moment of awkwardness that neither one of us is particularly enjoying. I'm petty enough that I'm enjoying watching Eli's bewilderment about the arrangement on the counter. On the other hand, I'm annoyed that he doesn't immediately think that someone would want to send me flowers. Someone other than him.

"We're ready to start on the front counter," says the woman with green hair.

"We'll be out of your way in a minute," I tell her.

"I'm going," Eli says. "Are you staying here tonight?"

I frown. As if I have a reserve of cash just for premium—or non-premium—London hotels. "Why wouldn't I? I live here."

"Because of all this…whatever this is." He gestures around.

"They're not filming in my flat. Their voyeurism only goes so far."

He's quiet. "If you need anything, or if they do take over your flat, call me."

"You'll chase them out?" I laugh.

He brightens at that, his expression softening. The damn man is too attractive for his own good, and he knows how to use it. "I just might."

I swallow. "You can't be my defender anymore."

I hate saying it, acknowledging that truth out loud. If only I could swallow this moment down, keep it in a private place away from light and scrutiny. Granted, he's got a track record of Aubrey defense. From dealing with arseholes at school to uni shenanigans together at UCL, Eli was always predictable and reliably in my corner.

"I suppose you're right."

And for a moment, Eli looks a bit deflated, slump-shouldered with his hands in his trouser pockets. Of course he looks handsome as ever, golden hair slightly disheveled from the heat, a hint of stubble along his jaw. There's always something appealing about him, no matter how irritating he is at times, even with the past championing.

"Ryan'll be waiting," he says.

"I know."

About then, there's another sort of commotion at the door. Thankfully, I don't hear any more about safe—or unsafe—words. Which is something to thank some higher order of deity for, one who manages texts and looks over hapless booksellers.

Gemma's too-cheerful voice rings through the chaos. "Of *course* Aubrey would love to help you."

Both Eli and I turn as if we're one to see Blake Sinclair weaving his way easily through the upheaval, deftly striding toward me through the builders and their kit, under Gemma's gleeful watch. Even her new BFF, the security guard, watches with interest.

Oh shit.

Blake's tan has only deepened since I last saw him, his tropical flamingo shirt cheerful as though we're in Florida or somewhere deeply exotic and not at all like central London. Behind him, feedback still shrieks over the guard's radio. The heat of the day rolls in through the open door. As he walks, the black lanyard around his neck swings with his filming ID. He grins at me as he approaches with an easy nod at Eli.

"Hey." Blake stands with easy confidence, slightly shorter than Eli but somehow even more of a presence. His gaze goes from me over to the flowers then back to me with a slightly wider smile.

Beside me, Eli stiffens ever so slightly, his expression quickly covering any hint of surprise with cool lawyer facade. Not noticeable to anyone else, but enough for me to pick up on that he's recognized Blake Sinclair at the very least. And that Blake's looking at me in a way that's not entirely the sort of usual way customers do.

"Hi." I gulp, palms already slick with sweat. Unobtrusively, I attempt to dry them on my trousers. Dear God, let's hope he spares us the round of awkward greetings. What do Americans do? Especially in already awkward social encounters, the dreaded post-blowjob-bolt-and-apology-flowers gaff.

Eli's eyes narrow ever so slightly at Blake.

My face burns. Meanwhile, Blake is the epitome of cool despite the oppressive heat of the day and my unfortunate unraveling.

Please, on the deities that watch over booksellers, don't mention the flowers right now.

"How can I help?" I manage, somehow keeping my voice from breaking like a teenager's with emo angst.

"Shop's closed," says Eli abruptly, who evidently gives no fucks for celebs and is getting weirdly...possessive?

I frown slightly. "No, no," I say to Blake. "I'd like to help."

Regardless of Eli's terribly unsubtle attempt to brush Blake off, I'm not going to be influenced by his bad manners. My gaze flits from the flowers to Blake.

Blake's smile widens ever so slightly. "We all ought to

make proper introductions, don't you think?"

Oh shit, the awkward greetings of doom. Here we go.

"I suppose. Since you're becoming a regular," I acknowledge awkwardly.

God, is *he becoming a regular? Better not focus on that.*

"Blake Sinclair." He sticks out his hand, looking at me in a way that melts my insides.

With a hard gulp, I dare touch his hand and it's everything I can muster to keep from yanking my hand back with the thrill of touching him again. My body betrays me. I open my mouth and have to try twice for words to come out. It's highly unlikely this theater is convincing Eli, who obviously knows something's up, judging by his arms folded tightly across his chest.

"Aubrey Barnes." It takes all of my powers of concentration to remember my name and not just echo Blake's.

We stare at each other for a moment too long before Eli coughs.

"And, ah, this is Elliot Gladstone," I say quickly.

They shake hands in a slightly aggro manner, some sort of reluctant acknowledgment on Eli's part and undaunted good cheer on Blake's. If Blake's surprised or caught off guard, he doesn't show it—but then again, he's an actor.

"So," Blake says, focusing his devastating gaze on me. From the corner of my eye, I swear Eli's glowering at the flowers. Could be a trick of some feral, hopeful part of my imagination that wouldn't be sorry to see Eli jealous. Is that so wrong? "You said you could help?"

"Um. I can try," I say, with complete confidence, as though my shop isn't in shambles and my ex-boyfriend isn't shooting proverbial daggers at him. "Yes. How can I help?"

Perhaps better luck with round two. Standing tall, I keep my ground, ignoring Eli.

"I've come for a poetry book," says Blake eagerly.

Part of me, a big part of me, suppresses a groan, sigh, or some sort of visceral poetry-related physical response. "Not the one you returned, I hope?"

I sincerely hope that's not what he's after, amusing himself at my expense. Also, there's the simple and practical fact that the poetry section's been boxed up and carted off to who knows where—and Alice Rutherford's team has the box list in their care.

"Oh no. I've actually come for poetry recommendations." Blake gives me a hopeful look. He glances around what once was a nice shop, if I can say that much. "But I see things have taken a turn."

"Evidently," I say wryly.

"Well. Guess I'll need to come back another time. Try my luck then."

"I suppose that's a sensible plan," I say gamely, as though I'm totally up on sensible plans, especially around poetry supply and demand for American customers.

"Great. Better get going, then." Blake grins. "Nice flowers, by the way."

That does it. Words escape me. I do my best to channel the endearing on-screen charm of, say, Hugh Grant or Timothée Chalamet, but there's no such luck.

"Who sent them?" he asks. If I didn't know better, his eyes widened ever so slightly.

The cheek.

"Er…the kind people at *Horse and Hound*. They're dedicated to their retailers, you see. Fine British magazine, actually," I say. "It was either that or send round a gift pony. And you know what they say about looking gift horses in the mouth. They're also terribly behaved in shops."

"Good intel. I'll need to check that out. I mean, who doesn't like horses? Or hounds?" With that, Blake nods at

Eli, but he can't stop smiling either. "Nice to meet you."

"The pleasure's all mine," says Eli neutrally. Unfortunately, I can't elbow him without it being obvious. With any luck, he can feel my invisible elbow in his pancreas.

Blake beams and heads out, head held high. Also a fine opportunity for me to admire his arse in faded blue jeans, but that's neither here nor there. Something Eli doesn't need to know about, certainly.

Once Blake's safely away, Eli hovers for a few more minutes till he finally takes off for home.

Taking a deep breath, I gather up Blake's bouquet and head upstairs to my flat, which does indeed smell of paint fumes and freshly sawn wood. I set the bouquet down on the desk, staring at it.

My stomach twists at the thought of Blake potentially being in my shop again. For poetry. Or…even on set.

If he's even in this scene.

He won't be.

I flop down bonelessly into the sofa in front of the fan that puffs air. I'm not sure how I feel about the possibility—disappointment or relief.

Chapter Seven

By seven o'clock the next morning, my shop's tarted up. Not in an unbecoming way, for the record. Yes, it's still my shop, but a posh, film-friendly version ready for the limelight, and even the odd close-up.

The film crew's taken out half of the usual shelving, which ordinarily leans tall and close, instead leaving shorter oak bookcases in the middle of the room. The sunlight pours in across the red area rug, a bath of light. The shop feels warm and inviting. Every surface has been touched up, repaired, and painted. The wood floors have been polished, the carpets washed, the windows gleam. The deep aubergine paint smells fresh. And it looks expensive, with that color saturation. They haven't started scenting paint yet like exotic perfumes, but *eau de la bookshop* could absolutely become a thing.

Having given Alice a key to the shop yesterday, I start my day by hearing voices downstairs, which spurs me into action. After a quick shower, I join the gathering crowd in the shop. Different people, talking logistics and filming angles and the like, all broad gestures and sweeping arms.

I hang back. Alice joins me, handing over a takeaway cup of coffee, with a sleeve from the café down the street.

"Flat white for you. And, by the way, please feel free to use the catering tents since we're causing no end of disruption. It's the least we can do." She gives me a lanyard with my own laminated identification card on the front. "You'll need this to get back inside if you leave. If you stay for the filming in the afternoon, you'll be let back in between shots. You'll have to be absolutely silent, but you're welcome to watch them film."

I stare at the card. There's the predictable photograph of me: reddish hair in unruly waves, a hint of my nose ring, full lips. At least they've caught me rightfully looking skeptical as one might expect when a camera appeared uninvited in my face yesterday, like a snap from the ID paparazzi. Clearly, I'm not ready for the media or social media or, frankly, any sort of press. I'll leave that to the professionals. I hang the lanyard around my neck and taste the coffee. It's excellent. Maybe this won't be so terrible after all.

"Thanks."

She smiles. "What do you think?"

As I gaze around the shop, I can't help but notice in prime view is the artful arrangement of the green books they purchased on one of the low oak bookcases. At least they're getting a moment in the limelight.

"It's actually not bad." I give her a wry smile and shrug of my shoulder. "Any damages?"

"None to report. Don't worry, I'd tell you if there were."

Relieved, I nod. That's something, at least.

We hear new voices from beyond the open door, laughter ringing out.

"Come on through." Gemma's voice carries from outside, where she's refereeing traffic at the front door with security. She was here before I came down to start the day, giving anyone who would listen a full report of the breakfast options she'd already enjoyed at the nearby catering tent. I can just see her from where I stand, but not who she's talking to.

"The actors," says Alice. "On time for their seven-thirty call."

The actors troop in on schedule, a surprisingly rowdy set for the unholy hour. A couple of them are quieter, but the group of them are exceedingly awake. And there, in the knot of effervescent enthusiasm, is Blake Sinclair.

I scald my tongue on the coffee, splutter, and try to cover as Alice gives me side-eye.

"Wrong pipe," I manage hoarsely when I can speak again, not looking at Alice as my eyes water.

But I am, however, looking at Blake.

God, he's got that gleaming grin from his social media, the grin he unleashed on me last Saturday, which inspired me to unprecedented impulsiveness. He's in a navy jacket and T-shirt, looking photo-ready.

Someone calls for Alice across the room, and I busy myself by my made-over oak counter, which is looking far more posh than usual. Studiously, I shuffle papers and retrieve my ledger, which obviously is an integral part of my business that I need to deal with right now. I pretend to look things up, cross-checking with my planner for extra effect.

"Hey," says a now familiar Southern male voice very near beside me.

My head shoots up. I jostle my coffee as I reach to snap the ledger shut. Blake's hand is out like a shot to grab my coffee before there's disaster.

"*Motherfucker.*" I back up literally into the counter and jar myself to 110 percent alertness, my body so taut it could snap with a hint more strain.

Blake's grin is huge. "Good to see you too. I need a nickname for you, but I don't have one as catchy."

I flush scarlet. A furtive glance out of the corner of my

eye shows that the full-on filming shenanigans have everyone else busy enough that no one pays attention to me dying not so subtly of dire embarrassment.

"Shit. I mean, sorry. Fuck. I don't know what's wrong with me," I gasp, then force myself to take in one deep breath. Which leads to another, and another while I white-knuckle grip the counter.

Blake looks from my hands to meet my gaze.

God, he's devastating. The bluest eyes, and such an unrestrained grin. Not overblown, but as though he's genuinely entertained by my lack of suaveness. At least someone's enjoying it. As for me, I'm trying—and failing again—to keep it together in front of him.

Behind us, the din continues. The director's arrived, and they're gearing up for the rehearsal, bringing in and arranging chairs. But I don't register anything beyond that.

Instead, everything's Blake. The air. The sky. The swelter of heat that rises from the core of my stomach in waves, and beyond. My chest is tight. This is what suffocating must feel like. Euphoria. All of it, at once. Once, I was chill. Not now.

"Hi," I whisper.

"Hi." He's perfectly calm, letting me calibrate to his presence. Like he knows if he makes any sudden moves, I'll flee like prey, an impala bounding on the Serengeti to escape the lion. Or more likely, run out the front door into traffic. Or possibly up the back steps to go hide in my flat.

Even so, no more Animal Planet for me.

Shit. He's not smiling. Why isn't he smiling? It's got to be because of Eli yesterday. Eli ruins everything.

Or...maybe he just realizes this is all too strange. Him being an actor, and me being a bookseller.

"Thanks for the card," he murmurs, mimicking my pose by standing beside me at the counter, leaning his forearms on the edge. So near I smell his posh cologne. "That handmade flower was my favorite part."

I can't speak. Not for a long moment. Till I remember what breathing is. "Thanks. For the real flowers. Obviously. They're so...so—"

He peers at me, lifting his eyebrows at me in a way that's subtle and truly devastating, cursed things. "So—"

"—beautiful," I say in a rush, dizzy.

His grin is wicked. "Not as beautiful as you," he whispers.

"Fuck off with that," I gasp immediately, unbidden.

Jesus. What did I say? Like some other power controls my mouth and it's a nonstop litany of shit.

Blake laughs with delight, as if I'd said the most clever and witty thing. It's mortifying. Once, I was good with words. Supposedly they're my thing. Clearly, that's a pack of lies now.

I eye him warily.

"Tell me more," he says.

"I've got nothing."

"You've already had plenty to say in the last..." Blake makes a production of checking his watch. "Two minutes."

"You should see what I can do in five," I blurt. Oh God, the unintended innuendo. If only I could take those words back.

"I've already had a preview," he drawls, all southern silk.

Of course he's going to torment me now. And he's obviously thrilled at the chance.

I shiver. "I meant generally speaking. Not... Well."

Too late. We've both gone there again.

For a moment, it's nothing but us alone in his trailer, me on my knees and him decidedly elsewhere, and truthfully, in this moment, what I'd give to be back there right now—

"You wanna know something?" he asks.

"What's that?"

"I've been dying since then to know what you can do in two hours. For science."

I swallow hard. Obviously, he's messing me about.

"There's absolutely no way a film person would have anything to do with a book person. Because, you know, different media." Even when lewd acts are involved. *Especially* when lewd acts are involved. I flip open my ledger and scowl at the page. "Different business."

His chuckle, so near, undoes me. I do everything that I can to suppress any hint of that. I've already revealed far too much.

"Aubrey?"

"Yes, Blake?"

"Wanna go out for a drink later?"

I narrow my eyes at him. Is that a come-on? It's got to be. Bold. Hard to say as his eyes dance with mischief.

"We could discuss our separate industries. If that would make you more comfortable. I'd do that for you. It could even be cross-cultural learning," he says generously.

My face burns. Arsehole. "I don't know if that's a good idea."

Blake looks serious. "It could be a terrible idea, you're right. But I get it if you're scared."

"Scared!" I give him a stern look, straightening to my full height. What does he take me for?

Flustered, I adjust the cuff of the aviator watch from Eli. "I'm not scared. Are you?"

"Nope. Then—I dare you to come out with me tonight."

He can't be serious. Are we teenagers? He's obviously trying to provoke me into a reaction. *Don't give him that satisfaction.*

"A *dare*. How ridiculous. Is this what actors do?"

"Mm, it varies on the film genre." He's nonchalant. Damn actor advantage, schooling his expression like that.

"Fine." There's a competitive streak in me, usually deeply buried these days, that abruptly comes to the surface. I won't be outdone, shameless goading or not. "I'll see you your dare, then."

"You say it like you're gonna raise it."

My lips twist. "Dinner, then. Drinking on an empty stomach is a recipe for disaster. I've been told on excellent authority that crisps will only carry one so far."

He grins with delight. "Right, dinner it is. Mind you, it might be late, depending how it goes. Us film people have long days."

"So I'm learning about film people."

God, he better not be gunning for a Michelin-starred restaurant. Already, I'm torn between regret and curiosity.

The director claps his hands, whistles, and then calls everyone to gather for the rehearsal.

"Guess that's my cue," says Blake. He starts to leave, then turns back and flashes a smile that takes my breath away. "I'll text you if you're not here when we wrap for the day."

"'Kay." I can hardly believe what I've agreed to.

Then, it's all serious film business. I settle on the stool behind the counter, out of the way. Thank God, a chance to recover a slight distance from him. But even in the same room, goose bumps linger.

The actors gather. Scripts are shared. They talk blocking, lighting, logistics. And my heartbeat is faster than a sparrow, like this moment is something fleeting that could disappear in an instant.

• • •

There's only so long a man can pretend to work on the books or browse online while a film rehearsal goes on. They run through lines and camera angles and do other things. I don't know what exactly is going on. Warm-ups, possibly. I stay for some of the filming then retreat to my office after essentially swearing a blood oath to silence. Occasionally, I hear the wash of voices down the hall when they take a break, and then I know I can boil the kettle or run upstairs to get something.

And I do end up—mostly—working.

Filming goes late. They weren't joking about the endurance hours.

Around 6:00 p.m., Blake texts me. Clutching my phone, I reread the message several times.

> *Still want to meet for dinner? Cool vegan place nearby if you're up for that The Wholesome Pea*

I purse my lips, perturbed.

A cursory Google search tells me that Blake isn't pranking me. In fact, there's a legitimate new restaurant about a ten-minute walk away called The Wholesome Pea, celebrating the humble legume and bespoke seasonal dishes, according to its website. No Michelin star, but there's 4.5 stars on the reviews, which seems surprising for a place celebrating the triumph of okra this week. If that isn't troubling enough, the lack of appropriate punctuation in Blake's text before the restaurant's name has me twitching. A colon. A dash of some manner. Anything.

Rubbing my eyes, I tell myself to chill the fuck out.

I didn't used to care about those things so much. I used to be relaxed.

Don't judge people by their use of punctuation, Aubrey. Give the man a chance. Eli's always saying I need to relax. And the arsehole's right.

Fuck off, Eli.

Like I can't angst over the prospect of a first date without Eli interrupting my thoughts. Rude. Better go back to the series of lewd daydreams I've had about Blake since meeting him. The man is very effective at driving me to distraction and beyond. Like my new habit of flinging hot beverages around whenever he appears, like some visceral automatic response deep in my nervous system that can't be stopped.

Chilling the fuck out isn't in my nature when it comes to

Blake.

Instead, during the next break of filming I hurry upstairs to look in the abomination that is my dilapidated wardrobe, crammed full of clothes wilted with heat. God, why didn't I think about this problem hours before? Back when I might've had time to do something about figuring out something half decent to wear.

I flip through shirts hung on wire hangers in a haphazard way, in the empty hope that a shirt I've never seen before might materialize like a first date offering from a portal to Narnia. But no. There's no instant access to Topman or anything of the like through my wardrobe. Instead, I'm confronted with the reality of a series of unironed shirts for the simple fact I don't own an iron.

I find the least wrinkly option—a white shirt with a small gray bird print. With a frown, I hold it at arm's length. If only I could run the shower set to blistering to try to smooth the wrinkles out. I pat the shirt down ineffectively. The heat wave's done nothing for de-wrinkling fabric. But I don't dare run the shower with the shrieking pipes and faulty plumbing. I don't want the wrath of the director on me. But I haven't had a chance to get ready, not properly.

I give my Docs a three-minute polish to get the worst of the scuffs off.

The distant part of me that occasionally embraces reason knows Blake hasn't had a chance to get ready either. He's been filming all day.

I find my cleanest jeans, run a hand through my hair, and change my shirt. That's about as good as it gets. And, on schedule, I go downstairs as they wrap for the day.

Decidedly not ready, I shove trembling hands into the depths of my pockets. Reality dawns that I'm going on a date—a date!—with Blake Sinclair. Thrilling. Terrifying.

Here goes nothing.

Chapter Eight

At 7:30 p.m., the evening's still warm. The sky is soft, light sliding toward twilight. I meet Blake outside of the shop. He leans against the building by the front door, dressed in dark jeans and a fresh shirt. Blake's bright-eyed, and there's nothing about him to suggest the man's worked the last twelve hours straight. His hair is perfect and he gives that devastating grin, which proves to be my undoing.

I do my best to give him a confident smile. Laughable, if he knew how nervous I am. Hurriedly, I busy myself by locking the door to the shop.

Act cool. Pretend you're cool. Also: has anyone ever thought me cool?

"An idea occurred to me." I slide the key in my pocket, followed by some fidgeting with my watch as I glance up at him. So close. He's slightly taller than me. Scented of cedar, like something woodsy and wholesome, but I know better about how gloriously not-wholesome he can be from firsthand experience.

"Tell me." He hooks his thumbs into his jeans pockets.

Still leaning, like he owns Soho.

"Is it fine for"—I wave a hand vaguely—"for a famous person to go out to dinner, just like that? Without being bothered?"

"I'm not *that* famous." Blake chuckles, watching me in an entirely unnerving way. His gaze isn't exactly intense, but he's taking me in far more closely than I'm comfortable for anyone to do. "They're interested in the leads. Not me."

"You're in a film," I point out.

"But I'm not a lead actor, not by any stretch of the imagination."

"What's your role, then?" Curiosity gets the better of me as my glaze flickers over him.

"Understudy to the bookcase."

"Very funny."

Blake laughs and straightens, all long limbs and perfect teeth. "I'm in a supporting role. The best friend to the lead. Which is a very noble and important role, by the way. You'll see me for at least two seconds."

"And in those two seconds everyone goes to the bookshop?" I ask, raising an eyebrow, unable to keep the skepticism from my voice. "It doesn't seem like the place for a rom-com. Just think of the dust."

"People happen to like reading, you know," he chides lightly. "And don't you vacuum in your shop? I know for a fact you do." Blake beams at me. "Besides, we're in London. In the film, as well as now, obviously. For work. And we take a break in a bookshop from work and the romantic leads meet by chance. Sparks fly. She's into business, he's into romance. They bump into each other."

I frown at him. This is where he's getting his inspiration for literally bumping into me around Soho. "So this date is method acting, then. You're having me on."

He laughs, holding his hands up. Wide-eyed, he's terribly

appealing, the shameless arsehole. "Oh no. Just serendipity. Honest."

"Hmm. Serendipity." Unconvinced, I gaze at him. Maybe that explains the flowers, his eagerness for our impulsive encounter in his trailer. How can I explain this otherwise? Return a poetry book, pick up a bookseller? Odd tactic otherwise. Perhaps this is what they do in America.

His expression softens. "I like you, Aubrey. You're intriguing."

Gulping, I give him an uncertain smile. "You must say that to all of the boys. In all of the London bookshops."

"Oh no. Believe me, I don't. I keep my personal life low profile. And you're the only bookshop date I want." He reaches out to touch my arm, which instantly brings goose bumps, traitorous body. "Ready for dinner? It's supposed to be a small place."

"'Kay."

"'Kay," he agrees, and we walk.

It's not long before we reach the restaurant. Blake's made us a reservation at a table toward the back, tucked away in a quiet corner. I haven't been here before, but Ryan's mentioned it in the past. The waiter brings us broad menus printed on unbleached recycled paper. The room's high-ceilinged and bright. The tabletops are decorated with assorted mason jars holding flowers. Paintings and illustrations from local artists hang on the wall. I recognize the work of a couple of them from cards in my shop.

The walk was long enough to let anxiety run riot with my stomach. I have no idea how I'm supposed to eat anything, legume or otherwise, under such conditions. Gingerly, I sip my glass of cold water once we're seated at a reclaimed wood table, a thick varnish over dark planks, including part of a hand-lettered crate.

We gaze at each other across the table. I swallow hard.

What have I done, agreeing to come out with Blake, a man I know next to nothing about? My track record for actual dating is disastrous, and Eli's shadow looms over everything. At least Lily's dating disasters don't have the shadow of her longtime ex lurking in the background.

Don't be daft. Plenty of people date after their relationships end.

"You all right?" he asks curiously.

I gulp and nod and immediately stare at the menu, trying to pick something. Anything.

Just don't think too much. You always think too much when you're nervous.

Blake's looking at me. I flush.

"Braised kale?" I ask gamely over the menu. "Does that have cheese?"

"Unlikely in a vegan restaurant," he says easily, smiling.

"Oh."

My face is on fire. It's warm in here. Too warm. Like I might faint. I gulp down water.

"Sorry," I say. "I suppose I'm not up on veganism."

He chuckles. "Plenty of people aren't. There's vegan cheese, but it's not quite the same. No dairy products. Or any sort of animal-based food."

"Not even eggs?"

"Not even. Vegetarians eat eggs and cheese, though."

Chewing my lip, I give him a wry look. "Not off to a good start, am I?"

"Don't worry, it's fine."

God, I have kale-related anxiety and Blake-related anxiety and all of the anxieties that are there to be had in a vegan restaurant at the best of times. Forget about the first date part. Faux cheese faux pas are only the beginning. Never mind the nut pilaf, a quandary of squashes, and then the greens. We haven't even gotten into the okra or the noble chickpea, the namesake of this place. What was it again? The Whimsical Chickpea? The Whodunnit Chickpea?

"I think I'm doomed, actually."

"Not at all. I can help." Blake looks eagerly at me. "What do you like? Pasta? Burgers? Pizza? Looks like they do it all."

I gulp. "I do..."

"But?"

"I didn't even say but."

He laughs. "It's written on your face. Go on, tell me. You secretly eat mushy peas and pies every night. Or what is it, fish and chips?"

"No. Wrong and wrong. On a good night, a sarnie."

"What's that?"

"A sandwich."

"And on a bad night?" Blake leans in slightly. "If you're naughty."

Transfixed, I couldn't look away if I wanted to. "A cheeky kebab. Or two. Eaten in the street. After a night out."

"When was the last time you did that?"

"Haven't the faintest clue. I don't keep track of these things."

"Interesting."

"Busy running a shop and all that."

Somehow, I break away from the intensity of his gaze to study the menu as the waiter approaches for our order.

Blake goes full-core vegan with said braised kale and collard greens nestled on a bed of wild rice and chickpeas. Not to be outdone, I go for the tempeh curry which calls itself a summer celebration of vegetables. My body's about to come into a shock.

"How about you?" I dare ask. "Your last mad night out?"

He grins. "Saturday night, maybe?"

I shake my head. "See, different worlds, yours and mine."

"Well, you know. I flew in from America and met up with

friends here already in London. So I just didn't go to bed to calibrate with London time. Figured it was the sensible thing to do. We went straight to a party."

"Is that normal for you?"

"No, not exactly," Blake admits. "But I'm not one to turn down an invite. You never know what might happen. So we had a night out. And just kept going the next day. I did need a couple cups of coffee to keep going but it was fine."

My bravery ends at asking who the "we" might be, but I don't think I want the answer to that. In case it's not the answer I'm looking for.

"Have you been to London before?"

"Nope. First time."

"And how do you like it?"

"It's cool. A British New York."

"Hmm. Does that mean New York's American London?" I could get used to the way he looks at me, like I'm someone special. I'm hardly mysterious, I don't think.

Blake laughs. "Sort of. I don't know. Obviously, London's older. But New York's twice as big. Trade-off."

I've never been to New York before to trade notes, aside from what I've seen in films and read in books.

"How long are you here?" I ask. "You can make more research happen."

"About two weeks? Depends on how it goes with the filming. If we stay on schedule. With a couple of days off at the end to chill out."

"Difficult in a heatwave."

"Very."

"You can't even have ice cream."

"But I can have vegan ice cream."

We contemplate each other as the food arrives. And it's surprisingly good, despite some of my deeply held suspicions about vegetables beyond potatoes in deep-fried form, the bloodletting of beets, and the slime of okra. The curry's excellent. I'll never confess to anyone else about the lentils. As for cooling down, it's tough to imagine how that might happen, as the temperature steadily increases between us.

"It's good?" Blake searches my eyes, seeking approval. Eager to please. Unexpected.

"It is," I admit. It's hard to focus on eating when he looks at me like that. "It actually is."

For a moment, we're both engrossed in food. Hungrier than I thought, my meal's disappearing in a hurry and I make myself slow down. Wolfing food down like a man who hasn't eaten in a week probably sends the wrong message, like I'm getting ready to bolt. I mean, I might, but not yet. I still can't reconcile the fact that I'm here with Blake in a corner over candlelight. Him, me, and a promenade of legumes between us.

"How was the filming today?" I ask curiously. "I made myself scarce so as not to interfere. Or make some interruption."

"Good. Rehearsals went as planned, no hiccups. I mean, we've rehearsed before but it's always a bit different when you're on set and filming."

"Do you…normally do romantic comedies?"

"I'll do anything that I can. Rom-coms are fun, though. I had a small part in a superhero film in the winter, another in a historical drama after that. And a rom-com before this one too."

"Sounds busy."

"Yes and no. Some parts are bigger than others."

"What's the best part about rom-coms, as you say?" I study him, setting down my cutlery in favor of water.

Blake purses his lips slightly. He sips water too. "The kissing."

I gawp.

He laughs at my expression. "Sorry. Couldn't resist."

"Now you're making fun."

"You give such good reactions, though. But to answer your question… I don't know, they're playful."

"Playful?" I say this like it's a foreign word that sits awkwardly on my tongue.

His lips quirk, some secret delight. "Mmmhmm. You wanna play with me?"

"Oh—"

Oxygen vacates my lungs in a rush. I'm in a permanent blush by this point and I look anywhere than at him.

"Filthy boy," he teases. "That wasn't even what I meant."

"It…wasn't?"

"I mean…what do you do for fun, Aubrey?" He savors my name, soft on his tongue. Like something worth lingering over.

It's entirely unnerving. I avoid his gaze again in favor of chasing a wayward lentil around my plate with my fork, one of the last survivors. Giving up, I set the fork down and twist the unbleached, hemp, bamboo something-or-other—or is it linen?—chic vegan napkin in my hands.

"Fun?" I ask weakly. God, he would have to bring up fun, wouldn't he?

"How do you relax?"

"Oh. I don't."

Blake's eyebrows shoot up as he frowns. "What do you mean?"

"I mean…I don't have time. Not with a business," I say a bit too fast. I stare at the napkin. Maybe it's linen. I glance up at last and continue to fidget with my napkin. "Not with trying to keep the shop afloat. I work all of the time. There's always more work to do than there is time, running a shop."

"No fun ever?"

"Nah. I'll leave that to the other punters who deal in fun.

Fun-free, me."

How to say the last time I dared to have fun was with Eli? That fun didn't work out for me. Now, I've got loads of responsibilities with a struggling shop. Somehow, I've turned into uptight Aubs, a target for Gemma's humor, and an occasional source of worry for Eli.

Blake's expression tightens with shock. Clearly, he's a man who has time for fun, a man with time for shenanigans and whimsy.

"Fun, I think, is something for other people. Like maybe those who have the luxury of time. I guess I'm…I'm just a serious person?" I tilt my head.

A slow smile spreads across his lips.

Blake rests his arms on the edge of the table. "Uh-uh. Fuck that. I saw some hint of fun there the other day. And today."

"You're seeing things." I lean back in my chair, folding my arms across my chest. Despite my better instinct toward reason, I'm smiling. "Like, you're hallucinating fun. Or, maybe, projecting?"

He laughs at that. "Yeah? A fun projector? I think you're projecting your fun aspirations on me."

"You're saying you're miscast? A man who's into rom-coms clearly has a Venn diagram overlap with fun. Fact."

"I wouldn't say miscast. But you don't know anything about me."

"You're anti-romance, anti-fun, anti-comedy?" I counter without missing a beat.

Holding up his hands, Blake laughs. "Shit, Aubrey. I'd hate to get on your bad side. Ouch."

"Sorry." I relent into a twist of a smile. Despite myself, despite my misgivings about fun and things that run in its orbit, here I am. Possibly enjoying myself. I thought that part of me atrophied some time ago. Life lately doesn't usually have much of anything approaching fun, its ilk, or a reasonable facsimile. But tonight with Blake, I'm letting my guard down a little, letting myself be swept up in his easy enthusiasm. It's so easy.

"Hey." Blake leans in, lowering his voice. "I have an idea."

My eyebrows lift ever so slightly, a smile lingering. "An idea? Ideas are the worst. God knows what they might lead to."

"You up for showing me a Londoner's idea of fun? Show a newbie the ropes?"

I crack up hard at that. "That's as bad as your dare!"

"What, you want to call it a night at nine o'clock?" Aghast, Blake shakes his head while I check my watch.

"It would be sensible," I tell him. Sensible's already left the building to have me out on a date with this gorgeous man, like I'm in some upside-down universe, because things like this—hot men like Blake—don't appear out of nowhere keen to spend time with me. "You have no idea. Transport gets decidedly more shit from this point out. Less service. Then, if you miss the last tube or train, you're caught on the horror of the night bus. Or worse, waiting for the night bus. Or even worse, dawn." I shudder.

His face lights up. "I'm already in."

"You're not serious."

"Dead serious. And…"

"And?"

"Don't make me dare you again. Because I totally will. Whatever it takes."

"Oh God. You really mean it."

"I think you're sitting on excellent insider info that's just dying to come out. A wild side."

I snort. Who does he think I am? "I have no wild side—"

"Evidence to the contrary."

"But—"

"—you realize it's ridiculous to call it a night at nine," Blake finishes, laughing as he sprawls back into his chair. "Or you're about to have a friend call with a pseudo-emergency."

"You think I have friends? Bold assumption."

Blake can't stop laughing. "I suspect so. Unless you're a total recluse."

"How do you know I'm not?"

And that's when my phone comes to life in my pocket. Lily with the inevitable out, always ready for an art emergency that she might need rescuing from. Truly a brilliant friend, if ever there was one.

"You gonna get that?" drawls Blake.

"Nah. Not yet. I need to show an American the city, I think."

• • •

Half an hour later, on board the tube, I check the flood of texts from Lily. She's unleashed a litany since 9:00 p.m.

> *HAVE YOU BEEN MURDERED TELL ME YOU HAVEN'T BEEN MURDERED AUBREY. RESPOND POST HASTE. I AM ASWOON WITH WORRY. Lxxxxxx*

Laughing, I text back. *That escalated quickly. You've also shed punctuation. xx*

> *You're so predictable Aubs. Lxxxxx*

> *Going to Lucky Bar with a man. Maybe JJs after. xx*

> *OOOOOOOOoooOOOOOooo*

I slip my phone away.

Blake peers at me, hanging on to the handrail as we

ricochet noisily through underground London. He gives me a curious smile. It's fucking hotter than the sun down here, closer to the molten core of the Earth. The heatwave persists at subterranean levels. Like Lucifer's cranked the heat to welcome my folly.

"Canceled the scheduled emergency," I say smoothly. "Ready?"

"Born ready," Blake sings, turning a few heads. He has a brilliant singing voice. A man near us sleeps on the seats. An elderly woman is unmoved.

As we exit, I leave my inhibitions behind me on the carriage. Till later, till my return to ordinarily scheduled sensibilities, like a regular stocktake. Right now, London's calling, like I'm leaping off some cliff into an abyss.

Chapter Nine

When the tube spits us out in the swelter of King's Cross Station on our adventure, we go up via the escalators to the concourse level. Even at this hour, the concourse is busy, flowing with travelers coming and going. Digital signs announce departures and arrivals, cancellations and delays.

"What are we getting? You can't be hungry yet." Blake chuckles. "Please don't tell me you're pit-stopping for meat snacks."

"Oh no, we're stopping for something much better than meat snacks," I retort, making a beeline for Boots before the shop closes in a few minutes. With a gulp, I take Blake's hand, hot in mine, a gesture that sends a ripple up my spine. "And I can't say I'm confident that's not some sort of American innuendo."

He laughs with glee. "No! I quite literally meant meat snacks."

"Well, you're in for a surprise, then."

Oh God. I'm in. All in.

He squeezes back, a surprised—and if I didn't know

better, but who's to say at this stage of our current non-relationship status—yet terribly hopeful grin on his face. "Condoms?"

"Guess again."

We go immediately to the beauty section. Everything glimmers with promise, from eyeshadows to nail varnish. "We need makeup for a night out."

I give him a challenging look as we stand before a display of eyeshadows in an expanse of colors.

Intrigued, he gazes from me to the stand and back again.

What does he think? This is probably a terrible idea. I haven't done this sort of thing in a dog's age. Probably not since back before dogs evolved.

"What are you planning?" he asks, squeezing my hand.

"We're going dancing. And we need to look the part. Up for that?"

He laughs with delight, moving closer. "Oh yes. So not only do you make things, but you make over people too. I'm totally game."

So I get to work, giving him a critical eye and then picking out colors. In cruelty-free makeup suitable for vegans. Particularly a vegan that I suddenly, strangely, want to impress. In a way beyond books or earnestly flailing my way through my non-existent knowledge about pulses and veganism in an effort to make a lasting impression. Now, I'm digging deeper into the dormant skills of a past Aubrey. With mineral eyeshadow and liner, red lipstick, moisturizer, and foundation, I insist on the purchase since he bought dinner.

And once we exit, I pull him into an alcove. He catches my jaw and kisses me in a way that promises to be my undoing, something fierce. When his hand rests on my chest, my heart thuds a rhythm beneath his touch.

• • •

I orchestrate an efficient makeover in the toilets at King's Cross. Apparently there's such a thing as muscle memory when it comes to remembering how to put on makeup. We're in and out, no muss, no fuss.

"Genius." Blake marvels at his reflection, the color on his lips striking with his dark hair, a smoky eye. In theory, it's supposed to be kiss-resistant. We may put that to the test later.

We better.

"No one will recognize you so easily now." My reflection's all rumpled reddish blond waves, a softer pink lip, eyeliner, and shadow. If only my shirt wasn't quite so creased, but oh well.

"Talented *and* thoughtful. You're a great catch," he jokes as we head out for the short walk to the rock club. "Now, where *are* you taking me?"

"Lucky's."

"Ooh, I like the sound of that."

Unable to keep a smirk from my lips, I hurry him along. At night, the heat's only a fraction less than the day, waves still rising from the pavement. I've texted ahead to my mate who works at the club, saving a couple of tickets for us at the door.

The hipster woman at the box office efficiently completes the transaction. The bouncer waves us through soon enough. We find ourselves in a wash of dappled club lights, the roar of the show already underway. The dance floor writhes with movement. Ecstatic energy of the dancers bounces off the walls.

We get over-the-top cocktails, and once they're finished and before I can protest, Blake's led me onto the dance floor, his hand hot in mine.

On the dance floor, it's a sea of bodies moving with the music. Blake's hand sears my skin as I grapple with the shock from the impulsive decision to get out here, rather than skulk sensibly by the safety of the bar. That would have been the more dignified, tamer approach. My usual go-to spot in a club, well away from the dance floor.

Out here, Blake's rhythm takes over, the way he gives himself over to the music. Head back, eyes closed, he's the beat of the drum, the bassline, resplendent under dappled lights. Like this, I have a chance to admire his beauty, the comfort in his movements as he dances with ease.

And when he opens his eyes to catch me in mid-gawp, he laughs and pulls me tight against his body. Like this, I'm officially on fire, between his closeness, the heat of the club, and the hundreds of dancers where we're insignificant.

I slide my arms around his waist. The way he glows at that makes me smile too.

"What are you making me feel?" I breathe against his ear, a playful nip for good measure.

With the thumping music, I don't know if he hears me, but he pulls me against him to dance tight together. This euphoria, this closeness, takes over my usual restraint. Possibly also helped by the cocktail.

Out here, we lose ourselves to the moment, the simple pleasure of dancing so close—so carefree—with someone.

Not just someone. Blake.

One song leads to another, and another. Eventually, parched, we have water and fresh drinks at the bar. There's a long, tentative moment where we gaze at each other, quite unlike the way we danced with abandon only a few minutes before. He's flushed.

Finding some courage drawn from Aubrey of days long since past, I slide my hand along his jaw, rough against my fingers, to draw him close for a kiss that claims us both. Then, there's no club, no angst. For a moment, a glorious moment, I'm lost in the simple, pure joy of kissing a man who wants to kiss me right back.

When we straighten, I see signs of people making a move to leave seating at the back in a shadowy corner. Leading Blake by the hand, we snag the table as they go, setting our drinks down.

Dead impressed by my table-hunting prowess, which is admittedly formidable, Blake leans over for a flirtatious kiss. Of course I encourage this naughty behavior, tucked in our corner away from roving eyes. It's still too loud for non-shouted conversation, so we go on with kissing, because our mouths say plenty without words.

Despite the thudding bass, I hear—and taste—a throaty, blissful groan from Blake. Of him pulling me slightly closer. Of me pressing over, the heat of my leg against his as I slide over.

Our kisses are greedy. Hungry.

This is about when I slide my hand over the front of his jeans, confirming that yes, he's actually hard as I suspected on the dance floor.

Because of me. God, what an idea.

Blake shudders, eyes half closed with pleasure. As I suck on his earlobe, he shivers.

And it's my turn to groan as his hand rubs my stiffening cock through my jeans. And fuck. It's impossible to think straight.

With a glance around, we clumsily snake hands inside each other's jeans. It's impossible to know who's more undone, our bodies electric with the current of music and each other.

It's everything I can do to keep myself from climbing on top of Blake in public, but beneath the table, our hands rove without mercy. My hand's inside his button-fly jeans, over the cotton of his boxers, moving rhythmically with the beat we started on the dance floor.

"Ohh fuck," manages Blake, biting down on his crimson—

remarkably unsmeared—lip, as I work him to the brink, back down, and increase the tempo again. And he shudders hard, thrusting in my hand as he comes, hot and sticky. I tease him till he can't take it anymore. At last, I wipe my hand inside his jeans against his boxers.

He kisses me thoroughly.

Which only makes him work me without mercy, holding my gaze when we sit up. My fingers press against the edge of the table. Gasping, it's all I can do not to cry out, breathless.

Club lights dazzle. The music pounds. His touch burns.

And then it's too much, the firm press of his hand, the shudder of skin as his hand takes my cock.

Unable to help it, I muffle a cry in my mouth, half smothered in my throat. And thank fuck for the noise in the club, drowning me out.

Blake's grinning, gaze fixed solely on me, our separate debauched world a few galaxies over from the rest of the club where everyone else is.

And then he eventually retrieves his hand, making a show of licking his fingers with unabashed glee. "Mmm."

My face burns as he then licks my fingers. I try to remember how to breathe, sides heaving, spine tingling, legs sprawled against his under the table.

"Fucking hell." I lean my head against his shoulder, reeling. Blake laughs with delight, sliding his arm around me.

And then, right then, everything's brilliant.

• • •

By the time last call happens and everyone's subsequently shooed out of the club, we're both loose-limbed with drink, giddy as people pour out into the street. In a dark corner, we kiss, Blake's fingers gripping my arse. My fingers slide against his chest, tracing muscle under the suggestion of fabric.

God. This man. Perfection, or as close as a mortal can get.

Then, inconveniently, my stomach rumbles. Dinner was a long time ago.

"Would you be mortally offended if I had a kebab now?" I ask, light-headed with the euphoria of the night. With the taste of Blake's kisses still light on my lips.

What is this strange, warm feeling? A big night out, beyond reckoning. The first in an eternity. Or is it an eon? Even nights out with friends don't see me feeling so relaxed by the end of it.

We're kisses and air, fingers and goose bumps. Part of me is sorely tempted to drag him back to my place to carry on.

Except I can't.

I can't show him how I live. Where I live. Not a chance.

"These are the meat snacks you want?" Blake's entirely irreverent.

"Chickpeas and kale aren't the same at two in the morning," I protest. "But now I feel terrible. Selfish of me."

"Oh no. I want you to have your kebab fix because you deserve it." Blake smiles.

"Would you eat chips, at least?"

"I just might. Fries, as we say in American."

"Cute. Let's go."

We don't have to go too far to find people queueing for kebabs at a nearby shop, the spillover from the club. Before terribly long, we have our food and it's beautiful in its deep-fried glory. Blake's happy with his falafel and chips. I have my favorite kebab. We alternately walk and pause to eat.

We've definitely missed the last tubes and trains. Taxis are scarce, empty ones even more so. We could try to find a taxi rank but taxis are too expensive anyway. Which means—

"Are you staying near Soho?" I ask once we finish eating.

Blake nods. "Do you..." he falters, searching my eyes,

"want to come back with me?"

Part of me screams a "yes, fuck yes, right now" sort of yes. I'm having far, far too much fun with him tonight, even more galaxies over from my usual problems—and fuck me if it's not a terrifying idea. The greedy part that wants more fun fights with the part that's nervous for more.

Because if there's more, what does that mean?

I hesitate. "I…"

"No pressure," Blake says in a rush, tripping over his words in his eagerness to put me at ease. "I mean, we've had a lot to drink. And eat. And…"

I gulp, gazing at this entirely too beautiful man, like nature made him to torment me and his legions of Instagram followers. He's all angles, eyes a soft blue beneath the streetlamps.

It would be very easy to lick my way along his jaw right now.

Not. Helping.

"Would you…" I take his hand, gulping in a steadying breath. Or something like it, from back when oxygen and I were friends. "Be offended if I said not tonight?"

His expression softens. "Of course not. I mean, I want you to be comfortable."

"I know I'm being weird. I'm like the anti-Grindr right now. I'm kind of mortified, actually. I don't know why I'm like this."

Reasons pop up. The shock of our impulsive tryst. Self-consciousness. Too much to drink tonight might lead to another freak-out—and I definitely don't want that.

I don't want to ruin this thrilling, fabulous night.

"It's fine, don't worry. I've come out with you because you're interesting and funny—and hot—and I want to spend time with you. You don't need to come back to the hotel with me… I just want you to know I've had a lot of fun with you tonight."

We stand in a bath of light cast by the streetlamp. The heat from the day still lingers at 3:00 a.m., close to the skin and sultry. Like Blake's hand in mine.

"I still feel like a numpty," I confess.

"I don't even know what that is, but I think I get the idea," teases Blake, all nighttime sleek.

"I can try to make up for being daft by attempting to navigate the night bus to get us closer to Soho again." With that, I retrieve my phone from the depths of my pocket, lost in schedules and maps. I'm fucked if I'm too drunk to figure this out.

"How about this one?" Blake squints into the distance at an approaching double-decker. "It's at least headed south."

"How do you know that?" Aghast, I stare at him. A newbie in town, and he's already a pro at public transport. Meanwhile, I flail around rather uselessly, especially for someone who should very well know the night bus routes like a second heartbeat, having grown up in London. But the honest truth is that I've had far more nights in with books than mad nights out, no matter what Gemma thinks of me and my quasi-rocker looks.

It's been years since I've had big nights out on the regular, going to gigs with friends. When I did, often enough, we were in stumbling distance to someone's flat. Or the gig *was* in someone's flat.

At any rate, I better not reveal how much of a recluse I've been lately if I'm going to save any face at all.

He's still looking at me while I have a moment of internal Transport for London existential despair. I'm fairly confident this is the right bus, but—

"Well," he says, lowering his voice, "wanna know a secret?"

"Of course." Impatient, I look at the bus as he flags it to

stop, the official stop just ahead.

"It's in the southbound lane." With that, Blake winks and boards. We tap in and join the jostle of travelers trying to negotiate London at an unholy hour.

"We could end up absolutely anywhere," I say. "Shit, Croydon if we're unlucky." Not that Croydon's particularly unlucky, just that it's very much not where I want to end up tonight. "How about we go to the river for a walk? More of the local tour. Show you some more of the city."

His eyes dance. Neither of us wants to call it a night quite yet.

We cling to the handrails.

"That's part of the fun." Mischief in his eyes, his hand brushes mine, and it's all I can do to hang on. "Not knowing where we might end up together."

That's how we find ourselves along the Thames sometime later, watching the sky shift through a cascade of pink-orange clouds at dawn. We've found tea despite all odds and the unsociable hours. We walk along the promenade in easy company, relaxed. The city is ours.

"Wait, wait." Blake tugs at my hand to stop. We're at Waterloo Bridge, with the makings of a fantastic sunrise to the east.

Pausing, I take the chance to study him as he marvels at London looking its best with the golden promise of morning light. He pulls out his phone for a couple of pictures, and I follow suit.

"I wish I had my proper camera with me, but it's amazing what phones can do," Blake marvels. He glances over at me with a broad smile.

"You're also into photography?" I ask, surprised. And

then I feel rather silly, because it's obvious that he's into it to some degree, given the fabulous catalogue of images he has curated on Instagram. And they're not all selfies, but brilliant photos too of city life and the occasional foray into nature.

"You bet. You too?" Blake looks intrigued, lowering his phone as he studies me in a way that's thrilling.

I nod and give him a wry smile. "I do, when I can. I have a couple of old film cameras that are fun to play with, see what they can do."

He brightens at the surprise of this common ground between us. "Oh, I'd love to see your photos sometime. I mean, if you don't mind."

"Of course I don't mind." The words come out before I have a chance to hesitate, a thrill running through me. "I'd be happy to show you. I mean, I don't have a fancy setup or anything like that."

He waves my belated backtracking off, clearly not dissuaded. "It's not about a fancy camera. Just the way you see things. And I'd love to see the way you see things."

And we stand on Waterloo Bridge in a pink-gold haze, unable to stop grinning at each other even if we wanted to. Like the promise of everything that might be hanging between us. As though the countries and worlds between us don't mean a thing at all.

"Oh, and just look at that. It's the perfect amount of cloud." Blake sighs happily. "Would you stand against the rail so I can get your photo?"

"Me?" I ask, startled, glancing up at the spectacular skies shifting overhead.

"You," confirms Blake with confidence. "You're the most beautiful part of today."

Somehow I don't swoon or mock him, which I'd like to think is some kind of growth. Instead, I just laugh and shake my head at his hopeful look, phone in hand.

"Please?" he entreats, in the most appealing way possible—which, for the record, is essentially impossible to say no to for such a simple thing. And I definitely don't want to say no, even if he is entirely mad to think I'm more beautiful than the sunrise.

"Just this once," I tease him, leaning against the rail. Over us, the progression of dawn transforms London into something stunning, all warm tones over historic and glass buildings.

Blake grins. "Awesome."

And I admire him, my expression soft. Thinking how I can be falling into serious like for someone I only met a few days ago. That for all of the differences between us, there might be some common ground too.

He frames the shot, his expression thoughtful as he does. The wind teases us, fresh before the swelter of the day, a fine morning. The river glistens. Traffic trickles past.

We swap places, because it's only fair. And it's my turn to take a photo of Blake, his stunning grin and open expression just for me, attention rapt.

Goose bumps cover my arms beneath my light jacket, riding the euphoria of the last few hours as if fatigue is a thing that only other people worry about.

He pulls me in finally for a quick kiss. "Selfie," Blake declares. With his arm around me, he stretches out a long arm to capture us both, with him trying to sneak in a kiss while we laugh.

"Those'll be dreadful," I assure him.

"Pure gold, these." Delighted, he shows me the photos of us laughing, unguarded. My hair's tousled by the wind, Blake's dark hair in compliance due to the skillful application of styling product. Some unstressed Aubrey lives in Blake's phone. Where did he come from?

"Filming's going to be tough tomorrow. I guess today,"

I say gamely. "You think you'll be able to get some sleep?"

"Maybe. Sometimes it's better just to keep going. It's totally worth the missed sleep, though. This night out with you."

He gazes intently at me and I meet his gaze just as intently. Then, he brushes his lips against mine. And we melt into each other for a stolen moment beneath the awakening city. We're all pink-gold sunrise too. And right now, here, Blake is all mine, in a private moment just for us.

Out here, in this early morning London, everything's ours.

Chapter Ten

When I collapse—alone—onto the creak of my sofa bed, I'm light-headed with exhaustion. And something like joy, if I'm completely honest. The room reels. Morning sunlight spills into the room from the gap between the curtains where they're not fully drawn.

As I drift off, my last vision is that of Blake, following a furtive peek on Instagram.

Social media isn't entirely terrible, after all. It's my last coherent thought before passing out.

By the time I open my eyes much later, the room swelters. The angle of sunlight creeping up the wall tells me it's far later than I usually wake. With the filming chaos downstairs rumbling through the hardwood due to shoddy soundproofing between floors, I have the luxury of a rare lie-in.

Downstairs, it could be a break in the filming, given the noise. Which means I'll have a chance at the kettle to temper the dull thump in my head. Too much fun, not enough water.

But God, it was worth it. Something dangerous like euphoria still lingers, the secret thrill when I look at the picture we took together at dawn. Imagine relaxing with Blake, a day spent lazy in bed.

Lying sprawled on the bed, it's terribly easy to think the whole thing last night was a very vivid dream. I imagine being in Blake's arms. Dancing. With me, his mouth brushing my cheekbone. Later, we shared teasing kisses along the river.

That had to be some other Aubrey. Some other Blake. And reality borrowed from someone else who isn't me.

Right now, all I need to think about is tea.

Something tangible. Something real.

• • •

The day passes in a rare lazy idyll. As the sunbeam shifts through my bedsit, me and my cat chasing the warmth, I spend the day alternately reading and drowsing, with a couple of trips out to the catering tent to bring out food. I haven't seen Blake amid the filming today.

There's a fair bit of waffling that occupies the hours.

Should I text? Do we have a texting sort of...well, certainly not relationship. Status?

Even friendship seems far-fetched. Though all evidence points to more than a one-time hookup, if vegan meals and midnight kebabs are any proof. And—the dancing. Plus, there's the lust that took us in the corner of the club.

I still can't get over being so close with him, our bodies pressed in the swelter of the dance floor. Or his hands teasing me despite being surrounded by people. And God, how much I liked it.

What kind of text is adequate after all of that? Instead, I skip the lame *how are you today* text to send a shameless photo of a chickpea and a simple text. Even so, I wrote and deleted three versions of awkward texts. After all, the photo of a chickpea should alone be at least worth a thousand words.

Double word score given how wholesome and ethical that is.

I had fun with you last night. xx

Okay. Simple. Too earnest, though. God. Why did I send that?

I'm revealing way too much. Fun leads to liking. Liking leads to my certain downfall. And I can't fall for him. Too dangerous. And he's only in London for a short time anyway.

Be practical, Aubrey. This can't last.

Can it?

Yet, I lose myself to the agonizingly hopeful wait for a response.

To pass the time, I text Gemma from my sprawl on the bed. She reports spinach and strawberry salads in the catering tent, fruit salsas, and more that they've just brought out. The shop still stands. She says she only made out once with the security guard. We've had a few messages to the shop about our closure, about when we might reopen for business.

If only I knew. It's terrifying to think of the lost sales, even with the daily rate I'm receiving. What if those customers never come back?

The problem is that when life goes back to normal... well, life will be back to normal. Which means no Blake, or dreamy first dates.

Hours pass. And my phone stays silent and dark.

• • •

The crew wraps filming a little earlier today around 4:00 p.m. The stillness and quiet that follows is unsettling after the steady commotion downstairs over the last couple of days. Which gives me all the more reason to angst about not having heard from Blake.

In my bedsit, I've pulled the curtain against the slant

of the peak of the afternoon sun in an attempt to make a shady refuge, but it's admittedly suffocating in here. I retrieve the pitcher of iced tea from the fridge. Cross-legged on the velveteen sofa, the bed folded away, I sit between the floral cushions that my mum sewed for me.

He's busy. Clearly. He's working.

That's the reasonable chain of thoughts. Versus:

Oh God, he hates me and is full of regrets and woe after being up last night with me and I'm full of cringe and I'll never hear from him again.

So much for fun.

Lily sends texts during the day demanding an update, and it's safe to call her as I eat the last of the pizza I brought upstairs from catering.

"Hey, Lil."

"Thank God. I was starting to think Blake stole you to become his husband."

"Ha. No. Fuck, no." My face burns with the inevitable blush when I think of Blake. "I'm fairly certain that doesn't usually happen in America."

"Well, he'd have to get through me first. You deserve a good price. And I deserve my commission."

Relenting into a smile, I laugh. "Glad you've got my back at least."

"Of course I do. Now you've kept news from me for *hours.* I figured that maybe your date carried on into today..." Lily teases, her voice light. In the background, there's the clatter of a café, full of steamer screech and the rattle of crockery.

"Not like that," I spill. She can't have found me out already, can she? Possibly she has spies everywhere. Worse, what if Gemma knows? "I mean, we were up all night but—nobody went to anyone's place or anything rash like that. That way lies scandal."

There's silence. I swear I can hear her grin over the line.

"Into hijinks in public places?" she drawls.

The perma-blush is back. "No! It's not like that. *Definitely* not. I would *never.*" I cough.

"Oh yeah? What was it like, then? I'm dying to know."

She's onto me, I swear.

"Er..." How to put last night into words, all transcendent and full of some light-hearted feeling that leaves me a bit unsteady. Also the filthy bits I'm keeping entirely to myself. Like the world shines brighter today. How odd.

"Please tell me," she coaxes. "I won't even judge you if you say you had a good time."

"Well, in that case..." I gulp. "Amazing?"

"That's wonderful! Tell me everything."

"We had a vegan meal and we went dancing and..." I skip over dark club corners with a blush I'm glad she can't see, and some regrets that I'm no longer in that corner with Blake. "We were up all night. Dancing. And walking around. I didn't get home till very early. Or very late, depending."

"You deserve to have some fun. And I'm so glad you've connected like that."

"He's kind of addictive," I admit. "I don't get what he sees in me, but the more I find out about him, the more I want to know, and...maybe he feels the same way too?"

"I'm about to cry with joy over here. There's so much to see in you, Aubrey. I've years of study on the topic. I'm, in fact, a world-renowned authority."

"Ha."

"I'm serious."

"Now I'm terribly embarrassed."

Aside from a couple of disastrous post-Eli dates, after enough pressure from family and friends to get on with things, I reluctantly tried to get on with things. Spirited efforts—disastrous results.

My heart back then wasn't in it, still shaped for Eli.

There's no guide on how to move on from something like that. My first real relationship. We got together young, still in school. Eli, I thought then, was the man who was my future, or so I believed, along with my past.

If only Barnes Books sold books about how to exorcise exes from our past. That'd be brilliant late-night reading. God. Why don't I stock titles like that?

"Just enjoy this," Lily tells me. "That's all you need to do. Don't think about it."

"That goes against my nature. Enjoyment, pleasure. Work needs doing. You should know that by now."

"I know. But try. For me. For you, more than anything."

"'Kay. Fine. I'll think about it."

"Excellent. You should listen to me more often. I'm very wise."

"Very modest too. There's one problem, though."

"What's that?" Lily's concern radiates over the line.

"I haven't heard from Blake today. At all. What if he… regrets it? Being with me?"

She tuts. "How could anyone regret being with you?"

"Oh, easily. Because I'm ten flavors of awkward, that's how. But I appreciate the vote of confidence."

"Well, he must be busy. And, like you said, if you were up all night, he probably needs to catch up on sleep."

It sounds reasonable. It is reasonable. Except—

"He said he wasn't going to sleep because he had work to do straight away."

Lily's quiet for a moment. She's probably going to say something terribly logical, rather than saying I've already fucked this up. "Then he's working and probably crashing out right after. Simple. Just try not to worry. If he was out with you all night, clearly he's into you."

What a thought. Perma-blush is back, all July-hot and close. On the floor, my cat lies on her back sunny-side up, stretched out in the crack of sunbeam spilling onto the rug between stacks of books. She has to be right. Blake's collapsed with exhaustion somewhere, trying to restore himself.

"You'll hear from him soon enough. Just enjoy a night off. Shop's still closed, right?"

"Yeah. I should be working on something, though." Relaxing isn't second nature to me, not by a long shot. Like, it's missed the mark by several shots, actually. Especially not when I think of Blake. My face reddens.

"Try."

I relent. "'Kay."

"'Kay."

When we hang up, I go back to reading the last of *Maurice*, and start on my next novel.

In the privacy of my flat, nobody knows if I'm reading a rom-com. For research. Customer recommendations and all that. Not because I'll like it. No one will ever know.

Hours pass, and I hardly move from my sofa sprawl, absorbed.

Eventually, a text comes with a photo of a small green bean in the palm of someone's hand—must be Blake's?—along with a brief *catch up later.* At least, it's got to be a bean, though I'll be damned if I know what it is, well out of my bean comfort zone, which admittedly lingers around the baked beans mark.

Can't wait, I text back.

And, after a futile search for beans, I give up. Who knew there were so many kinds? What do the different beans symbolize? Like some kind of Victorian flower code. Except for violets and tulips, we have legumes.

I fall asleep again.

Later comes. And goes.

I don't wake up with any bean or Blake-related insights. Or any texts, aside from the reminder I programmed to place a grocery order.

The evening technically stretches into tomorrow; it's just past midnight when I wake again. Again, there're no messages on my phone. Glum, I check the shop email, and then because I can't help myself, Blake's Instagram for the latest post.

Unfortunately, there's no recent update—but the last photo was posted over twelve hours ago, showing a spectacular sunrise over London's skyline.

Chapter Eleven

When I wake up in the afternoon, everything's still. There's no commotion downstairs.

Dust motes hang in the filtered sunbeam through the mostly drawn curtains. My cat sleeps beside me. It's early for the filming to have wrapped. For a while, I stay there, unmoving, in case they're in the middle of a quiet shot.

Eventually, I sit up. Bare-chested with the heat, my skin's so ghostly that I'm practically translucent, an indigo dragon winding from my shoulder to my arm, its tail and talons around my bicep. I reach for a black T-shirt and pull on my jeans.

I find my phone to check for any more texts. Unfortunately, no texts from Blake, with or without bean banter. Disappointed, I tell myself he has to be busy, getting on with things. He's only in London for a few days before he has to go back home to America.

Don't get too invested, I try to tell myself. There's some niggling worry that it might be too late for that.

After thirty minutes of creeping around my flat, I decide

no one's downstairs after all, and I go to investigate.

Everyone's gone, along with all of their film equipment. Shelves are out of order. Books are also out of order. Most troubling of all, there're deep gouges and chips in my hardwood floor.

I gawp unhappily. Furniture's clearly been dragged over the floor. To add further insult to injury, there's a hole cut into one wall, including through the wood lathing—a hole that has absolutely no business being there, where no hole existed before.

There's an envelope on the counter addressed to me. I open it and pull out the letter.

Dear Aubrey,

My sincere apologies about the damages to the floor and wall. We've finished with this location for the filming. We will arrange for repairs. We see that the floor is quite old and has previous repair patches. I'll send you an email tonight and let's chat about how to proceed before bringing the lorry back with the rest of your shelves and books. We received your post while you were away today, which I've placed on the back counter.

Kind regards,
Alice

I want to ball the paper up and chuck it against the wall. Or scream. Or do something else dramatic as I stare at the obvious chunks taken out of the floors. Sure, the floors are old and worn in places, but they had done a great job in refinishing them a few days earlier, making them look as good as they could. Now it looks like they put even more effort into wrecking the floors than buffing them to mirror polish.

These were the floors my father installed. The damages make me feel like I'm letting him down. That he'd be disappointed in me. Plus, there's definitely no money for repairs. God, I can't even afford to fix the damn kitchen sink properly, never mind replace all of the floors, which would probably cost a small fortune. Or a mid-sized fortune.

Sure, the film people say that they'll cover the cost, but will they cover all of it? Would the floors be as nice? Plus, the disruption in sorting this out means more delays in reopening the shop, and all the time to put it back together again. Which means lost sales.

Lost sales leads me to thinking of reopening. Reopening leads me to—

Gemma.

She was supposed to be watching the film people.

I text her.

The shop's been wrecked. What happened?

If nothing else, she's a prompt correspondent. But then, she lives between apps and scrolling, so I shouldn't be that surprised.

Shit yeah meant to tell you Mercury's in retrograde bad for communication and floors and all of that don't worry they'll fix it soon. x

Does that explain what happened to Blake? The lack of punctuation in her text? Mercury in retrograde? Is that really a thing?

Frowning, I shake my head to clear it and respond. Focus.

I don't care what celestial events were unfolding. You were meant to watch them.

A moment later, my phone lights up.

They dragged a metal cabinet and scraped the floors but if it makes you feel any better I yelled at them. Gx

It doesn't.

I rest the cool phone against my forehead like I can will Blake to message me. Also this is probably a good way to fry my brain. So much for Mercury and communications.

In a daze, I venture out into the blaze of the late afternoon sun, going for a walk to try to clear my head. At the café, and a flat white later, I see my barista friend Charlie, who asks if I'm all right.

"Yeah, good," I say.

I should never have said yes to the filming. It's just brought disaster.

When I check Blake's Instagram again, I scroll through his feed, full of images of him looking all too gorgeous.

He certainly won't remain a C-list celeb for long. Everyone will fall into serious like too, and then be laid to waste like me. At least then we can all be ruined together when he's an A-lister.

In my misery, I walk the streets around my shop.

It's too hot for food. Too hot for anything. I don't want to sit in my tiny bedsit for the evening quite yet. I don't want to look at the ruined floors.

Instead, I turn to go to the photography shop a couple of streets over, to admire cameras I can't afford in an effort to cheer myself up, which probably is a bit twisted. Occasionally they get in some cool vintage cameras, which are more my budget. I have a few back in my flat. Even though they don't cost as much as a new digital camera, the vintage cameras are all the more unattainable now due to the shop's problems, like everything else. The shop and my dating life, it's all a disaster.

As I reach for the door handle to go in, the door swings open and I nearly collide—yet again—with the person I least want to see when I'm out of sorts like this: Blake.

He didn't text, which must mean he regrets our date.

Sometimes, Soho doesn't feel any larger than a postage stamp, especially when trying to avoid someone.

"How can you possibly be everywhere at the same time?" I blurt. Frustrated, I manage to keep my balance this time and not end up flat on my face. My face is on fire.

"Aubrey? Are you all right? I was going to call you when I got back to the hotel. What are you doing here?"

"What are *you* doing here?" I retort sharply, crossing my arms tight across my chest. "This is *my* street."

Blake's eyes widen. He holds up his hands. "Hey, what's wrong?"

"Everything's wrong!" I practically vibrate with all of the pent-up rage and frustration and please don't let me burst into tears or totally lose my cool at him. But who am I fooling? Because I don't have any chill and he's nothing but. "No thanks to you and your stupid film."

He steps onto the pavement toward me. My scowl is so fierce on him that it's incredible he doesn't burst into flames with my fury. Like everything is his fault. Concern is plain across his face.

"I don't understand. What happened?"

"Of course you don't." I scowl. "You didn't text back, for starters."

His expression softens. "Aha."

"Aha?"

Blake droops. "I'm sorry. I should've stopped by. Or left a note, or something. I was thinking of you, I promise. It was a long day of filming, and then I fell asleep. And then I think someone on the crew 'borrowed' my charger and I couldn't text."

I grunt a grudging acknowledgment. That's probably all very reasonable. Except I'm not quite in a reasonable place. "The film people ruined my floor."

We consider each other. Blake's face is creased with worry.

"What do you mean they ruined your floor?" he asks at last.

"I mean exactly that." Relenting slightly at his expression, I sigh. It's not right to take out the shop's problems on him. "I mean, of course I know that's not your fault."

Blake gives me a hopeful look. "Could I...come see? Maybe I can fix it."

I give him a wry smile. "It's not your job to fix things. Your job is the acting bit. I'm sure it says that in your contract."

"You'd be amazed at the things I can do," Blake says cheerfully.

About then, a customer skirts us trying to get into the shop.

"What...what're you doing here anyway?" I ask.

"Heard there was a good photography shop nearby from someone on the crew. So I came to check out the cameras before they closed for the day. They have some nice stuff in there."

"They do," I acknowledge. Somehow, I feel awkward in front of him, under the midday sun beating down on us. There's not the magical light of dawn around us this time.

"Actually, I planned to come by your shop to show you what I got."

Startled, I stare at him. Whatever I expected him to say, it wasn't that. He actually planned to come see me? With a camera kit, no less? Which means he was thinking of me. Goose bumps cover my arms, with that, and the earnest way

Blake looks at me. It's thoroughly devastating.

"I mean, I don't want to keep you from what you were doing—" he blurts.

"I don't want to make you go back in—" I blurt at the same time.

Then we laugh. Blake reaches to squeeze my hand. My heart pounds at the thrill of his touch.

"Let's go back to my shop, then. I'm not buying a camera today," I confess. Spending time with Blake is a far more exciting prospect, even if that means looking at ruined floors together. We walk through Soho, darting tourists and narrow pavements, passing ramen places and tattoo shops on the back streets as we shortcut back. The street looks bare without the catering tent and caravans.

At Barnes Books, the bells on the back of the door ring as we enter, the only thing back in place in the shop.

Blake blinks in the darkness of the shop compared to the dazzle of bright outside, also startled by the changes and damages.

"Well, that's bullshit," Blake declares, as we stare at the floor together for a long moment. "I can see why you're mad."

"I can't put the shop back in order till this is sorted." Glum, I shake my head. "But you don't want to hear about shop problems."

"I'd love to hear about your problems. Shop or otherwise."

I glance over at Blake, who looks intently at me, his expression soft. And then I realize belatedly I didn't have a plan for us other than staring at the floor together, which is a rather shit second date idea, if that's what this is. Though our first date was long enough to be three dates combined, so this is probably date four, and who knows what the hell people do on date four.

"Are you sure?" I shake my head at the idea, but relent at a smile. "They're terribly dull. Would you like some tea? I can offer that, at least."

"Sounds great."

Who knows if Blake normally drinks tea, but if he doesn't, he's not confessing.

We navigate through the shop and past the office and into the tiny kitchen. I fill the kettle, set out the teapot and cups, and make my way through the usual tea-making routine, then lean back against the counter to wait.

Blake's trying very hard not to openly stare at my sink, but his gaze keeps going over. And then I remember and about want to die at my random tape repair, which admittedly is rather shit. I flush. Also, it's unbearably hot in this kitchen, especially with Blake adding to the hotness factor.

"Ah, it had a problem. Emergency repair," I offer by way of explanation. And for an emergency repair with no end date in sight due to the finances issue, it's holding up admirably. Seven layers of tape might do that. No leak would dare.

"I see that." Blake comes over to peer at the faucet. Experimentally, he turns the tap off and on.

"At least it's a mixer tap," I offer in its defense.

"A mixer tap?"

I nod as he glances over at me, his expression now shifted to all plumbing business. "You know, where hot and cold water come out of the same faucet?"

"Isn't that normal?"

I laugh. "No. Not in old buildings. I have separate taps for hot and cold water in the bathroom."

His eyes widen slightly at that. "Huh."

"Welcome to England," I say wryly. "To be fair, those taps aren't leaking. Admittedly, this was something cheap but I didn't expect it to break so soon."

"Huh," Blake says again.

The kettle boils. I fill the teapot. And smother a yawn, worn from the heat of the day.

"I can totally fix this for you," Blake entreats, looking at me. "I mean, I'd love to fix this for you."

"You don't need to worry about that. I'm admittedly embarrassed about my repair job."

Blake shakes his head, coming close to give me a kiss, his mouth warm on mine, but it's the best sort of heat, the heat that warms from the core out, the heat that transcends everything—especially dodgy plumbing repairs.

"Mm," he says happily when he straightens, both of us reeling. The fact Blake just kissed me in my tiny kitchen only makes the room spin more.

Sheepish, I gaze at him, Blake-addled. He's too bright to look at, all golden promise. And everything he says seems perfectly believable. And, if he didn't care about me, he probably wouldn't be here. "I'm sorry."

"For the kiss?" Blake teases me.

"Oh no," I say immediately. "I'm definitely not sorry about that. For acting like a jerk earlier."

"You weren't a jerk," Blake assures me. "I was off the radar longer that I meant to be and I left you hanging. And you were upset about the floor."

"I was," I admit. Blake wraps his arms around me and I snuggle against him. God. Even with the heat, it's comforting to be held like this.

"I'm sorry for not being in better touch. That's my mistake. By the way, did you get my mung bean?"

"Is that what that was? I did get a gratuitous bean pic." I relent into a smile, gazing at him. "I'm not up on my hipster beans."

He chuckles, taking my hand. "It's a favorite."

"You realize it rhymes with dung."

"It's nothing like dung, I swear."

"Promise?"

"I do solemnly promise," vows Blake.

"That's important to clear up."

I put the tea on a tray with some biscuits, cheese, and fruit to go along with it. My nerves continue, realizing I'm about to show him where I live.

"Don't expect anything posh," I warn him when we go up to my tiny flat as he trails me upstairs. The wooden steps squeak.

Luckily, I can't see his face when we walk into the small room. I set the tray down on the desk and turn. He's gazing at an excess of books everywhere, the desk that's a mix of crafts and account books, the rumpled sofa bed in the corner, books on the other sofa.

He's gorgeous, flushed slightly with the oven-like temperature here in my flat, even with the windows giving a tease of a cross-breeze. And the way he looks at me makes me shiver, despite it all. "This is perfect."

If I wasn't about to swoon like a Victorian heroine before, I am now. He thinks my flat is perfect? Probably he's overcome with the heatwave. However, it's in my favor and I'll take it without question.

"Would you come closer?" I whisper. "I need to show you something."

Obligingly, he comes closer, sliding those well-muscled arms around me, sending a series of shivers down my spine. And when he comes as close as he can, I brush my lips against his, a heat of our own between us. Of course he's glorious. And we kiss lingeringly, till I draw him down on the bed with me to continue our exploratory kisses before I feel a bit dizzy again like I did downstairs. And stop.

"Okay?" he asks gently.

"Just…a bit spinny, having you so close," I confess. Which is true, like the room won't stop moving. Or that somehow I'm orbiting the dream of Blake in some alternate universe where meeting someone like him could happen to me.

"You have no idea what you do to me," he murmurs. "If you had any clue."

Smiling into his neck, it thrills me to hear that. "Can you tell me more?"

"I will. And I want you to tell me more too," Blake murmurs against my skin, his breath tickling my ear. Held tight, close and safe, I feel cared for. Wanted.

Chapter Twelve

Later, it's cooler. And I'm alone. Twilight hangs like a veil beyond my window, the curtains still left pushed back for airflow.

Sleepily, I roll over. Something's missing. Or someone. As my brain awakens, two things are obvious: Blake's no longer in my bed, and in the distance, there's some sort of metallic clanking and the sound of intermittent running water.

Shit. What if the pipes have gone too? One of my fears realized, water damaging the books.

That would be fucking perfect. At this point, I'd believe anything, including that having Blake in my bed was a fantasy in a fevered dream.

Except I see a couple of books on the table next to the sofa that weren't there before. The romance I'm reading, open facedown, half read. I scowl. And also facedown beneath it, I discover *Ten Steps to Personal Growth.* Two book atrocities in one go. I find a couple of bookmarks and place them, saving the books from their terrible spine-cracking fate.

How long was I asleep?

Sitting up, I push my hand through my hair and get out of bed. I find a T-shirt again before padding downstairs on bare feet, following the sounds to the kitchen…where I discover Blake at work, testing the tap, and a scatter of tools on the counter and floor. My eyebrows lift at the unlikely combination of Blake and my pocket-sized kitchen, and the fact that he's in the throes of some manner of DIY project. The duct tape is noticeably absent from the faucet. And God, he's distracting, with or without DIY, but it may have made him even hotter.

"Blake?"

He turns, his face brightening at the sight of me.

"You're up," he says, pleased, like I'm the best thing he's seen all day. Meanwhile, I'm at a loss about how much time I've missed where he could half read two books and play repair man.

Except he's obviously not playing.

"Check this out." He turns on the tap. Water pours as it should. When he shuts the tap off, it doesn't drip. Clearly, I must be standing in someone else's kitchen and not mine. "You had everything I needed under the sink to fix this."

"Witchcraft," I remark. It's the only reasonable explanation. Who knows what sorts of incantations and rituals are needed to repair aging plumbing without divine intervention? I've ordered bits and bobs from internet searches, but I would always get overwhelmed about actually going through with the repair.

"And this." Turning the faucet from side to side, it moves smoothly, even with the water running.

"Show-off," I tell him, matter-of-fact as he crows with delight. I give him a wry smile. "You've probably put two and two together and figured out that fixing things isn't exactly my specialty."

Blake flashes that grin that melts my insides like ice

cream left out, a bit squidgy. "Well, your secret *is* kind of out of the bag."

"Mm. I didn't realize you could fix things too."

"Not just another pretty face for your roster. I have skills," Blake says lightly, coming over to slide his arms around my waist and giving me a kiss. And God, I've never felt so turned on about plumbing of any sort before. Or maybe it was the witchcraft. It's so hard to tell when I'm, in fact, hard.

"My roster is..." I manage between increasingly urgent kisses, "surprisingly short with the number of pretty faces. Show me what else can you do?"

"Oh, plenty of things," he growls, cool hands sliding against my belly. I shudder with the shock, then lean in as his hand snakes lower to cup my balls. Groaning, I lean my forehead against his shoulder. "If you want."

"Believe me, I want." Pulling him into greedy kisses, my reformed kitchen fades from my awareness into a new reality that only has Blake in it, along with his teasing, which leaves me weak-kneed. "Let's...take this upstairs."

"You're sure?" he murmurs against my ear.

"Very sure."

And we go upstairs before my legs buckle. My go-to would be clothes off and a hasty dive under the covers, safely shielded from view. Except it's way too hot for even a sheet. Very soon, I'm standing in only my boxers and cuff watch. Blake traces the tattoo over my shoulder, the dates inside my other forearm of my father's birth and death. His fingers trace the map of my body, tweaking a nipple ring as I shudder.

He pauses long enough so I can help him out of his T-shirt, and my God. The man is built like something out of a magazine. Not like everyday people. But then again, film people aren't everyday people.

"Are you a unicorn?" I manage, gawping with plain admiration.

"No, you shameless letch," he teases, drawing me into a kiss that only makes me hunger for more. Then it's a stream of eager kisses and we're both impulsive and desperate. "But...I see you're a dragon."

"Possibly," I breathe as he presses me down onto the bed. His mouth works up my inner thigh, making me shudder, to breathe hot through the fabric of my shorts, already tenting with the strain of my hardness. Because my body doesn't miss a chance to respond to him.

And then he pulls my boxers down, and I'm entirely naked before him. Self-conscious, I gulp, daring to gaze at him. Blake's admiring me most appreciatively, much to my surprise, because I'm definitely no actor, just ordinary me with an ordinary body.

Blake teases my cock with his tongue and then I'm definitely floating outside of my body, because he feels so damned good, and his mouth should definitely have some kind of Interpol ban or watchlist at the very least, leaving me all quivers and gasps. I go from clutching the bedsheets to gripping his shoulders, my fingernails digging into his skin, my animalistic urges imprinted on his body.

"Holy...shit..." I reel, unable to take the all too heady combination of the day's heat and Blake's nearness and care and the absolutely incredible way he's working me with his hand and mouth like there's a million ways to tease me, and let up, and on it goes till at last I can't stand it anymore. With a shudder and moan, I erupt hot and fast into the sear of his mouth.

Then the room spins and blood pounds and Blake's kissing me and kissing me and I don't want him to ever stop. And I'm clumsily helping him out of his jeans and boxers, still far too clothed for my liking, and his cock is magnificent when sprung from its confines. I stroke him as he murmurs into my ear words that are only for me to hear.

And I'm begging him to continue, his hands skimming my body, like there's a thousand sunsets in his fingers, and he pauses just long enough for a condom and lube.

"Please, Blake," I beg, unable to wait any longer. Like I've been waiting since the dawn of time for this, quite frankly, and I kiss him fierce, biting his lip.

Then, he's pressing inside me and I'm truly undone, my arms and legs around him as I sob with the weight of him on my body, the press of him inside. And he keeps saying my name in my ear and how can I be hard again so soon, his endless teasing.

It's incredible, being together like this, a tangle of limbs on cotton, the sunbeam creeping up the wall. There's a universe inside this room, the ecstasy of him and me and our rhythmic union. And God, he's so hot, all sleek muscles under my fingers and against my body.

There's no way to describe this feeling, our shared lust, but it's becoming more than that, like there's some kind of promise being made, like there's a future beyond right now. Like there's a day beyond this one for us, and maybe a day after that. It's hard to know, but for once, I see possibilities.

"God, Blake—"

"You're so fucking hot—"

And then there's quite possibly begging between kisses and a lot of groaning and I clutch desperately at him as I urge him on for more, uttering complete nonsense.

He pins my wrists down and I groan with the thrill of him, lost in a sea of pleasure as he finally comes with a cry. He moves with me and that's about when I come too, drowning in his nearness, the way he's holding me down, watching me with obvious desire. When he collapses half on me, we're sticky, and God I'd do this all again in a second.

We gasp together.

Blake eventually lets up on my wrists, shifting just

enough so he can unfasten the cuff of my watch. And then he discovers the heart tattooed beneath, a legacy from a lifetime ago. And he gazes at me and kisses it reverently before catching my jaw, kissing me so thoroughly like we exist only to kiss each other.

And we lie there kissing till exhaustion's claimed us again.

After I awaken again, it's proper night. The curtains and window are still wide open. Coolish air washes over my skin, a sheet around my waist. Blake traces my shoulder, with the small bedside lamp casting a soft glow. He's backlit, in shadow.

"Hey," he whispers.

"It's some unholy hour, I know it," I mumble into my pillow, all crinkle and fluff. He's taken away my watch and who knows where my phone is at—God knows what time it is, but it's definitely a time meant for sleeping. That is, sleeping for the sensible, which clearly he isn't. It's every man for himself. I can't save him but I can try to save myself. I squeeze my eyes tightly shut.

"I have to go before long. I have a six o'clock call. I was torn about what to do, to let you sleep or not, but I didn't want to sneak out either."

"Mmmph." I press my face deeper into the down pillow. Reluctantly, I soon shift to look at him, curling my body around his. He draws me into his arms and this is so perfect I could live in this moment forever, skin to skin. It's been so long since I've been held like this. Since—

Not going there. Not now. Don't ruin the moment, brain.

He kisses me lingeringly. "I want you to know I had the best time."

Sleepy, I smile into his shoulder. "For the record, I'm mortified that you've seen how I live but…I had a great time too."

And I really do mean it, against all odds of letting myself have any fun. He's been entirely delicious and I'm not sorry for indulging in some vegan dessert.

"Does that count as a second date, fixing your sink?" he asks, nipping my ear.

I hook my leg over Blake's. "I think that's the natural progression. Vegan restaurant and meat snacks straight to sink repair. Seems about right. Imagine what date three will be like."

Blake laughs with delight. "Can't wait."

His fingers continue to trace my skin, the pale freckles, the outline of the dragon that lives in indigo on my shoulder. Goose bumps rise. "Tell me about this tattoo. It's great."

I shift slightly, better to look at him over the pillow. "It's a dragon," I say lightly.

"I can see that. Don't make me tickle you," he teases with a growl.

"Oh God, please no. I'm not into that."

Blake grins. "'Kay. No tickling, but I'm curious. It's really nice."

"Thanks. It was a splurge," I admit. "Before everything with the shop. I used to read a lot of dragon books. Especially when I was a teenager. And so did my dad. He got a matching one, because he read dragon books too. Actually, he got me into them. And now whenever I see that tattoo, I think of him. He…he died a couple of years ago."

"I'm so sorry you don't have him anymore," Blake murmurs, his gaze soft.

"Me too." I sigh, reaching to trace his jaw, the comfort of stubble beneath my fingertips. "He was a brilliant dad. Cool. Funny. I miss him a lot. I just wanted him to be proud of me, you know?"

"Of course." Blake kisses me then, and I don't feel alone. Comforted. Like I can be vulnerable in front of him and it's okay. "How could he not be proud of you? You're amazing. Funny and cool too, by the way."

I give him a wry smile, thinking of the shop struggles. And a wash of earnestness that I had to admit I rather liked. "I try my best, but sometimes I'm not sure it's enough, you know?"

"Life has ups and downs," Blake admits. "And family can be complicated. I don't know what I'd do without mine, though. I totally hear you about wanting your dad to be proud of you. I'm the same with mine. And sometimes it's complicated. But they mean everything to me."

We share a smile, another kiss. It's scary how easy it is, talking with him like this. Like it's something we've done before. Something we might do again.

"Your family must have some fancy house like we see on the programs from America," I say at last into the silence.

It's his turn to laugh. "Oh no. I grew up poor, in the south, on a small farm that probably costs more to run than it's worth. My dad raised us, or tried to. Me and my two younger sisters, Lexi and Leah. They're still home. It was the hardest thing I've done, leaving home and leaving them. I'm working to help support them too. So I get when you're talking about how family's so important to you. 'Cause they're everything to me."

"No mum?"

The corners of his mouth turn down and twist sour. "She took off a long time ago. And she hasn't been part of our lives since."

"I'm sorry..."

"Don't be, gorgeous. It was her choice. For the longest time, I thought maybe if I'd been better—a better kid, better student, better worker on the farm—maybe she wouldn't have gone. It took me a long time to figure out that it was all her and not me."

"You were only a kid when she left?"

"I was nine, the girls six. Twins."

"They're lucky to have you, though."

He gives me a sad smile, unexpected. "But, you see, I left them too. To follow my dream to perform. So, all of this doesn't come for free."

What he's saying makes sense, all things I didn't know or couldn't imagine from looking at him, or his sleek Instagram photos. "But you seem so glamorous."

Blake smiles. "Thanks. That's just styling, though. Marketing. Really, I'm just a simple guy, trying to make things work. I've been lucky enough that it's worked so far. This was my biggest break yet, as a supporting actor. So I had to take the chance. And I don't regret it. Especially not since it's given me the chance to meet you."

"Me?" Imagine, Blake Sinclair excited to meet *me*. What a mad idea that is. "I'm sure you could find men having a lark with bookshops closer to home."

"Yes, but"—he draws me into a lingering kiss—"they're not *you*."

The kiss is bliss, meaning more after making myself vulnerable before Blake by talking about my past. He didn't run, didn't bolt. Hearing a little about his background with his family makes him more real, like we've discovered some common ground between us. And now I'm literally tongue-tied and twisted with Blake, and I'm grateful.

"Any luck in the camera shop?" I ask eventually. "I never asked."

"Finding you there was lucky," Blake says affectionately, which leads to more kisses. He grins as I shake my head, laughing. "I was just in getting a couple of filters, no new camera for me either. Sometimes I take a few shots while we're waiting between scenes or on breaks. Beats sitting around all of the time. When I can, anyway. It's not always so simple. Depends on the shoot."

Intrigued, I gaze at him. "Would you show me any of your photos? I mean, ones not on Instagram?"

"If you're good. Or…not."

It's my turn to nip at him, and his shoulder is my target. He shivers and reaches to smooth my hair.

"I can be very not good," I promise solemnly.

He laughs, obviously pleased. "Only if you show me yours."

"Dirty man."

"Filthy."

We laugh and I lift my head slightly to peer at him. He's languid, a hand behind his head, looking entirely at ease.

"You actually slept in my terrible sofa bed?" I ask as we both sit up at last.

"I actually did. It's not so bad. And I finished your book, 'cause I've been up for a bit and didn't want to get caught out like a creeper watching you sleep. I do think you tend to sell yourself and your surroundings short. It's all charming, like you."

"You saw my sink," I point out. "That's a nightmare, not charming."

"Well, I *might* give you the sink." Blake laughs.

I gaze from him around the room. It's so small and so full of books, from floor to ceiling, us tucked in a corner on the sofa bed, the desk under another cascade of books, plus the books stacked in front of the tall shelves. The few bits of wall are covered in vintage prints and posters. A red acoustic guitar sits on a stand in a corner.

"Most people don't live in their stockroom." I shake my head with a sigh. "I mean, I didn't used to."

He takes my hand, squeezing it. In response, I shiver. "Well, I think you've got a perfect setup. Three-second commute to work. And entertainment too. Didn't know you played." He nods at the guitar.

"My dad's. I guess you're right, that it's convenient being here, but…" It all comes back then, after my suspension of reality, lost in this alternate universe with Blake, where time stills. Coming back to the real world is terrible. I'd rather live in this moment, because it can't last for a million reasons. And now I've got a damaged shop in disarray.

With a sigh, I rub my face with my hands. I don't want to deal with any of it.

"If you don't mind my asking, why do you live in your stockroom?" Blake asks curiously.

It's a fair question, an inevitable question, but a question that squeezes a groan out of me anyway.

"Because I couldn't afford a flat of my own after my last relationship ended." I look anywhere but at him. "I'm putting most of my salary straight back into the shop, because it's struggling a lot, to be honest. I own the shop, since my mum signed it over to me a couple of years ago, not long after my dad died. I can't let her down, because she's got too much to deal with already without me being the Barnes that makes the shop go under. Plus, I want to help her," I confess, daring a glance at him. "So everything's fucked up."

Blake's quiet, taking this all in. He's contemplating me, all angles in the low light, his hair delightfully tousled. Is he regretting this, regretting me? Spending time with awkward Aubrey Barnes in his disaster shop?

Instead, he draws me into a kiss. "That all sounds like a lot. And admirable too."

"Admirable!" I laugh, but I don't feel it. An old familiar feeling settles in the pit of my stomach, grief and loss and the lingering shadows of the past. "No. I'm trying to do my best after my dad died. My mum hasn't been well since then. Well, before, really. She can't work anymore. So I support her. And when things ended with Eli, it just seemed like I needed to focus on her and keep the shop going."

"Do you mind if I ask what happened with your ex?" Blake asks tentatively. "You can tell me to fuck off otherwise. I don't mind."

My head snaps up. I wasn't expecting that. God, what to say that doesn't sound all woe is me? There's the *I wasn't good enough for him* or the *I wasn't fun or sexy enough for him* or the *everything got too real once I left uni after first year.* What comes out is a bit different.

Stick to the facts. Brief, succinct, to the point, Aubrey.

"He left me for our best friend, Ryan." I do my best to keep my voice calm and even. There's no giveaway waver, or telltale pause. "Eli—you met him, that day in the shop, after you sent the flowers. He just lives up the road. We're trying to be friends but it's not always easy."

Facts. Just facts.

Blake gasps slightly with the surprise. "Oh no, I'm so sorry."

"It was over a year ago, so I've had some time to get used to it," I tell Blake with a sigh. It's not quite forlorn, but it's real, and carries weight. "It wasn't easy to get over, since we were together so long."

A separation I never wanted.

"Still…" Blake frowns. "That's really tough. Like, a double betrayal. Losing your partner and your friend."

Uncomfortable, I shift and inspect my fingernails. I've started chewing them again lately. Not an attractive habit. I try to hide my hands instead.

"It's complicated. And…we changed. I mean, we were together since we were sixteen. So we didn't know what it was like to date someone else as an adult," I try to reason.

"But, yeah. Ryan was my friend first, and then he became our friend. A couple of years ago, more now, he was hit by a car on his bike. We both helped him out after, while he got used to life in a wheelchair when he couldn't walk anymore. Then, I guess things developed between them. I mean, obviously they did. And I moved out and Ryan eventually moved into Eli's flat. And to be fully honest, moving on's been rough."

He looks at me in a wry way that makes me swallow hard, like he's seeing right into the core of me.

"Anyway, that's history," I say awkwardly. "And…here I am. In a stockroom." I wave a hand around. "The pro is I have plenty of things to read."

Blake takes my hand, overturns it to trace the heart tattoo before kissing it again, like I'm someone special to be fawned over. If only. I gaze at him as goose bumps track up my arms.

Blake considers me. "So I guess you live with a lot of ghosts."

"Guess I do, yeah."

We're quiet for a long time. Trust Eli to be a conversation killer.

Blake shifts, lost in his own thoughts.

"What're you thinking?" I ask at last.

"About my own ghosts," he confesses with a sigh. "We all have them. I mean, a couple of my ghosts are exes too."

I trace his arm as I listen.

Blake shakes his head. "I had a long-term boyfriend who left me to go back to his ex. And, well, it hurt. I couldn't live up to whatever they had, I guess. It felt like he was living more in an idealized past than the present, you know?"

"I'm really sorry."

"Thanks." He squeezes my hand, gazing tentatively at me. "I was cheated on a couple of times. Once was bad enough. The second time, with another boyfriend, I was sure

I was cursed. That there was something wrong with me."

It's hard to imagine Blake going through something like that, when he seems so together. Who wouldn't want Blake? I wouldn't say he's perfect, because no one is, and that's a lot of expectation to live up to, but he's sexy and funny and kind. And the way he looks at me is a way I never thought anyone might look at me again.

"I promise things are over with Eli," I say softly to him. "I wouldn't dream of cheating on you. Or anyone."

He swallows hard, his expression momentarily raw before he smooths it over again. "'Kay. You're sure? 'Cause... Well, I really like you a lot, Aubrey. Even if it hasn't been that long. If...if it doesn't work out between us for whatever reason, please be upfront with me."

"I will." I hold his gaze. It's hard to breathe when he looks at me like that, so vulnerable. And with longing too. Like we're not together for a handful of days before reality takes over again and he has to go home. But, maybe we can figure out this long-distance thing. Maybe that's a thing people do. "I want you."

"I want you too," Blake murmurs.

And again we're lost in each other, kissing with reverence.

"You're brilliant." I gaze tenderly at Blake. Imagine a couple of weeks ago, my life pre-Blake, pre-filming and rom-coms. What a dark time. Now, it's like I've got hope again.

"So are you. From what I've seen."

"You hardly know me," I murmur teasingly.

"I know, but I'd love to get to know you more. If you'd let me."

I gulp and nod.

His answering smile warms the room. And me. "Besides," Blake drawls, "you need some serious bean education. Who else is going to provide that?"

"Nobody else," I say with certainty, because that's a plain

fact.

"I really like you, Aubrey."

"I really like you too," I confess sheepishly, my face warm. I can't quite look at him. There's tumult in my stomach at the realization that Blake actually does mean something to me. Something important and unexpected.

Blake considers. "You want to do something rash?"

A laugh escapes me. "Like what, aside from being up at a ridiculous hour for this long without tea? Go all out at the organic grocery store? Buy mixed nuts?"

He grins. "Nope. Let's get away together on the weekend. Out of the city, away from anything to do with films and media. We can even take our cameras. Your shop's still closed, right? And by the look of things, they need to do repairs before you can put anything back in order."

I open my mouth to protest. To say no, I can't, I couldn't possibly. There are the floors to repair, the shelves to restore, and never mind what promises to be days of sorting out books into their right places. He's got to be mistaken, like he's got some read on me that I haven't, because I feel like someone who's far from living up to my potential. Everything I wanted was put on hold for Mum and the shop. There's no place for me.

And yet. His eyes are a deep blue in this light, his gaze steady and unwavering and hopeful. It does something melty to my insides, and I'm going to blame that for what happens next.

"'Kay, all right," I find myself saying to my complete shock. "Let's fuck off out of town for a couple of days, then."

Chapter Thirteen

There's still a day of filming ahead of the weekend. Blake goes off on his filming call at the unholy hour of 6:00 a.m. or whatever horror he said. It's no kind of hour for a bookseller, and instead I go back to sleep and aim for a more reasonable later start to the morning.

When I go down for tea a couple of hours later, I admire my newly repaired kitchen sink. The new faucet gleams. At a touch of a lever, water runs smoothly from the spout. Water doesn't squirt at alarming angles or from strange places.

Terribly pleased, I can't stop grinning as I fill the kettle. Thinking about Blake repairing the sink only leads to me thinking about the invitation back to my place upstairs, the tryst that followed, our confessions to each other.

He didn't run away. In fact, he left with great reluctance, lots of sleepy kisses, and the promise to catch up later. It's a rash thought, but what if we could actually make this work? Despite everything, including some small matter of distance.

Humming, I go about my morning. Fortified with tea and some breakfast, I retreat to my office and do some work on the accounts and orders. I even go out to the damaged shop to sigh at the floors without spiraling into deep, existential despair. It's still bad, but this can be fixed, right?

The door's open for some fresh air as I sweep up the debris left behind. If I clean up, maybe it won't look so dreadful. As I work, there's a knock at the door, and I pause to turn.

The courier peers at me. This time, it's not the flower delivery man, or my usual courier. She gives me an intent look, only momentarily thrown from her game with the complete absence of my bookshop's interior.

"Mr. Barnes?"

"Yes?" I ask, leaning the broom in the corner and going over. Sunlight spills across the half-swept floor. The gouges admittedly still look terrible. It's not the usual day for a book delivery, and she doesn't have any boxes with her.

I frown slightly as she hands me an envelope and a clipboard.

"Sign here." She taps at the bottom of the page, and obediently I sign.

"What's this?"

She gives me a look like I'm especially thick before she leaves. "A letter."

I grunt an acknowledgment, turning the envelope over to see the return address from the borough. A scowl comes immediately. Whatever this is, I don't like it already.

As she disappears out of the shop, I stand by the entry, the breeze promising a hot afternoon. My good mood's rapidly disappearing as I open the envelope with a satisfying tear. And—it's worse than I thought. They've reassessed the bills for my flat and my shop.

Dear Mr. Barnes,

Please remit prompt payment immediately upon notice. Our recent calculations indicate that you are owing on bills for over the past year due to the incorrect council tax band, given the attached flat...

My mouth opens. I make some kind of hiss.

There's no financial way out of this, even if I could afford the bills, given what the shop takes in. The recalculated taxes are a nightmare. This would have never happened if my father still ran the shop. And if the shop fails, and I disappoint him even though he's gone, how can I live with that?

It's even worse than I thought. The shop's truly fucked now.

After a round of rage sweeping—which is nowhere near as satisfying as it sounds—the damage is fully revealed, adding to my foul mood. A fine cloud of dust hangs in the air. I sneeze.

I stare at the inexplicable hole in the wall that someone's cut in for who knows what reason. Unable to bear it any longer, and not sure what to do, I call Gemma.

"I need answers," I blurt when she picks up.

"God, Aubs, don't you have the decency to text first about a call?" she mumbles, obviously half asleep. "I thought someone died. *Nobody* rings me. Not even my mum. You should know better. This is hardly a psychic helpline."

"No one's died," I confirm. "And I don't need any kind of reading. Or seance. Yet."

I hear the sound of rustling and mumbling and quite possibly the voice of someone else, but who can say for certain other than Gemma.

"'Kay, I'm up, I'm up," she says while smothering a yawn.

"It's nearly noon."

"I'm not scheduled to work today." She pauses, the frown in her voice. "I don't think. I mean, the shop's not in order yet, is it? I haven't slept for a week."

"A divine intervention did not, in fact, occur overnight," I concur, raking my hand through my hair. Though that does raise an intriguing explanation about what happened with Blake last night, but I'm definitely not bringing that up to Gemma, no matter her passing familiarity with celestial events, both scheduled and unscheduled.

"So what's happening?"

"The floors," I say darkly, gesturing at them widely in my despair, even if she can't see. "They've been murdered."

"Old news, mate."

The arrival of the fresh crop of devastating bills was just the nail in the coffin that I hardly needed for the shop. I'm not mentioning that to Gemma either. Instead, I pace.

"I don't know what to do," I say.

"Obviously, you fix them. Or somebody does." She tuts. Water runs in the background. Then she half covers the microphone and there's some half-muffled conversation on her end about tea.

"Of course, but how?"

"Call a builder, silly. Call the film people. Is there a meeting? I don't know. You worry too much—it'll be fine."

"I worry the appropriate amount, thank you very much."

Gemma laughs, obviously unperturbed because it's not her ruined shop. "Maybe you need to have some fun and take your mind off things," she advises.

I open my mouth and shut it. "Fun," I blurt, reddening, "is *not* the issue."

"Are you quite sure?" Gemma sighs. "Look, did you want me to come by and try to fix the floors?"

A shudder runs through me. "I hate to underestimate you, but no, I don't need you to come fix them."

"That's good, because I have things to do today," she says brightly. "But I can come tomorrow. If that helps. Just let me know."

"I'm going—" I catch myself, hesitating. Tomorrow means going away with Blake. We haven't exactly figured out where we're going, mind you. That's something for us to decide tonight. "I will," I promise instead.

"Perfect. Talk soon. It's going to be fine, Aubs. You'll see."

"Is it?"

And she hangs up. I scuff unhappily at a gouge in the floor, aged wood splintering under my sneakers.

Later, Blake rings me on a break from filming. His voice cuts through the gloom of my day, holed up in my office where I'm trying to make miracles happen with the accounts. In truth, it's more like shuffling papers around and pulling at my hair.

"Hey, gorgeous," drawls Blake teasingly in my ear. "Miss you."

Even with the impending financial ruin, my spirits lift at the sound of his voice. For a minute, I can close my eyes and pretend we're still wrapped up in each other.

"Hey. I miss you too." Even with being happy to hear from him, I can't entirely keep a shadow from my voice.

"What're you doing?"

"Nothing exciting, I promise you." Unable to keep a sigh at bay, I shake my head. "It's tedium."

"Tedium? That's serious."

"Unfortunately, yes."

"You're not arranging a private bean collection alphabetically or anything terrible like that, I hope."

I laugh. Something frees up inside my chest. "No. I'd be useless at that without you. Even if I had a bean collection."

"Give it time," he teases.

Something in me leaps at the idea of more time with Blake. He says it so casually, like of course we have unlimited days before us, unlike the current clock ticking on his days before going back home to America. It's a thrill to think of doing anything with Blake, even organizing a hypothetical bean collection.

God, I have it bad.

"'Kay, so no bean organization. Book organization?"

"Well," I say glumly. "You're close with that one. Except my shop's still mostly cleared out from filming, my stock in boxes somewhere on one of your film crew's lorries. And the problem—one of them—is the floor. Apparently my assistant, Gemma, saw the damage happen. Alice Rutherford left an apologetic note, but I have no idea if they will actually fix this. Or how much it will cost me. Or how long it will take. Because every day the shop's closed is a day I'm losing money. They're not filming, so I don't think I'm getting any money for the location, either."

"Shit." Blake's frown is audible. "That's fucked."

"Yeah."

"Well," he says with authority. "Let me help."

"Blake, it's brilliant that you fixed my sink, but the floors—"

"I'm not going to fix the floors, don't worry—but I'll talk to Alice to make sure they do right away." His voice is tense. "They should have fixed it already."

"Well..."

"Leave it with me," Blake assures me. His easy confidence provides some comfort. I'm not used to letting anyone help me. Everything always needs to be sorted on my own. I want to protest, but it's a strange, comforting feeling knowing that he wants to help me.

"Are you sure?"

"'Course."

"'Kay." I draw a deep breath. I'll give him a chance to sort this out. "See you later to make plans for the weekend?"

"Wouldn't miss it. And don't worry, I'm going to talk to Alice right now."

With that, I hang up and sit back in my office chair. I'm still stressed, but with Blake's help, I feel less overwhelmed. Like maybe this is fixable after all.

When Blake arrives later, the shop has heated to the surface temperature of the sun. The usual curtains that cover the windows were packed away during the filming prep, and the curtains for filming taken away. The door's propped open for any hint of a breeze. A couple of ancient fans attempt to circulate air.

"Aubrey?" Blake calls into the mostly empty room, his voice echoing.

I emerge from my office to see him standing just inside the open door. He puts down an overnight bag against the wall.

Behind him, traffic's snarled with the Friday commute. A steady flow of foot traffic passes. This would be prime time for book sales. If only I had books. Never mind.

Instead, I thrill at the sight of him, lifting me again from the glum of the day's problems. Blake's in a form-fitting sky-blue shirt, a great contrast against his tan. And, thankfully, showing his well-toned arms. He takes off his sunglasses and grins. He draws me close, and we kiss to make heat of our own.

When we straighten, it takes a moment to bring me back.

"You all right? I've been worried. You sounded so down."

"Well..." I'd rather pretend I don't have problems with the shop and disappear into the fantasy of Blake. But he's looking at me so intently. "I'm mostly okay. I suppose. Except for the bits that…aren't."

He frowns. "Well, tell me. But first, look what I found. It's rare in your country."

Blake produces cold beer and crisps from another bag. "Let's have a picnic for now and then order something or go out. What do you think?"

"Brilliant."

I lock up the front door, turning to see Blake scowl at the damaged floor. He's crouched, running his fingers along one of the deep ruts.

"I'm so sorry," he says.

I sigh.

"But I have good news."

"Oh?"

We walk through to the back and climb the stairs to my flat, which is also hot. At least the air moves more up here with the open windows. Blake sets out our picnic. The cold lager's refreshing.

"I talked to Alice," Blake tells me after opening the crisps. "And I got mad that they hadn't fixed things already. She promised me that they would have someone come tomorrow—"

Disappointment knots in my stomach. So much for our plans to get away.

"Thanks." Unfortunately, I sound more disappointed than thrilled.

Blake frowns at me, worried. "Is that not good? I just wanted to help."

"No, no, it's good. Thanks. Just…I was looking forward to a weekend mini-break with you," I confess sheepishly. Though that will cost too, but I don't want to be a drag either. "Obviously the floors need to be fixed as soon as possible."

Blake's expression softens. "I'm looking forward to going

away too." He's quiet for a moment. "Could your assistant help? Like, could she supervise?"

"Her supervision is how this happened in the first place." I sigh. "Maybe. I can ask her."

He brightens. "If she can help, the weekend's saved."

The only problem is that Gemma's help comes with a price tag.

"This is all so expensive. I just…maybe I shouldn't." I reach for the crisps set on the coffee table. Blake's beside me on the sofa.

"On that note," Blake says, "I have some news."

"Oh? What sort of news?"

Blake's smile gives me hope.

"Yeah, news," he confirms. "Great news. The production company's covering not only the cost of all repairs, but every day you're closed too. Original hardwood floors better than the ones you had. And they're paying for every day till you can fully open again."

I brighten a little at that. "Really?"

"Really." He squeezes my hand.

"It sounds too good to be true."

"Apparently it's in your contract you signed, Alice says."

"You're right." Despite the heat, I lean into him. Blake wraps his arms around me. Like this, there's some hope.

"Thanks for looking into all of this for me." I give him a kiss, but I can't shake off my worries, even so. Not entirely.

He frowns. "You still have that look."

"What look?"

"A stressed look like you're thinking of fifteen different things all at the same time. What is it?"

"It's not what you've done," I assure Blake. "That's brilliant. It's just…well, I'm behind on the shop's bills and now the flat too and…all of this might not be enough. I mean, I shouldn't spend more money on anything, really."

Blake gives me a kiss. "Listen. The weekend escape is my treat. If you still want to escape with me, that is."

"Of course I do," I blurt instantly.

He laughs, looking relieved. "Oh, good."

"Sorry. It's just been so much worrying about the shop, you know? I'm behind on a lot and the film's helping short-term, but I don't know how I can get out of this hole. Or if I even can, how I won't end up in the same place six months from now."

It's a lot to think about. I'm mad at myself for even thinking about any of this while Blake's here, just wanting to enjoy the very limited time we have together. Anything beyond this is a dream, no matter how much I want him.

He squeezes me lightly. "I'm very glad you're telling me. I want to know about you. And help."

"You're fantastic, did I tell you that?" I sigh, leaning into him.

Affectionately, he nuzzles me. "All you need to worry about this weekend is relaxing."

"God, I'm going to miss you." That tumbles out before I can help it too. That's the problem with Blake. He's so disarming I find myself saying all kinds of things I don't say to anyone, not even Lily.

"I'm not going anywhere yet, gorgeous. Now. Let me spoil you and take you away this weekend, if you'll let me?"

"'Kay. What did you have in mind?"

"I hear the Lake District's beautiful. We can grab a rental car and do some hiking. Or hillwalking, as I hear the locals call it. Get a little cottage for a couple of days. What do you think?"

Part of me wants to stress and protest at the cost. The other part of me thrills at being taken care of by Blake, his careful attention. In response, I kiss him. And he kisses me.

Then, we spend the evening making arrangements.

Gemma agrees to come help with supervising repairs at the shop. Blake and I scroll through cottages and book one.

It's wonderful, the idea of having Blake to myself for a few days in a world of our own.

Chapter Fourteen

We fuck right off on Friday morning, as Blake's filming breaks before their last push before wrapping, all the way up to the Lake District. It's an expanse of a palette of greens and sweeping skies and brooding clouds over mountains, a respite from the heat island of London and a break finally in the relentless heat wave of the last week.

But first, there's the getting-there part. We pick up a hire car and we set off on the motorway north, fueled with plenty of vegan snacks and a buffet of crisps by way of cultural introduction. A couple of times I white-knuckle it on the *oh shit* handle as he gets used to right-hand driving, but luckily he's a quick study. At any rate, he's a confident driver, like everything else he does.

We've got enough clothes for a couple of nights, along with my dad's guitar. Knowing my dad, he probably wouldn't have wanted me sitting around getting too precious about it. Last night, I did my best to condition my old hiking boots, which are more or less in shambles and past ready for retirement. They're from the days when Eli and I would take off to the

South Downs or further afield for a change of scene. From the times I would stomp through tall grasses for the perfect shot or during frosty mornings or with fog rolling through broad pastures.

We have a holiday cottage, a private getaway as promised. Blake at least lets me pay for petrol and the snack buffet. To compensate, there's also plenty of veggie crisps, dried seeds, mixed nuts, and wasabi peas that I picked up from the organic grocer's while Blake picked up the car. We stop to collect the keys to our cottage after hours cooped up in the car.

When we pull into the gravel lot by the low stone cottage, the afternoon threatens rain. It's a relief after the scorching few days. Out here, I feel like I can finally draw in a deep breath, even with the adrenaline of this rural idyllic escape with Blake. It's uncharted territory, just him and me, away from film sets and damaged bookshops, and the ghosts that chase me.

He parks and we step out into a fine mist.

Blake outstretches his arms broadly, smiling with his eyes closed. "Oh, this is perfect."

I can't help a grin at how blissed out he is. I tug on the hood of my light jacket. "This is the normal weather in my country. I'm glad it's finally delivering."

He returns the grin and comes close to draw me into his arms, into a deep kiss. There's no one around, just rain and grazing sheep off in the distance, and the rustle of leaves in the light breeze from the nearby trees. A bird sings, and there's a stillness and peace I haven't felt in a very long time. The sort of peace that doesn't exist in the heart of London.

Blake catches my face between his hands, gazing affectionately at me. "We made it."

"We did," I confirm, and greedily I steal another kiss. It's him and me and Cumbria is all ours this afternoon, without another human in sight. It's perfect. And then I smother a yawn and he laughs.

"Am I boring you already?"

"Oh no. It's just I'm not used to long car rides. Long anything, really."

"Really? I might have something for you that you'd be interested in," Blake teases, pressing into me with promise. "Well, we can have a nap and a lazy night."

So we go in and check out the quaint cottage from an era gone by, all traditional furniture and paisley print cushions and matching curtains. There's a working hearth with fire, if it gets cool enough later. A small kitchenette is off to the side, with the all-important kettle. Being me, I've brought along a selection of tea in my pack. A bowl of fresh fruit sits on the counter along with a welcome note. It's all quite perfect and Blake draws me down on a proper bed. And we make out till we finally give in to the drowsy, lazy afternoon and fall asleep to the patter of rain, held in each other's arms.

The evening passes quietly, with us holed up in the cottage, and both of us getting an actual decent night's sleep with the cooler temperatures. For me, the cottage also means the luxury of a real bed.

Today, the sky brightens. We put on our hillwalking gear and off we go tromping about through farmer's fields and windswept paths and along green tracks. We come across few people along the way, eventually rewarded with vistas over villages and expanses of lakes. Our reward at the end of it when the next squall rolls in is putting our feet up in a local pub and drying off.

We kick off the mud from our boots and hole up in a corner together, in a mix of locals and other hillwalkers. Everyone is happy to be dry inside.

After I return to Blake with two ales, we reward ourselves for our efforts and clink glasses.

"Not a bad way to spend a day," Blake says, still smiling from our adventure.

"Not bad," I agree, and I could happily spend a lot of days tromping about with Blake outdoors. We both brought our cameras and enjoyed some photography along the way.

"I've got the bean of the day for you." Light-hearted, I smile affectionately at Blake, unexpected brain chemicals making me happy, almost giddy. See, I can do new tricks.

"Bean of the day!" Blake beams over his ale, looking a bit like a mountain man today in his thermal top and five o'clock shadow, a bandana around his neck and sunglasses on his head. "You've got my attention."

"I've got a clue." I give him an intent look. "It's white."

"Ooh, let me guess: navy bean, broad bean, the actual white bean."

I make a face at him, wrinkling my nose. "That's cheating. There's no such thing as an actual white bean. Cop-out."

"There really is such a thing," he assures me with an irreverent sparkle in his eye. Was there a time when I was Blakeless, without any bean banter in my life?

"Another clue."

"I'm all ears."

"It's got a black bit."

"Oh! Black-eyed bean." Blake looks at me, triumphant. "Easy."

I gawp. "Seriously? How did you guess that so fast?"

"I know my beans, remember? Runner-up would be the pinto bean, but those have brown spots on them."

Harrumphing, I sip my ale to nurse the abject loss of stumping Blake over beans. Really, I ought to know better than go head-to-head with a vegan over legumes, but sometimes I go a bit off the rails.

"They're one of my favorites." Blake looks at me hopefully. "Great in soups."

"Yeah?" I give him a skeptical look.

"Delicious, in fact. I'll make it for you sometime."

I blink. "You'd cook for me?"

"Of course I would. I love cooking."

"Imagine." It's hard to imagine, actually. But seeing as Blake has a handle on things, from beans to DIY, why should cooking come as a surprise? Somehow, I've generally failed to adult appropriately. The idea of being taken care of by him, though, sends a ripple up my spine. Even if it's bean-related care.

"Well, I didn't see a ton of vegan options on the menu," I tell him. "But there's green salad and chips, if that's all right. Maybe they can make a sandwich with veg instead. I don't know how well cut out country pubs are for vegans."

"Don't worry, I'm very adaptable." He grins.

I feel my face growing hot. "Good to keep in mind for future reference. What else should I know about you?"

"Oh, you think there's more to know?" Blake teases.

"Could be," I drawl back. "Who knows what else you've got."

"Ideas. Loads of ideas."

"Ideas about what?" I peer at him, smiling.

"Not just filthy ideas." Blake's grin warms me. "Even practical ones."

"Go on. I'm intrigued."

"For your shop, even."

Now he has my attention. "What sort of ideas?"

"Well, you said it's struggling. If you want, I can help you come up with a plan to turn things around."

"This isn't a snake oil salesman trick?" I smile, but even my hope is tempered against the current reality of the shop.

"Oh no. I'm fresh out of that. I'm actually qualified to

help."

I laugh. Blake looks so earnest. "Tell me more."

"I'm a marketing major. But I never used it. But I've taken business courses too. I can help you come up with a business plan. Like, a short-term plan helping toward a long-term plan. You know, one-year plan versus five-year plan. We can look at your publicity and marketing, online sales, things like that."

I just stare at him. Blake's talking some other language. Things I should probably know about, but frankly, don't.

He grins. "See? I'm totally the guy you need."

"Holy shit, Blake."

Blake laughs with delight. "Really, I'll help if you let me. And you?"

"I definitely don't have a marketing degree. Obviously."

"What did you study?" he asks.

"Two guesses and the first two don't count."

"I'm gonna go with English?"

"Literature," I agree. "Predictable me. Surprise, surprise."

"Hardly. But I know you love books. When did you finish?"

I cough and glance away. "I, er, didn't."

Blake looks surprised. "You didn't? You love everything to do with books from what I can tell."

"It wasn't that I didn't want to finish. Just...well, life happened instead. I needed to work, to help my mum after my dad died. So, I stopped going." I hold his gaze, feeling a familiar heat in my face whenever the subject of uni comes up. Which inevitably makes me think of my dad. And thinking of my dad usually makes me sad. I carefully steer my thoughts away from him. There's a time and a place to feel his loss, but today isn't such a day.

"Sorry. Didn't mean to make things awkward. Ask me

anything." He squeezes my hand.

"So why didn't you use your marketing degree?"

"Acting," Blake says simply. "Instead of getting a real job, I worked odd jobs after graduation, because that works best around auditions and parts and moving around the country all of the time for roles. I'd already landed a few small parts by the time I finished college. My dad thinks I've made a mess of my future. Joke's on him—I can wait tables anywhere now."

"Sounds like a useful degree, at least," I say wryly. "Strangely, the world isn't clamoring for lit grads. At least your degree will always be there if you ever want to work in marketing. If I had actually taken any business training, I'd probably be a lot better off than I am now."

"The world is making poor choices, and there's plenty enough people with business degrees," says Blake firmly, glancing at me. "We need more readers and artists and creatives. They're the real visionaries. The rest is just capitalism. And if you really want, you can still take business classes."

"I wouldn't call myself a visionary."

"I would," he says cheerfully. "From what I can tell, you have lots of talents."

"Rumors."

We grin at each other. Feeling buoyed, it's easy to feel optimistic about the future with Blake's encouragement. With Blake. Like we'll have unlimited time to figure everything out.

Like America isn't next week. But America's out of mind now. Instead we dine and tease and joke the evening away.

When we're back at the stone cottage, seated together in front of the fire, we take turns playing on the old guitar. Of course Blake's brilliant. How could he not be? The way he looks at me as he sings undoes me and my worries.

And after the liquid silk of his voice, his unwavering gaze,

Blake sets the guitar down. A sultry moment hangs between us. In the twilight, his eyes are deep blue, his mouth slightly parted. The way he savors me is my undoing. It's amazing how quickly he's become so important to me.

I reach over to brush his lips teasingly with my fingers. He nips, holding my finger between his teeth a moment till release.

"Naughty," I drawl, sliding my hand along his jaw, safely out of teeth range, savoring the shudder that ripples through him. Shifting, I slide onto his lap to straddle him and wrap my arms around his neck. He's already stiff. I can feel that. Like I'm already hard too.

Blake's fingers grip my arse.

When I brush my lips against his, he shudders in my arms.

"I wouldn't mind," he murmurs between our teasing kisses, slightly breathless, "seeing more of your talents."

"Is that right?" My mouth travels to his jaw and throat as I work to unbutton his shirt. He returns the favor with clumsy fingers. Under my hands and kisses, his chest rises and falls with his quickening breath. I lick a path along his collarbone and he moans.

Like I needed more encouragement, unwrapping this gift of a man. Of course, I pause for a moment to admire his well-built physique. He gasps when I tweak his nipple, slide my hand down to tease him through his jeans.

With a growl and in one fluid motion, Blake scoops me up in his arms. Wrapping my legs around him, it's my turn for uneven breathing as he places me on my back on the sofa. Urgently, he yanks open my shirt. A button skitters across the hardwood floor while I make short work of unfastening his belt and fly.

"God." Blake's gasping hard.

"It's Aubrey. Aubs if you're cheeky."

I kiss him hard as he slides his hands against my ribs, and

then I'm helping him with my belt and jeans. Once I'm free, he hauls off my boxers and jeans with some effort, frowning.

"Fucking skinny jeans."

I grin at him, how focused and urgent he is—and so incredibly hot.

The rain drums against the window as he pauses just long enough to go over to his suitcase for a condom and lube. It's a great opportunity to admire him, mussed dark hair, flushed face, rigid cock reaching to the sky.

"C'mere," I demand. And in a moment, he's back in my arms, and we're caught tangled together on the sofa, the rub of his cock against my arse. Lube-slick, he presses in, burying his face against my neck and shoulder with a shudder.

"Oh— Blake—"

I'm begging and urgent and feral. Our kisses are fierce. My cock strains and…fuck. Just, *fuck*.

"You're so hot." Blake's arms are powerful and his mouth blazes on mine. And as the summer storm thunders overhead, there's no one around to hear our cries. There's Blake and there's me, and our urgency while he rides me.

"I want you." Grasping at him, it's the last coherent thing I say.

Blake mutters nonsense against my ear. His stubble's rough on the side of my face. And I don't care, because I don't ever want him to stop.

And when I can't take it any longer, the amazing feeling of him inside me, I make desperate, incoherent noises as his hand works my cock. Arching, I spurt messily all over us. We're pressed together, sticky with cum and sweat. Then he comes, bucking against me, holding my wrist roughly with his other hand.

He thrusts a sharp rhythm of my heartbeat, of the beat we make together. And eventually, Blake sags against me, his face still pressed against my neck. And we are left quiet and reverent. He's trembling, from effort or emotion, I don't know, but it's fucking hot and I wrap my arms and legs tighter around him.

At last, he lifts his head. His face is soft by the firelight. He kisses me reverently, like I'm to be cherished. And I do the same. And we forget about the world beyond the cottage, or the ocean between our homes. Because all that matters right now is that we're together, far away from the frenetic energy of London, where time's suspended. Out here in Cumbria, it's just us, together.

Sometime in the dead of night, there's a ringing by my head. On the bedside table, my phone comes to life, incessantly bright and buzzing. I should have shut the stupid thing off before we went to bed.

But then a thought comes to me through my disorientation. I'm not in my bed. There's a man beside me. Blake—and not a Grindr offering. Or my ex.

I groan sleepily, determined to ignore the phone, but what if it's something important?

What if it's Mum, and something's happened? Or even Gemma? A cold fear grips me and gives me a sharp kick to wakefulness.

I reach for the phone and answer in a half-alert state, sleep still thick on my tongue while my brain scrambles to make sense of what's happening. "H'llo?"

"Aubrey?"

And it's Eli.

Why is Eli calling at 3:00 a.m.? My stomach knots with dread.

Even in that one word—my name—I know him so well that I know he's out of sorts, all jangled, and something's wrong.

"It's me," I say. "Just give me a sec."

I sit up and push hair out of my eyes. Through the slightly open door of the bedroom, we left the cabinet lights on in the kitchen as a nightlight in an unfamiliar space. Not wanting to disturb Blake more than I have already, I find shorts and a hoodie in the dark and head out into the chill air away from the heat of Blake and our bed.

Along the way, I pause to dress and try to wake up a little.

"Right, you've got me now." I gulp, bracing myself. Something's definitely wrong for him to call at this hour. It's not his style. It would make more sense for Mum to call, but obviously it's not her. Ryan, maybe? "What's happened?"

A nervous laugh. Have I ever heard Eli get nervous before? Probably it's genetically impossible for him.

"Eli?"

There's silence and a sigh. "Me and Ryan had a fight."

I blink. "No one's dead?"

"Jesus. No. Why would you—"

"Because it's three in the fucking morning, that's why," I retort, pacing the length of the cottage, passing by the kettle, pausing long enough to fill it and turn it on. "No sane person calls another at this hour unless it's an emergency. Or you're really, really drunk."

"Well, it's an emergency to me," says Eli, wavering. Emotion is all caught up thick in his throat. "I didn't realize the time. I had a few drinks and…I didn't know who else to call."

I groan, shaking my head. "Where's Ryan? Can't you spend this time working things out with him and I can go back to bed? Because, honestly, you lost the right to call me at stupid o'clock a long time ago."

Awkward silence drops like a lead weight.

"I deserved that," Eli says. "Sorry. To answer your

question, Ryan's home. I've come to the office."

"Your other home." At the kitchen counter, I fidget with the tea mug I've pulled out. What sort of tea is good for 3:00 a.m. drama when I should be sleeping? I have a peppermint tea sachet in the small tin I brought and set that out for when the kettle's ready.

"I guess."

"Soo..." I prod at Eli as best I can over the line. "You called me to announce that you had a fight with Ryan. And what can I do about that? What did you fight over? Also, can't we have this conversation in daylight hours, like normal people?"

Fuck knows who's normal these days, or what that even looks like. But five past three is, at the very least, an antisocial hour ripe for kicking. He should have the decency to be at least a little embarrassed by the hour, but nope.

Eli's swallow is audible on the line. "Like I said, I didn't know who to call. And you're always good at listening, Aubs."

Part of me bristles at the nickname he has for me, an intimacy he doesn't deserve. Not now. Not after leaving me. Another part of me is flailing madly in the dark, desperate to hear more. What is wrong with me? There's a strange vindication and satisfaction in knowing things are going pear-shaped for Eli. There's another part of me that hates that he's hurting.

"You still there?" he asks.

"I was...thinking." A quick cover. "Tell me about this fight."

"I don't know. We were grousing a bit at each other all evening. You know, one of those nights where everything goes wrong. It's all trivial stuff, but it added up. We went to the restaurant where I had made a reservation. They had no record of it. Then they didn't have space for Ryan's wheelchair so we had to wait quite a while for a table. Ryan wanted to leave, I wanted to stay. So I try to make it up to him by ordering food: the wrong meal comes for me, they forget his order. The waiter spills our wine—"

I can't quite help but laugh as I pour the water over the tea to steep. "Jesus, Eli, did you take him to the most shit restaurant London has to offer?"

"Hey. It had excellent reviews." He's defensive.

"I could be petty and say that I'm happy you had a shitty time."

"I know you're hurt—"

"You have no fucking clue what I am, actually," I say coolly. "So how did you get to the fighting part?"

"Then we had to get home, and the taxi was difficult about his wheelchair and that's when we had a terrible row in the street. And he said I wanted an able-bodied boyfriend and not him and his inconveniences, which is definitely not true, but then we kept fighting. And then things got really heated."

I sigh, the momentary joy for his misery going just as suddenly as it came. I feel bad for Ryan, who faces enough shit already, and it does sound like an epically crap night out. "What were you *actually* fighting about?"

"Aside from each of us saying the other's impossible to please?" Eli swallows again. A gulp of liquid, I think. Hopefully water and not booze.

"Don't fuck me around more than you already have."

Silence. Then—

"We fought about you, Aubrey."

"*Me?*" It takes a long moment. "What the *actual* fuck?"

"Ryan's convinced he's living in your shadow. That I'm comparing him to you. And it's not the same, it isn't. No two relationships are the same, of course. I know that. But... maybe he was a little bit right."

I rub my face wearily. Hot tears spring to my eyes, and

I white-knuckle grip the edge of the counter. "So then you fucking call me? That's fucked, Eli. You know it is."

"I didn't know what to do."

"I don't know. It's definitely not my problem. Go for a run? Do yoga? Work things out with Ryan?" I say pointedly. "And stop being an arse."

He's quiet. "You're right. Of course you're right. It's totally unfair of me to call and dump on you like this, in the middle of the night—"

"Damn right." I sip my tea through my tears. My voice, thankfully, doesn't give away anything. Not till one small snuffle as I sit quiet on the line, taking refuge by the embers of the evening fire. "I probably should go. I've got stuff to do."

"At three in the morning?" Eli asks blankly. "You starting new shop hours? Or is it because of the filming?"

"Well..." Indirectly, I suppose. The filming led me to Blake. Unavoidable Blake, who I kept crashing into, like some sort of gravitational osmosis that I couldn't escape. I'm far from one to believe in fate. More like forced proximity due to the small patch of turf between my shop and their filming setup.

And part of me bristles at the fact Eli thinks I just sit around in some sort of void, waiting for his call. Like I don't have anything else in my life. Or anyone. Like that afternoon in the shop when he stopped by and saw the bouquet.

"I'm out of town," I confess, emotion caught in my throat this time.

"Fuck, and I'm going on. Sorry. But—" I can hear Eli's frown over the line. "Why are you out of town?"

"Mini-break," I say simply. "You might've heard of them?"

Eli had delighted in out-of-town trips. Usually, I had to work Saturdays, which is how Gemma came to be hired as the weekend help, so we could occasionally get away. Then, maddeningly, by the time we broke up, I had come to rely on her to let me make the odd weekday errands and have the occasional weekend off, back when the shop was doing a little better.

Back when I was with Eli, and I had places to go.

And again I feel a wave of irritation that he thinks I wouldn't want to go anywhere on my own. "You don't think I like taking a break now and again?"

"I'm sure you do, but"—there's a long pause—"you don't really have the spare money, do you?"

"Fuck you, Eli," I snap at last, irritation reaching a flashpoint. God, he knows how to provoke me, and clearly he wants to fight with everyone tonight. "I'm out of town because I have a life that exists beyond you. Hard to imagine I'm not sat alone in my bedsit forever, I know. I'm not in some vacuum, waiting for your call. I need to go now and get back to bed. I suggest you go home and do the same."

"Sorry, sorry. I shouldn't have rung; it was a mistake."

"Obviously."

More awkward silence. We exchange some agonizingly awkward goodbyes and hang up.

I wipe my eyes on the cuff of my oversize hoodie. Stupid arsehole. Focusing on my tea instead, it's grounding, some familiar comfort, though I'm hundreds of miles from home, with a man that I'm only starting to know. A man who doesn't have the weight of history like Eli does, for better or for worse. Eli, who knows what buttons to push, how to play me till I'm wound like a top careening wildly.

Fuck, I really hope Blake didn't hear any of that. Once the tea's finished, I slink back to bed. If he's awake, he shows no sign of stirring, and so I curl up around him.

Sleep doesn't come for ages and I'm left far too alone with the agony of my Eli-related thoughts.

Chapter Fifteen

The next morning is cool and rainy. Dark clouds hang low, practically scraping their bellies on the woods that surround us. In our waterproofs after breakfast, we head out early to take advantage of the beauty outside of our door before we have to return to the reality of London later tonight. We walk a track along a small, meandering creek.

"Are you going to tell me about that 3:00 a.m. call?" Blake asks after we've been walking for about twenty minutes. We've already gone through a lightning round of bean trivia: *a bean named after an organ*—kidney bean. *Bean with an identity crisis*—fava, faba, or broad bean, the Janus of beans.

I cringe and give Blake a sidelong glance. He's in a black waterproof, hood up, wearing a wry expression. My heart's in my throat or quite possibly caught in my mouth at this point.

"I was hoping you'd missed that," I confess. "There's not much to say. It's not important. It was a round of stupidity, to be honest."

"It sounded…heated."

"I guess, by the end." I pause and sigh, shifting my pack

on my shoulder. I'm in everything blue: blue waterproof, blue bag, even blue thermals underneath it all. And, to be honest, I feel lost this morning in a bit of a blue place. Trust Eli to provoke me, to stir things up that I thought had been put to rest last year. "It was just my ex. Being stupid."

"Oh?" Blake's expression is hard to read. Remote.

"He had a fight with his boyfriend. Eli apparently decided calling me was the appropriate response." I roll my eyes. "The man made his own bed and he should go lie in it. I told him to go deal."

"Makes sense." We resume walking, side by side. He glances at me again. "This is the same ex you told me about?"

My only ex.

"Um. Yeah."

"The one you got the heart tattoo for?"

Double cringe. I give him a sharp look back. "Well…yes. To be honest. I was young and dumb. Dumber than I am now. I'd like to think I've wised up with age."

More silence as we walk, the drum of rain on our waterproofs giving a staccato rhythm to the day. Before us, verdant fields give way to mountains. Our destination is a pub before we loop back on the higher trail.

"You were on the phone a long time."

"Longer than I meant to be," I concede. "I'm sorry. I didn't mean to wake you. I mean, obviously Eli called, and I answered. I should have cut to the chase immediately and told him to go fuck off."

He's looking at me. Still unreadable. And I'm definitely starting to feel like I'm failing at something important. "What was the fight about?"

"Hard to say, really. Him and Ryan were squabbling about things, from getting his wheelchair into a restaurant and taxi, to…well, me," I admit sheepishly.

Blake nods, digesting all of this as we walk.

"And that's it, really. I hope he went home after that to sort things out with Ryan."

I glance over at Blake. His profile, like the rest of him, is striking. His lips twist.

"Aubrey?"

"Yes?"

"Why didn't you tell him about me? That I was the reason you were out of town."

And now I realize what that expression is: hurt.

I don't know how to process that. "I didn't realize we were at that stage of telling people about…things." I wave a hand helplessly.

Shit.

We stop again as the rain comes down harder, and of course we're having this conversation in a downpour, because why wouldn't we?

He frowns at me. "Aren't I important to you?"

"Of *course* you're important to me. I mean, I'm here, right? With you."

"But you didn't tell him. Eli. The man who broke your heart."

"Well—I know you're private or, I guess, selectively public about things—" And true, he's put a couple of scenic shots onto his Instagram, but certainly not of us out here.

"It's a cop-out," he counters, giving me a hard stare. "You need to figure out who you're protecting in this situation. Him? Me? Or yourself?"

I open my mouth to protest. And it stings. "All of the above, I guess? I don't know. I mean, what are we doing, exactly? Maybe we should figure that out."

"Maybe you've already figured it out if you're fielding intense calls from your ex in the middle of the night and giving space to that?"

"Don't tell me you're jealous of my daft ex—"

"Why wouldn't I be jealous, or hurt, or whatever you want to call it, when you get a call like that and don't think it important enough to tell me about it yourself? Like I don't matter in your world, like I don't even register," Blake retorts, arms folded tight across his chest. He's glorious but angry, and it's hard to know if that's just rain on his face or tears too. I could probably say the same for myself.

"Of course you matter!" I stare at him, pushing wet hair out of my eyes. "Blake. God. Listen. I've never met anyone like you before. You're hot, sexy, funny. And you see a lot more in me than I see in myself. I didn't tell you about the call because Eli was just jerking me around. Not because there's anything there."

"Are you sure?" he asks gently. "Because I think you're holding on to the past pretty tight."

I open my mouth again to protest, but once more, he's nailing truths into my heart that are altogether too true. "I'm sorry. I should have told Eli about you. That we were away for the weekend."

"I think..." says Blake slowly, dragging a scuffed toe of his boot through the grass. He looks hurt. "You need to figure out why you didn't."

"Who have you told about me?" I counter, stung. As if I'm someone to talk about. As if Eli deserves to know what's going on in my life anymore.

Blake's eyes widen. His mouth opens and shuts. "I haven't...yet," he confesses.

With a sigh, I nod. Of course he hasn't told anyone about me. Why would he? "To be honest, I'm having a hard time believing any of this is real. That someone like you would want someone like...well, me. Ordinary Aubrey. And yes, you're right, I have too many ghosts, and I didn't handle that call well, and I should have set some fucking limits, but I didn't. And I'm scared to actually like you too much, because you're going to go back to America next week, and where does that leave me? Alone yet again, that's what."

It all tumbles out, messy and hot, words that won't stop, my mouth going faster than my brain. And it's visceral, this pain. Like I'm already grieving a future loss. Steeling against the inevitable loss when Blake comes back to his senses and he sees me for who I am—just some guy running a shop that's basically doomed, and like Eli pointed out, a guy who's totally broke to boot. Yay, me. Winning hearts and minds.

We stare at each other.

His mouth twitches again. "Most of this is on you. I told you—I really like you. You need to sort your shit out, Aubrey."

So we stand in an awkward silence for an excruciatingly long time, a stalemate where we're both hurt, where everything's all wrong.

"What're we even doing?" I manage eventually, shaking my head. "You're going to have to go home—when, exactly?"

He straightens, holding my gaze. "Actually, I got a text from my agent that I need to go to L.A. for an audition."

"L.A.?" A cold shock hits my stomach hard. "As in, Los Angeles?"

He nods once. "Yeah, L.A. Tonight."

"What?" My face burns as we stare at each other. "Tonight? You—you weren't going to tell me?"

Blake deflates. Runs a hand over his wet face. "I don't know. I was trying to forget. Trying to extend things if I could, checking to see if I could go next week instead." He hesitates. "But it could be a chance at a breakout role. My agent said I shouldn't wait."

"It's what you've always wanted," I say, flat.

Blake looks defeated. "I guess. I mean, of course. I've worked so hard for it. And my family..."

"Then you should go," I manage. "And live your life like

you've been doing before we met. We can…we can meet up when you're back?"

"Yeah."

We stand and stare at each other. How did something so brilliant fall apart like this so quickly? My stomach twists. If only I hadn't answered that phone. If only I'd told Eli where I am, who I'm with. If only I had told Blake right away about the call.

Once back at the cottage, we pack up early.

"Would you take me to the station?" I ask softly in the car after we drop off our keys.

Blake looks at me, startled. "I can drive you back to London. I don't mind."

"I think it's better we went our own ways, don't you?" Listless, I gaze at him. "It's a long drive. Spare us a whole lot of awkward. I can give you some money for the petrol. It only seems fair."

How can it be two days ago that I felt light and free on the car ride up, like we were embarking together on some grand adventure, the two of us? Like maybe we were characters in the film he was shooting, like some fairy-tale rom-com where someone gets swept off their feet in a whirlwind romance? Except Blake's not a prince and I'm not a princess. There're not a lot of queer romances out there to model after, though I've always been one to forge my own way. But right now? Disaster.

"I don't know," Blake says unhappily. "I mean, I don't care about the petrol. But you can ride back with me. I don't mind."

"Please," I whisper, barely keeping it together. There are too many crashing thoughts in my skull, overwhelming me. The promise of Blake and the history of Eli that's always getting in the way of everything. And the obligations of my life, one that I haven't had a chance to live on my own terms, not really. "I think…I need to be alone for a while."

And at last he takes me to the station and I can't bear to kiss or hug him goodbye. It's going to be a long ride setting out back south to London, left alone with tears and two images on his Instagram and nowhere near enough on my camera to prove the whole thing ever happened outside of my own imagination.

Chapter Sixteen

The wait on the platform in the blustery afternoon is lonely. When I finally settle in my window seat on the train, the long ride to London is even lonelier. At least I have the two-person seats to myself without anyone beside me. My bag's been stashed by my feet. Something's missing—not just someone. And then I remember: Blake has my dad's guitar. Even if I resolved an hour ago to never see the man again, obviously I'll need to see him again to get the guitar back.

A headache squeezes my skull, an ever-tightening band around my forehead and temples. I've skipped lunch and won't get to eat something decent for hours yet. Somehow, I'm the one who ended up with the mixed nuts in my bag, and so I scavenge those and munch away while gloomily staring out at verdant views.

How could everything go so wrong, so fast? What's wrong with Eli? What's wrong with me that I didn't tell him to fuck off right away? Worse, what's wrong with me for not flat-out saying I was there with Blake?

Stupid, Aubrey. And now everything's fucked up.

Miserable, I sulk for a little while before pulling out my phone. In the train car, there's a pack of laughing teens at one end, others talking or on their phones. I'm hardly adding to the din if I make a call too.

My fingers hover over Blake's number, but no. I can't. Instead, I call Lily. She's probably busy. She's always busy. It'll go straight to messages and that's fine, because who rings rather than texts?

Of course she answers after the third ring. I can hear her frown on the phone. "Aubrey. What's wrong? I thought you were still away."

"Level five emergency." I crunch a nut to punctuate my unhappiness, a sacrificial almond.

"Obviously, because you're calling. Hang on. Let me get back to my office."

Right, work. Of course she's working. Selfishly, I didn't even think about that, that she might be doing legitimate things rather than waiting to field my drama. And it hits me that I'm calling to unload like Eli did to me, except with two important differences: one, it's not 3:00 a.m., and two, Lily and I haven't ever been in a romantic relationship.

"Sorry, Lil. I'm calling at a bad time."

"Nonsense. They have to wait for me anyway, and there's enough going on for them to do without me there for a few minutes. The show install is going as well as can be expected."

"That's good." I can only imagine Lily behind the scenes at her art gallery, calling the shots while people shuffle the art around to her specifications. "This isn't the Spain stuff, is it?"

"No, no. That's still in development. This is all about the influence of street art and punk rock in fashion. Very Alexander McQueen, plenty of skulls. Goth rating, ten out of ten."

Despite myself, my lips twist into a smile. "I didn't realize you were gothic, Lil."

"Want to come to the private view next week? Might cheer you up."

I hardly feel festive. "Maybe. We'll see."

"I'm back in my office now. Tell me everything. What's wrong?"

A groan escapes me. "It's stupid."

"Let's not make me drag things out of you again. I do need to get back before too long."

"Right, sorry. Well, Blake and I went away like I texted you. And we were having a great time hillwalking and relaxing in pubs. Till Eli called me in the middle of the night, having a crisis."

I hear Lily sucking back air. "He *what*?" Then a sharp exhale. "The jealous arsehole."

"No, no. He doesn't know about Blake. I haven't told him."

"You haven't told him?" she asks, incredulity in her voice. "Why not?"

Isn't that the question? "I don't know. Because this is so new? I mean, not telling Eli about him is part of the problem." I sigh. "Eli went on and on, upset after a fight with Ryan, with the punchline being that their fight was ultimately about me."

If I was there, I could imagine her wide-eyed gawp. Instead, I hear clicking. Probably some rapid-fire pen fidgeting, knowing her.

"You still there?" I ask.

"I'm so mad at Eli!" she explodes. "Why doesn't he deal with his own shit rather than bothering you in the middle of the night? Are you *sure* he doesn't know?"

"Mm, I didn't say anything and God knows I've kept Blake a secret from Gemma because I would never hear the end of it, which is easy enough because the shop's been a tip since the filming, and she hasn't been in. But Eli did stop by the day that Blake sent me an incredible bouquet of flowers, and then Blake came in. They met…somewhat. So, maybe on some level he knows something's up."

"I would dearly love to give the man a swift kick in the ankle. I mean, I would never actually do it, but I can't believe it," Lily moans. "Level five indeed."

"Then, I fucked things up even worse by not telling Blake about it, because I thought he slept through the call, but he must have heard at least part of it. And he brought it up the next day. And one thing led to another. I, er, didn't tell Eli about Blake and now Blake's upset. Course, he hasn't told anyone about me, like I'm some guilty secret. Which, fair, I'm nobody on the celebrity scale. *And* his filming wraps next week, and then he goes back to America and his regular life, and all of this is for nothing, anyway, right? To make things even worse, he has an audition in L.A. like right now and it's even worse than I thought, because he's leaving tonight. For a couple of days. So, he won't be back for long and then he's gone for good. So, you see, everything's ruined." I'm breathless from my monologue.

Silence. More pen clicking follows.

Meanwhile, I chew my lip as we pull into the next station. There's an announcement over the speakers, and through the mutterings of passengers, I can hear that the train is abruptly terminating service. And that we all need to wait for the next one. Nothing can be straightforward, can it? Not trains, not men.

"Sorry, this train's given up the ghost, I'm afraid. Bear with me while I get onto the platform."

And I do and she does. At least there's a bit of shelter from the rain. I go into the cramped waiting room, with its foggy windows from the muggy day. The clouds are low and gray outside, like a storm threatens but hasn't delivered yet.

"What a mess," Lily says at last.

"Hard agree." My unhappiness comes through my voice.

"I'm sorry. I want you to have good things. And some fun."

"It was surprisingly fun, till then. We'd actually been getting on and, er, getting to know each other—"

"So the sex was hot," she teases without mercy.

"Never you mind and maybe it was," I say hurriedly, flushing, "but we were on the same wavelength and finding out maybe we weren't entirely so different after all, and then...Eli and geography and timing. I'm on the train back alone. He's driving."

Lily tuts. "You didn't even ride back together?"

"I needed some time on my own. Plus, I thought that would be the end of it between us, but he has my dad's guitar. I need to see him to get it back." I groan.

She considers. "Maybe that's a good thing. You'll both be calmer by then, have had a chance to think. You can talk things over then, if you want."

"Doesn't change the simple fact that he's due back in short order to America, with the audition of a lifetime by the sounds of things. And my life is here with the shop. Which, by the way, has damages from the filming that I need to deal with when I get back, but it's just making my headache worse."

I chew my lip, watching as another train approaches. Everyone watches the board to see if this is the train for London. It is, and it'll be here in three minutes.

"Damages? What damages?" Lily's frown is in her voice.

"The floor. There're gouges and things. Some splintered bits. They're talking about fixing things this weekend. I don't know."

"That's not right, Aubrey. They should compensate you appropriately and make the repairs. It's their fault there's damage. That should be out of their pocket, not yours. Including compensation for the closures. And never mind the patching. Isn't there an agreement?"

"There is," I acknowledge, fidgeting with my pockets. "I guess...it's not just the shop disaster. There's everything with...a man that's not right either."

"Promise me that you'll talk to Blake too?"

I gulp as the train glides to a stop at the platform, and I weave my way outside. The angsty butterflies in my gut are having some sort of riot, though I'm not clear if the riot is over Blake, Eli, or far too many vegan snacks in the last three days. Or possibly not enough. At any rate, I'm out of sorts, but to be honest, I'm feeling resentful toward Eli. Like, Eli's had a whole year to get his shit together. It's as if by some finely honed instinct, he knows I'm starting to make moves toward something good and happy and mine, and then he appears like some sort of villain out of the shadows like some B-grade film that Blake would probably know about.

"I'll need to, won't I?" I say, getting onto the train and finding a seat.

"Hopefully with more enthusiasm than that," Lily says drily.

"Sorry, I was thinking about what an arse Eli is." Which is fair, because he is.

"God, I'm so mad at him. I'm tempted to give him an earful when I see him at Ryan's birthday—"

I groan at the reminder. "Right, Ryan's birthday. Shit."

Grimacing, I stare out at the sheep across the way, with all the lush pasture their woolly hearts could desire. Maybe I should start living out here too, away from everything hectic that I have to face in the city. The train glides through the countryside.

Of course I want to say, fuck no—to avoid Eli—and bail like a champion. Because awkward. But I feel a sense of duty. Ryan is my friend too. It's not his fault Eli's an arse.

"I don't want to ruin Ryan's day. How responsible of me," she laments, woeful. "You *are* coming to Ryan's birthday, aren't you? Would you bring Blake if he's free?" she asks hopefully. "I'd love to meet him."

"Yeah," I acknowledge. "I'm going. We'll see about Blake."

My stomach's still in knots from Cumbria and our abruptly ended getaway.

I can't believe I ruined things with him. Over stupid Eli.

"See you at the party?" she asks.

"See you then."

"Perfect." I can hear her grin over the phone.

I hang up and spend a few minutes chewing my lip, sighing wistfully and alternately scowling. I need to send an apology. I also need to send the bean of the day. I'm sure this is how mature people adult and make up, through legumes.

The train travels for a while and then glides to a stop in the middle of nowhere. Because of course it does. If the first train back had carried on as it should, it would have been an express service to London. Now I'm stuck on the milk-run train that doesn't even want to deliver milk.

While we wait, I scroll through an image search of unusual beans, wanting to stump him. Wanting him to know that I'm interested in things that matter to him, even if beans are a symbol of that.

I want him to know he matters to me.

And then I text him with a photo of exotic black and white dry beans, along with:

> *I'm sorry about our fight and not telling you about Eli's call. I understand you're angry and hurt. I realise that you have my dad's guitar—could we arrange for me to pick it up before you go? Also: gratuitous bean du jour. xx*

A few minutes later, my phone buzzes with a reply, much faster than I would have expected.

I'm sorry. You matter to me too. Where's your train getting in? I'll meet you. B.

I gulp. He wants to see me right away? Am I ready for that? He obviously made better time getting back to London with a car than my changes on the train and delays.

Euston Station in an hour. x

Silence. Then:

See you there.

When the train pulls into Euston Station, my stomach's tap-dancing, wrapped around my backbone from hunger. Nuts will only go so far. I down the last handful of them for courage. I have enough presence of mind to at least remember my overnight bag stashed by my feet, determined not to leave my belongings scattered across England. My bag's light since I'm still wearing my hiking boots, and I've only brought one slim book I've barely touched, rereading the same page several times over as my thoughts keep returning to Blake.

London's muggy and hot. Already, I miss Cumbria, especially the part pre-fight. Like greedily having Blake to myself. Or making out in bed like teenagers, all tangled up in each other's business, like we had all the time in the universe.

The sweltering day hits me as I reach the concourse, with a mix of emotions at once. Anxiety. Anticipation. Hope. Embarrassment. Okay, maybe not all the emotions on offer, but plenty enough to keep the adrenaline pumping. And enough to forget my hunger, at least temporarily.

Euston Station bustles with commuters and tourists. People drag suitcases and cluster in inconvenient places, while commuters deftly weave through the crowd on their familiar paths. Through all of this, somehow I spot Blake, holding the guitar in its battered hard case with familiar stickers. Definitely my guitar.

Definitely Blake.

Though I can't call him mine. Not quite. And maybe not ever.

There he is, gorgeous as ever, but uncharacteristically rumpled from the day of travel. Blake's got his backpack from the trip. He's obviously not had a chance to have a shower or get back to his hotel, but he still looks brilliant, tousle-haired. I don't think he could ever look terrible. He's in a light blue shirt, khaki shorts, Adidas trainers.

Blake looks at me anxiously, wide-eyed.

I gulp, approaching him.

Don't faint. Because seriously.

We stand facing each other. Blake grips the guitar case's handle like it's the only thing tethering him to Earth. As for me, I've forgotten to breathe again and the blood pounds in my ears as I gawp at him, the rawness on his face, the toll of the last few hours that have felt like a year and more.

It's too soon for someone to get all up inside my guts and mind and, worst of all, heart. And especially if that someone's from the other side of the planet. I shouldn't have fallen into serious like.

God, Aubrey, you're one sucker for impossible scenarios.

Too many fantasy books as a teenager has left me running full tilt to unreality, some secret romantic part of me. And that secret part of me seems to be all about the rom-coms, because I can't stop reading them lately.

"Hi," I say softly, searching his gaze.

It's Blake who anxiously chews on his lip.

"Here's your guitar," he says unnecessarily, making no move to hand it over. "I'd say it was a shameless ploy to see you again, but let's be real: I was too all over the place to take credit for that kind of planning."

He seems to be having the same sort of problem that I'm having. The unreality. Possibly the lack of breathing.

I swallow hard. "Thanks for bringing it to me. It means a lot."

You mean a lot.

Transfixed, we stare at each other. There're no adequate words to describe the tussle of feelings inside me. Thankfully, he's slightly more articulate.

"I know this sounds stupid, but I missed you like crazy. Even though it wasn't even a day." Blake's raw, open, the usual veneer of confidence gone, with someone much more uncertain in his place. Like a man who has everything to lose.

Except…how can I be that to him? So soon?

"I missed you too, Blake." His name catches in my throat, low and hoarse.

We continue to stare at each other like we're the last two men left on the planet, sole survivors of the zombie apocalypse. I feel just as raw as he looks. We're both, quite frankly, a mess.

"Where do we go from here?" I whisper uncertainly.

Blake shrugs, also looking lost. "I wish I knew. I wish… I don't know." He gulps.

Stupid Eli. Stupid me for giving Eli five seconds of my time and ruining this bright thing we had.

"If I had more time, I would've written you a song," Blake says, half joking, emotion caught in his throat.

I'm having that lack of air problem again. "You'd…you'd write a song for me?"

Startled, Blake looks at me intently. "Why *wouldn't* I write a song for you? You're incredible."

God, that does it. My face burns. I stuff my hands in my pockets, embarrassed.

"That's why I read poetry," he offers. "To help my songwriting."

I gaze at him, wide-eyed. "Probably past time for me to confess to writing poetry, then. To underscore my wanker credentials, and how I know firsthand poets are best avoided."

Blake's face brightens as if I've told him the most incredible secret. "You write?"

I look anywhere but at him. "Yeah. When I have time. And my poems are just short. They don't really count."

"Poems sound great."

When I dare glance back, he's beaming at me. Blake sets down the guitar case, opens it.

"What're you doing?" I blink at him. That's definitely my dad's guitar, cherry red, with old battle scars from his adventures back in the day.

Blake gulps. He pulls the guitar carefully out of the case and puts the strap around his neck. It's my turn to take over nervous lip-chewing for the pair of us.

Around us, people mutter at us standing in the way of everything and everyone, another knot of inconvenience to dodge. Announcements echo over the speakers, telling of cancellations and delays, train departures and platform updates. Nearby, a little girl runs shrieking with laughter from her mum. In the corner of my eye, I see a couple reuniting with enthusiastic kisses like nobody's around but them.

And, in all this, Blake's looking at me like I'm the only person here. Like the only one that matters. Gently, he plays a couple of chords, expertly adjusting the tuning. The guitar resonates through the buzz of the station. A couple of people glance over at us.

"You're...you're not about to do something horribly earnest, are you?" I ask breathlessly, the blood pounding again in my ears. I shiver despite the smothering heat even in the station, the din of the noise around us. My lips twitch into something dangerously near a smile. "I'm preemptively embarrassed. You should know that us Brits are experts in the indirect. In my case, possibly the obtuse."

"If we're talking angles, you're definitely acute," Blake says shamelessly with unbounded earnestness, making me laugh. He grins, buoyant.

And then, just as he gets my damned defenses down, he plays and sings without his gaze wavering from me, not even for a second, and I nearly die on the spot. His voice is melodic and the sap is singing "Crossfire" by Brandon Flowers, an indie-rock love song. I shiver, back in his arms in bed in the cottage, a summer storm rumbling overhead as we lost ourselves in discovering each other.

I'm...actually being serenaded? The attention's embarrassing, yes—but also *really* fucking romantic. Nobody's ever done that for me before. His voice fills the concourse and people stop to listen. He doesn't look away. I wouldn't dare. He's so incredibly talented, and I had no fucking clue. Not like this.

I can't breathe, all undone and wanting. Unsteady, I listen to him, wanting him, wanting a chance together. Maybe we can try again? Because I really do want to get to know him better.

What a strange, powerful realization. Against all odds.

And it's totally impossible, because he's going to leave, and yet he sings to me like I'm the only audience he cares about.

And it hits me that he's not singing *to* me—he's singing *for* me. Like a promise.

Then, I'm shaking, and when he's done, he puts the guitar down, comes over, and draws me into his arms while I hide my face in his shoulder. He smooths my hair and kisses me, and people applaud. I barely hear them, blanking on our audience because it's only Blake that matters as I lean into the comfort of his body.

"You're making a *scene*," I gasp inelegantly as he holds me and gives me a deep, lingering kiss that melts my knees, and who needs legs anyway? Overrated. "I can't believe you did that."

"I want you to know I'm awed by you," Blake murmurs. "You're someone I'm lucky to know."

And that does it. I tremble as he holds me tight, whispering things in my ear that only I can hear, and how can I be so unraveled, so quickly, by such a man?

"Why're you doing this, when you're leaving so soon?" I whisper. "It's only going to make things a lot harder when you have to go home for good."

"Because you matter so much to me, don't you see?" Blake's lips are against my ear. His hands are comforting in the small of my back, tracing my skin under my T-shirt.

"I think I'm getting the idea."

At last we straighten. I wipe my eyes on the cuff of my hoodie.

"L.A.'s only temporary."

I take a shuddering breath, straightening at last. L.A. may be temporary, but when he finishes filming for good, he'll be gone forever.

Is there some impossible way to make this work, despite everything?

Blake's grin is huge. "C'mon. Let's get the hell out of here."

I grab him, kiss him something fierce. And there's more thundering applause and whistles before we get away at last, laughing hand in hand.

Chapter Seventeen

In the late afternoon, the heat's still on in central London.

At the moment, I don't care, because I'm with Blake and we're kissing like teenaged fools in front of the British Library. Kissing in proximity to a copyright library can only be a good omen, right?

Out here, everyone looks a touch sunburned or sun-flushed. Traffic's snarled; honks and shouts are a familiar backdrop on the Euston Road. Buses steadily navigate up and down the street. The exhaust fumes from the vehicles catches at the back of my throat. As we walk, we pause occasionally under the shade of a tree, or duck against a building for respite from the sun.

Suddenly, Blake turns to look at me with worry.

"You need a hat?"

I laugh. Of all the things I thought he might say at that moment, that was not amongst them. "A hat?"

"I don't want you to burn. You're so pale, you're just gonna burn, right?" Blake frets. He's irresistible at the best of times, but even more so when he's worried about me. He digs into his gray backpack, pulling out a navy-blue ball cap with some symbol of American sports ball that I fail to recognize because I know nothing about sports ball in any country, and I know even less about American sports ball than the average person.

He plonks the hat on my head, looking pleased. "There."

"Am I a dress-up doll now?" I tug on the brim of the hat. God knows what sort of fashion statement this makes, but the shade is welcome.

"Don't give me ideas," he teases, and I swat at him good-naturedly.

"Cheers. I think." I make a face at him, but it does feel a bit cooler now. "Maybe I should put on sun cream."

"Probably a good idea," he agrees.

"The north clearly has its own weather system." Hard to believe only a few hours ago we had overcast skies, and that we were in the woods. I already miss it, our private escape into nature and mountains.

"It was refreshing, I'll give you that. And beautiful." Blake smiles, holding my bag in one hand, the guitar in another, as I find my sun cream and slather some on, having stuffed my light jacket away. Now, I'm bare-armed in a lavender T-shirt and gray trousers.

"Where are we headed, anyway?" I glance up at him, pausing in my efforts, arms streaked white.

"Maybe my hotel? It's not far. I mean, if you want." Blake uncharacteristically reddens into an appealing shade like some delectable summer fruit. "If you still want to hang out with me, after everything."

I roll my eyes, going back to rubbing the lotion into my skin. "Seriously? After such a public display, I think we're good for at *least* five more minutes."

He laughs. "I'll take it."

"Where are you staying?"

"The Pullman." It's not far from my old UCL stomping grounds.

"I went to uni near there," I tell him. "I could tour you around later, if you want."

"Sounds great." He looks pleased as we resume walking.

"The BL was my refuge." I nod at the library as we go past. "Well, any library, really."

"Not surprised," he teases me.

"Let me guess—you were always out on a sports field or something."

Blake laughs. "Only sometimes. I did my share of library time too, don't worry. Even by choice."

"Shocked."

"Don't typecast me," Blake says affectionately.

We make our way past couples holding hands, families with prams. A cluster of tourists pull suitcases behind them.

Blake steals a kiss, then tugs my hand. "C'mon. We're here."

"What?" I blink at Blake, confused. Belatedly, He's leading me into a posh hotel. I've walked past it a million times, but I never paid it any attention, because it was well outside my budget and daily routine. The air-con hits like a wall right away, sending a welcome shiver up my spine. "You're staying *here*?"

Obviously, I know where and what the Pullman is. But I never knew anyone who would be flush enough with cash to actually stay in the chic hotel. Other than Eli, of course. Even on contract, he definitely earns more than me as an indie bookseller. But he lives not too far away and has no need for London hotels.

"Yup. We get special rates. Don't look at me like that." Blake laughs. "It's just a basic room. No fancy suite for me. But it's big enough that we can gather in a meeting room if we need to, rehearse, and it's right by the tube and station too, 'course."

Stunned, I let myself be led by the hand through the broad lobby, past dark chic mid-century style retro furniture and dramatic lighting, including a huge dazzling globe light over it all. He takes me to a bank of lifts up to the suites, crossing plush carpets where dirt wouldn't dare land.

In the lift, Blake slides his arms around me. I lean into the warmth of his body as he holds me close and kisses me in such a thoroughly devastating way it's all I can do to keep upright. He's holding me in mid-swoon like I'm some sort of Victorian heroine in one of the novels I sell, and he's enthusiastically ravishing me.

"Yeah—" I beg.

His kisses are greedy as he claims my mouth. And I claim him right back as I wrap my arms around him, pressing my hardening cock against his thigh in a promise. My hand slides down between the buttons of his fly to press into his stiff cock, which is rigid and full of its own promises too.

"Gonna fuck you right here if you're not careful—" Blake manages.

"Dare you."

"Oh—"

Our kisses and seeking hands are abruptly paused when the lift stops to let a well-groomed couple on, possibly escaped from some kind aspirational lifestyle blog, who stand in front of us.

We both try our best to look normal. I tremble with the strain of not laughing, my overwhelming desire for him. A sidelong glance rewards me with the sight of Blake, flushed. Our fingertips brush. I take his hand in mine, searing hot, and place it on my arse.

He shivers.

The lift stops at our floor and we make our way out past the couple without incident, laughing because we can't help it. It's a great stress breaker. Dizzy with pleasure, I follow him down the corridor along plush carpets to his room.

Inside the room—yes, it's a room and not a suite, but a generous double especially for the heart of London—we pause long enough to wash our hands and faces from the grime of travel and down some water. Then, we pick up where we started in the lift.

Right now, I'm doing my best to shut off my brain.

I try not to think about Blake leaving tonight for L.A. and the audition of a lifetime. Or next week when Blake leaves for good. When I'll be alone, again.

That's the part of me that wants to stay guarded, keep safe, keep the walls fortified and gated. But they've come down with an epic crash after our trip north and Blake's song at Euston, putting himself on the line like that. For me. To prove to me that I matter, even in front of strangers. That he's not embarrassed by me, but proud. Maybe it's an act, because he's an actor after all, but even actors don't kiss like this, I'm fairly certain.

It's one of the last coherent things I manage to think before Blake's pulled me onto the bed with him. We manage to take off our shoes and immediately lose ourselves in each other. His hands are on my back as I lie half sprawled on him, kissing him back just as passionately. Blake tugs off my hat, peels my shirt off, and I return the favor.

We pause long enough to gaze at each other, bare-chested.

"You…you think we should do this?" I ask, breathless. I'm already hard, my body more than willing. My brain is unfortunately more reluctant, damn thing. Why can't it be quiet, even for one day?

"You don't want to?" Blake frowns with concern, tracing my indigo dragon.

"Of course I *want* to, but don't you think it'll just make

things harder?" A line of goose bumps appears after his touch.

A struggle crosses his face. "Don't you want me?"

"God, Blake. I want you more than anything. I just…" I reach out to trace his lips, and he catches my finger between his teeth, giving a tentative nip.

"Just?"

"I don't want to be thoroughly devastated when you leave, is all." I whisper my guilty confession as he runs a hand along my jaw and throat, along my chest, and skims my ribs till I shudder. "But I think I'm going to be regardless. So maybe… maybe we just need to make the best of things right now."

He gazes at me and nods, serious as he considers me. "You're important to me, Aubrey. Even in this short time. Sometimes, I think, life brings us people we're supposed to meet. Like there's something we're supposed to learn. And I guess, having been through what I've been through, the only thing I've learned is that it's better to take a chance than not. Even if it hurts after. Because not knowing would hurt worst of all, I think. At least this way we might have something to remember."

"Or maybe I just end up with another ghost," I murmur, words catching in my throat and staying there. And another broken heart. Then, I kiss him reverently, and he pulls me down on the bed.

"I won't ghost you," he breathes, kissing a path down my chest as my fingers grip his hair.

I shudder. "That's not what I mean…"

Blake gazes up at me, eyes soft. "I know, gorgeous." He kisses my belly. "I—"

"Don't stop. What you're doing," I beg finally, unable to bear his stop-and-start fitful teasing any longer, arching into him. Like my body belongs to him, even after such a short time. "Please."

And he resumes with his mouth and his tongue and his fingers, pulling me out of my boxers before long, giving me a blowjob that leaves me seeing the stars and the moon and the entire galaxy, and quite possibly the next galaxy over, till I balance on the point of coming, but then I beg again, this time to stop.

"I need you to fuck me," I manage, reaching for Blake. He's still decent in his jeans, while I'm the one in an entirely compromised state, hanging out of my boxers and jeans. I wriggle out of them.

He chuckles and stands, stripping down to reveal an athletic body, tanned and sculpted and…oh. Those abs. Seriously, though. I just stare openly at him, because really, a body like that is purely made for gawping.

"I love the way you look at me." Blake grins, sliding out of his boxers at last, his cock already eager. "It's so fucking hot."

"I want you right now…" I growl desperately, fumbling for my wallet. Without ceremony or hesitation, I fling a condom at him.

He laughs at my eagerness, taking moment to put the condom on before drawing me close.

"Is this what you do with all of the Hollywood starlets?" I say between increasingly ragged kisses. "Ravish them?"

Blake laughs with delight. "There're no Hollywood starlets! Or stars. And you—well, you're the only one I want to ravish." He bites my shoulder for good measure and I groan with pleasure. He's rubbing his cock against my thigh in a way that's only making mine harder and me more nonsensical.

"Stop. Teasing." I gasp. "*Fuck.*"

He laughs, reaching for lube. And then a moment later, he catches me tight, drawing my legs up, and he's rubbing and then presses in deep as I cry out with the sensation of him, even wanting him as badly as I do.

"Don't stop."

He holds me tight, rocking with me, mumbling things into my hair, nice things I can't bear to listen to, but I can't make him stop. And then I'm sobbing and he stops and I beg him to continue again.

"Just...don't be so kind," I gasp.

And then he's rougher—and it's a lot easier to take.

The bites. The scratches. The sharp thrusts.

The way he pins me down and rides me, sweat-slick and urgent.

There's nothing but us, here and now. No last week. Or next week. Or future or past. We're just two people, caught in something raw. Something real.

Something that will disappear far too quick. But I want him to know he means something. More than something—he means everything, in such a small time.

Right now, we're locked together. Fingers dig into skin. Nails leave marks. Blake's body is mine—and mine belongs to him.

And when he comes explosively, riding me while I cry out with the want of him, coming taut and messy and wild, my nails dig into his arse. I hold him there till he collapses on me, panting. Eventually, he kisses me, and I still gasp.

"Imagine if we could do that all the time," I say, breathless.

Blake grins at me, equally breathless. "Dreamy."

"You'd have to get used to my rather shit bed, I'm afraid. Nothing posh in my flat." I dare glance at him but he's still smiling. "As you've seen, there's plenty of DIY potential."

"A real fixer-upper," Blake teases. "You might need someone who's good with tools."

Smiling, I shake my head. "Scraping the bottom of the barrel for jokes already, I see."

"I've been very restrained without a single tool joke so far, in my defense."

"You're clearly a man of dignity and honor."

"You'd patiently put up with my terrible jokes in return for the sofa bed."

"The foundation on which all brilliant relationships are built. Mutual tolerance," I drawl. "It's some hypothetical future."

In truth, the thought of a future with Blake in it is too overwhelming to think about, too fabulous and too heartbreaking. And he'll be gone very soon to L.A., a test run before he goes for good.

Blake kisses me thoroughly. I melt against his mouth.

"How long before you need to leave for your flight?" I ask.

"An hour."

"Better make the best of it," I tease, running a hand along his admirable chest.

We start all over again, like our lives depend on our urgency, nearly frantic, trying to commit each other to memory before America steals Blake away again.

Soon enough, there'll be no glorious Blake, no posh hotel. Just me alone in a cramped bedsit, with more memories to keep with the old ones—alone with books for company.

• • •

Two mornings later, I stop by the coffee shop, which has sustained me since Blake left, thanks to my friend Charlie giving me his key for the loo. I get a flat white and a couple of pastries to take back to Barnes Books. My mini-break is over. Blake's flying back. I'm sorting out what's happened with the repairs, plus there's a courier delivery after 10:00 a.m., so I can't get to the airport to meet him, though I saw him off the other night. Nothing like swinging full tilt into reality once again.

Already, the morning sun beats down on the city, promising another hot summer's day. Other merchants on my street are opening up for the day: the antiques shop, a couple of doors down, has their door open for air, old things flanking the entry. A barrister's bookcase. Vintage wine crates. An oak table in the window.

There's also a design shop, and I go in for my last dash hope for a gift for Ryan. Otherwise, my backup plan is a book. The colorful shop showcases everything from industrial product design of household things—bespoke tea kettles, whimsical china, silkscreened prints—to the handmade. And amongst all of the things I find a small framed block print of a Soho streetscape not far from their home. This seems safe. So I buy it and have it wrapped, and with relief return to the shop in time for the courier.

Gus, the usual courier who brings me offerings, does a double take when he sees the empty shop gleaming with newly installed floors. A few empty bookcases stand in a corner, with boxes beside them. "Trying a new look, Aubrey?"

"Mmm, what do you think?" I gaze around, hands on my hips, sunglasses pushed up on my hair. A smile plays on my lips. What has Blake done to me that I'm so happy, even in this mess that needs sorting? "Should I keep it?"

Gemma supervised the installation. The wall where there had been a hole is now repaired, no hint of any troubles with the fresh aubergine paint.

"Only if you're into hardcore minimalism." He scratches his jaw. "I kind of like the purple paint, though."

"Yeah, it's grown on me," I admit. The way the sunlight floods the shop in its newfound expanse of space is somehow comforting amid the havoc. "This happened because of filming," I explain.

"Ah, say no more." Gus claps me on the shoulder. "Good luck sorting this out, mate."

"I'm going to need it." I shake my head. Gus gets on with the business of bringing in fresh stock that I have nowhere to place, so he adds it to my growing collection of boxes.

And with newfound confidence, inspired possibly by Blake's usual ease at moving through the world, I bring my laptop out to the front counter and perch. This, at least, is familiar. The wrapped gift for Ryan sits beside me on a stack of books, my flat white providing a caffeinated lift. The first croissant disappears quickly.

My phone buzzes. I pick it up from the counter.

Landed at Heathrow. Have we ever talked about black beans?

I smile and text back. *Don't think so.*

Important fact: I ate a shocking amount of black bean tacos while I was in L.A.

Laughing, I shake my head, even though he can't see me.

If you're up for non-Mexican later, would you come with me to Ryan's birthday? x

Course.

A thrill runs through me at the thought of seeing Blake in a few hours, along with nerves about introducing him to my friends at last. Most of all, I can't wait to see him.

At last evening comes around, which means Blake. Which also, finally, means Ryan's birthday. With enough angst about introducing Blake to my friends to make an emo teen quiver, I get ready and do my best to make myself presentable.

In the end, I find a short-sleeved blue linen shirt and

some non-falling-apart jeans for a smart-casual sort of look with a bit of spit and polish on my old Docs. When Blake arrives on my doorstep, he's all designer chic in a crisp white shirt and gray jeans and a light cotton jacket. Behind him, twilight purples the sky. We kiss.

He's still delicious.

"Mm, missed you," murmurs Blake, whose hand along my jaw makes we want to drag him inside and forget about the whole party, but reason prevails. Or maybe duty. Lily would never let me live it down if I failed to bring Blake for her to meet.

"Missed you too. Tell me about the audition on the way?" It's only been a couple of days, but even that absence felt like a lifetime. The gift's tucked under my arm. "Ready?"

"You bet. How about you?" Blake's gaze is appraising as he gives me a wry smile.

"Gah. But I'll live. At least it's not their wedding day." I shake my head. "Sorry, it's petty. Should get over this."

"I don't see why you should," Blake says frankly. "Going to your ex's partner's birthday is a big ask."

"Well, Ryan's also my friend," I point out. "Even with everything."

It's true that Ryan was my friend first, after that day we met, when he fixed the flat tire on my bike. After that first night out with Eli for drinks, Ryan would stop by the shop regularly for books and a visit around closing time, when we would carry on to the pub around the corner once the shop was shuttered for the night. He was always good to his word—the night he failed to show up as planned left me sick to my stomach with unease. Later that night we found out through another common acquaintance about the dreadful accident up the street where a cyclist had been struck.

The rest is too awful to think about, but the guilt still lingers, knowing that Ryan had been on his way to see me.

Instead, my grip's tight on Blake's hand, anchoring me in the present day.

We walk along the evening streets of Soho. Cars are parked on curbs, queues of the fashionable waiting for restaurants snake down pavements, and pub patrons spill out onto the street. The evening crowds are cheerful, the night young.

"How was L.A.? And the audition?" I ask.

"L.A.'s epic as ever." Blake grins. "Though, really, it's a blur between time zones and taxis. I think I showed up at the right place and did the right audition. Hard to say."

"I don't even know how you're awake right now," I say frankly. "Did you sleep on the plane?"

"I did," Blake confirms. "Which is lucky because that's a long flight to L.A. from London. And back."

"I can't even imagine." I shake my head. "I've never been to America. To be honest, flying terrifies me."

Blake gives me a wry look as we walk. "It's not my favorite thing. I hear you, though."

I smile back. "So, tell me. What's the part? When do you find out if you got it?"

"I think I find out next week. They'll call my agent. And it's for another supporting actor role."

"Another rom-com?"

"Drama. Something to do with being an adventurer."

"Hmm. Sounds like you might be getting into rom-com territory there," I tease. "Adventure's hot. Unless you're on a doomed expedition."

He grins, kissing me as I stop in front of our destination. "I'm definitely rom-com adventurer hot for you. And I sure hope this isn't a doomed expedition."

"God, me too." I give him another kiss for luck. Here's hoping Eli can behave himself tonight.

Ryan's birthday's being held at a restaurant in a private

room, at least sparing me the discomfort of returning to my old home with Eli and having to pretend even harder that things are normal when they're anything but.

Outside the restaurant, we pause and I draw in a long breath. "Ready?" I ask.

The stomach butterflies are going overtime. It's the first time Blake's meeting any of my friends. Well, it's bigger than that. The idea of introducing Blake to Eli again—this time as my boyfriend—might be the end of me. And my nerves are getting the better of reason.

Eli's just a person, not some sort of specter coloring everything I do. Or am.

It's one thing to think that—quite another to feel it.

"Ready. It's gonna be fine." He squeezes my hand, and we go in.

Inside, the lights are low, the restaurant intimate. We're led to the private party room, where mercifully about a dozen people are already gathered. That means I can do the human shield thing from Eli for a while.

Ryan and Eli are at one end of the room. Ryan looks great, sleek dark hair, a pink shirt, happy. Holding on to Blake's hand for strength with a rather vise-like grip, I approach tentatively. So much for using my body for protection in an authoritative way. Best laid plans and all of that.

Ryan notices me first and brightens at the sight of me. "Aubrey! So glad you could make it."

"Thanks for the invite." I gulp air. "Ryan, this is Blake."

He's obviously intrigued as he takes in the vision that is Blake, all good looks and ready smile. "Pleased to meet you," Blake says as they shake hands. "Hope you don't mind me tagging along as Aubrey's plus-one."

"Not at all. Glad you could make it."

"We have a small something for your collection." I offer the gift to Ryan, who accepts the package.

"You're spoiling me. Cheers, both." Ryan admires the package and wheels the short distance over to put it on the side table that holds a growing collection of gifts and cards. "Please, settle in and make yourselves comfortable. Lily's running late but should be here soon."

"I hadn't heard from her, so I figured she had an intense day," I acknowledge.

Eli's engrossed with a couple of other guests who I don't recognize, and I don't quite feel ready to intrude and go over to say hi.

We circle back to our seats.

Barely seated, Lily arrives in a rush of adrenaline herself. "God, I'm so sorry I'm late," she says to me, shaking her head. "Had a late art courier with a delivery that I needed to take care of, and then I needed to make my way over. Traffic was dreadful—"

Then she looks at Blake and does a double take. "Oh!"

Laughing, I take the opportunity to make introductions. "Lily, this is Blake."

Lily leans in to exchange air kisses with him and then me. "Aubrey's a dear friend of mine. And I'm so pleased to meet you. I've heard good things."

My face warms and even Blake goes a little pink at this acknowledgment that I have indeed told other people about him in my life.

I continue with introductions. "Lily's a curator," I explain to Blake. "She's constantly having an art emergency."

"God, it feels that way sometimes." She laughs. A waiter comes to take drink orders from us. "And you're an actor, Blake?"

"Yes," he says smoothly. "That's how I met Aubrey. Well, officially."

My face sears at the unofficial encounter in his trailer at the height of the heat wave a couple of weeks ago. It feels like a lifetime has passed since then. Plus, there were the other unofficial collisions before that.

"You both were away for a couple of days, is that right?" Lily asks. "It must have been so nice to get out of town."

"It was. It's my first time to England and I love how green everything is. We went north for hiking," Blake explains.

"Lake District," I add.

"That sounds wonderful," Lily says, glancing up. Eli joins us, and we all quickly stand up for introductions.

I die about a million deaths standing here between Eli on one side of me and Blake on the other. They gaze at each other in an appraising way, Blake more open and relaxed. Eli has a glint of the razor lawyer's edge in his eye. I know the look.

And trouble's brewing.

Chapter Eighteen

"So you're Aubrey's new…friend I've heard about," Eli says, considering Blake like he's a fresh offering for a sacrificial altar. The way he pauses before *friend* gives me mild heart failure. Obviously, Eli knows what's up. Unease grips my guts, squeezing them tight. Like Eli's the shark and Blake the proverbial chum—except Blake didn't get the memo to be daunted, and he grins shamelessly. In fact, Blake's positively buoyant, the gorgeous, flippant arsehole. It makes me want to swoon twice, having him here at my side.

"I am," Blake agrees cheerfully, squeezing my hand. "Great to see you again, man."

I meet Lily's eye and she looks guilty, a tinge of pink on her cheeks. "I told Ryan about Blake, actually. For arrangements for the party. I mentioned you were away."

So she was right that she didn't think Eli knew, but of course it was inevitable that Ryan would talk to Eli about me and Blake. I do my best to feign a confidence I don't feel. I'm caught between an alpha male confidence crossfire.

"I'm very glad you made it back in time, Blake," says

Eli simply. "It would have been disappointing for Ryan for Aubrey to miss his birthday."

"I wouldn't miss Ryan's birthday." Indignant, I lift my chin and stare Eli down. It takes a minute to realize he means the Cumbria trip and not Blake's trip to L.A. So, that's a dig at me.

"Whatever's important to Aubrey is important to me, too." Blake gives me an affectionate smile as he squeezes my hand.

"How codependent of you," Eli says drily, his gaze piercing.

"It's *thoughtful*," I retort. "Unlike calling people in the middle of the night."

Eli's mouth snaps shut.

Blake flashes a million-dollar grin, the sort of self-assured grin which would look brilliant on a feature film. Or, in blissful private moments, unleashed in full glory on me. His hand is warm in mine. He's entirely relaxed. "I just flew back from L.A. to make sure I could be here to support Aubrey."

"And, well, here we are." I take hasty advantage of the second lull of rounds between Blake and Eli. Are they actually having a pissing match over *me*? "Official lightning round of introductions for you all to meet my boyfriend, Blake Sinclair. Er, Eli—you've already met, of course. Right. Never mind. And this is Lily McEvoy. Blake, Eli's Ryan's partner and a lawyer. Eli, Blake's an actor who's in London filming. The film they filmed in my shop, actually."

Blake squeezes my hand again.

Mercifully, the waiter's brought us the promised alcohol, wine for Lily and ale for me and Blake. I gulp down some ale.

"Be right back," I blurt. "I'll be fine," I assure Blake before I make a beeline through the restaurant for outside.

I take a long moment to myself, pacing up and down the

pavement, trying to pull it together. *Think of Blake. He's brilliant and he wants you and you want him. Forget Eli and his games.*

For a moment, calm washes over me. Reassurance, even.

But when I turn to go back in, it's not Blake who's come after me, but Eli.

I stop short, eyeing him. Of course he looks incredible. Golden hair, tanned, blue eyes. He looks every bit the upcoming lawyer in his trim blue shirt, and I wonder how on earth we were together for so long, and what he saw in me. He's sophisticated in his business attire, while I'm a step up from torn jeans and a faded T-shirt.

"I said I'd come check on you," he offers.

I grit my teeth together, stuffing my hands into my pockets. My shoulders are tight. My chest is tight. Everything's too tight, including my skin.

"You seem out of sorts."

"I'm fine." I frown at him. "No thanks to you, by the way. What was that call about?"

"I told you—we had a fight. And I needed someone to talk to." His gaze is unwavering, that way he has of melting me from the inside despite my anger. "And like I also told you, you were always good at listening."

"You need more friends who're good listeners."

"True. But you're the best one. And the best listener too."

Rolling my eyes, I shake my head. "I don't know what's wrong with you. You're not even apologizing for that call. And— Did you know I was away when you made that call?"

He opens his mouth to protest, thinks better of it, and has the decency to redden. "I might've."

"Hmmph." I cross my arms across my chest. "So you're deliberately trying to fuck with something good I have going on in my life."

"I was drunk and not thinking clearly. Not myself."

I frown at him. "Wouldn't it be far more effective to talk to Ryan, the man you were fighting with? To resolve things?"

Eli's quiet, contemplating me. He looks deflated all of a sudden. And…sad?

I peer at him skeptically, not sure what ploy he's onto now. "What?" I snap.

"We broke up," Eli says quietly, staring in the vicinity of our feet.

Blood pounds in my ears as I try to absorb this news. Am I hearing right?

"What?" Startled, I stare hard at him. Stupid oxygen, leaving my body faster than I'm taking it in.

"After the fight. When we talked. I wanted to tell you. It's not official news yet. But I thought you should know."

I continue to stare at him. "What do you mean you broke up? Not—certainly not because of me."

Eli hesitates. "Maybe in part, if I'm honest."

My frown returns.

Is he actually serious? Eli's timing is absolute shit. If he was saying this to Aubrey of six months ago, my heart would be in my mouth over the possibility of getting back together. But current me has moved on. Even with the horrible fact that Blake's going back to America for good. Eli wanting me now that I have someone else is just classic. He's just bloody jealous.

"Eli, you need to sort yourself out. I'm seeing Blake, and we have something important. Something important to me."

Eli's face shifts to disappointment, his gaze lingering.

At last Blake comes out and makes a direct path to me, worry plain across his face.

Unable to say any more, I just look at Eli as Blake joins us, taking my hand.

"I should go back in. See you soon," Eli says, disappearing back into the restaurant.

I turn to bury my face into Blake's shoulder, needing his comfort. He smells of luxurious cologne. He rubs my back.

Clearly, the universe is jerking me around. Why can't things ever be simple and clear-cut? Why is Blake a limited time offer? How can I want someone I can't have? Someone who lives in a different world than mine?

"Hey, it's all right," he assures me.

Eli's news makes me feel worse, not better. In a week, Blake will be gone, and I'll have nothing to show for all of this longing.

Eventually, I lift my head from his shoulder and he gives me a soft kiss.

"You ready to go back in?"

"I am," I say, finding whatever courage I can scrape up. Drawing a breath, I stand to my full height and squeeze Blake's hand. "Let's go."

The rest of the evening passes without incident. Ryan's well-celebrated and well-loved, that's apparent. With good reason, since Ryan's great. I catch his gaze at one point and his wavers, looking away first. So, I take it he knows I know about their breakup, but no one else here does, not even Lily.

We have a few drinks and the evening slides by till it's time to go and goodbyes are made, with successful avoidance of Eli. After, Blake and I head back to my home, a ten-minute walk away.

Taking the entry direct to my flat, we tromp up the stairs and I finally let out the breath I've been holding all night. "Thank God that's over," I say with relief, sagging into Blake's arms as he smiles against me.

"It wasn't bad. Your friends are nice."

"Thanks. Sorry that Eli was being an arse." I hesitate

whether to tell Blake about Eli and Ryan's breakup. What good would that do, telling him? Selfishly, I want his last few days here to be like we live in some universe of our own.

Blake's unfazed. "He doesn't matter. *You* matter."

I melt against Blake's smile as we exchange kisses.

"How about I put on the kettle for tea?"

I perk up immediately, because the way to my heart is clearly lined with tea. "Yes, please."

He grins and goes off, trotting down the other stairs that lead to the back of the shop and the kitchen.

And, a moment later, I hear Blake calling for me.

"Aubrey!" Blake yells again from downstairs.

When I reach the kitchen, Blake's on his hands and knees, half under the sink, and in a pool of water.

"Holy shit." I look around with a sinking feeling.

"Where's the water shut off? It's not under the sink!" Blake calls out, almost banging his head as he scoots out and sits up. "Water's coming in through the wall."

"Fuck. Out front." I run to the hidden cover near the front door where the piping comes in from the street, shouting back over my shoulder, "The plumbing's fucked around here."

"I can tell," Blake yells back.

I find the shutoff in the bathroom and haul it closed before grabbing some towels and going downstairs to try to mop up the water and the damaged wall.

I suspect one my forever rattling pipes has at last given way. Blake knocks at the damp wall. "In here," he says. "Mind if I cut a hole?"

I sigh. "Go on. The wall's fucked. Along with the pipe. What's another hole in the wall around here?"

Blake finds tools in my stash under the sink and gets to

work. Meanwhile, I use all the towels and the mop and bucket to try to save the tiled floors.

"At least," says Blake optimistically, "none of your new books got wet. This can all be fixed easily enough."

"Shit, the books!" I dash off to go check the boxes delivered yesterday, but everything's dry. With relief, I return to Blake. "It's fine."

He gives me a reassuring smile. In the meantime, he's cut a neat but large hole in the wall, revealing the aged pipe that's given up keeping water to itself. "The culprit. Fixing that's beyond me, I'm afraid. I don't have the right tools or parts, but at least we can do an emergency patch with some duct tape, just in case any more water trickles down. You'll need to keep the water off till it's fixed though."

I groan. "I feel like my shop's cursed lately. If it's not one thing, it's another."

"It's not all bad." Blake's grin reassures me, despite feeling dejected about the amount of repairs needed for the shop and my flat. I've yet to see a pound for the filming and there's been no proper shop income in days, aside from a couple of special orders, which won't cover a thing. "We'll get things as good as we can manage here, then we can go stay at the hotel. In the morning, you can arrange a plumber to come here."

"There's still the whole situation with the shop up front." I shake my head. "From one disaster to the next."

"We can sort that too." Blake assures me easily, as if it's as easy as breathing. Probably for him it is in his charmed existence. "Bring your laptop tonight and you can follow up with the crew. We'll see where your books are at."

"Guess I'll need to, if we only have five more days." I slump. "And then, even if it's all back to normal, it might be too late. All the lost revenue. The bookshop runs on a very thin margin at the best of times."

"Hmm." Blake considers as we work together methodically, mopping up the floor and wringing out towels and the mop in the sink without even needing words to coordinate. Gradually, things are drying out in here. "Maybe I can help? I can take a look at your website and give you some ideas."

Startled, I give him a sharp look. He's all soft blue gaze, hair a bit rumpled with the effort, like it was out on our Lake District adventure. Like when he serenaded me in the chaos of Euston Station. "You'd do that?"

"Of course I'd do that for you. I can't promise anything, but I can take a look at your online sales strategy and give some pointers. Look at your demographics and target market. Things like that."

I purse my lips and start to laugh. And laugh till I'm on the verge of tears, whooping and holding my sides with the hysteria that's overwhelmed me, between Eli and a burst pipe the latest insult to my shop and home. "My...online...sales... *strategy*? Demographics!"

I can't.

Tears stream down my face. As if I offer online sales. The website might still be from the nineties for all I know, from back when the internet was invented. It's a step up from GeoCities. And the idea that I have some kind of strategy is the funniest thing I've heard in a long time.

Blake takes the mop from me and gathers me in his arms, rubbing my back. "I mean, only if you want—"

"I—you think I'm that organized?" I whoop with more laughter. "Oh God. I'm dying."

Relieved, Blake catches my face between his hands, brushing tears of mirth away with his thumb. "It's gonna be all right," he says soothingly. "Let's get to the hotel and get some sleep. It's been a long night."

Guilty, I realize he's half soaked from his cleaning efforts, and so am I.

I glance at my watch. It's after 11:00 p.m., and exhaustion hits me hard then. I give him a kiss. "'Kay. Let me get a couple of things. I'll text Gemma to warn her about the kitchen for tomorrow when she comes in. Let's get out of here for the night."

Blake orders a black cab to take us to his hotel, given that we're tired and it's late. I drowse, leaning my head on his shoulder as the driver navigates streets that are steady with traffic even at this late hour. Red taillights as far as the eye can see.

It's comforting to be like this, together. Part of me doesn't want to sleep, because waking up tomorrow means only four days left before he goes back to America.

Chapter Nineteen

Blake goes to have a shower. He emerges in a cloud of steam when he opens the door fifteen minutes later and steps out with a luxurious white towel secured around his waist. Of course, he's brilliant to look at, all slender muscle over his bones. He could have a very lucrative career as a men's underwear model if this acting thing doesn't work out. Or, in this case, towel model, which would probably do wonders for sales at John Lewis or whatever the American department store equivalent is. Nordstrom?

I'm sat on the bed, out of my jeans and down to boxers and a T-shirt, my scrawny legs hidden away beneath the fluff of the duvet, which is bearable given the substantial air-con in here against the summer's night. The hotel room is far more comfortable than my tiny bedsit.

I gaze at him. His hair is damp, water rivulets still tracking along his chest, which is lightly haired. Down soft, from firsthand experience.

We gaze at each other in the quiet and the glow of the bedside lamp.

"Come to bed with me," I whisper, leaning forward to kiss him. Brushing my mouth softly against his, and then again, I pull him down with me to the bed.

Together, we explore each other leisurely, hands roaming each other's bodies like explorers in the wilderness, charting new terrain. Then, we're kissing like our lives depend on it. Greedy, seeking. It's not long before Blake's towel and my boxers are history.

"I don't have any more condoms," I say breathlessly between hungry kisses, thirsting for this man. Blake's cock is rigid in my hand and God I want him more than anything. "But…my last test was clear. For STIs, I mean."

"Mine too." Blake pauses long enough to fumble in his bag, producing lube. He strokes himself, cock glistening. It's a gorgeous sight: Blake fresh from a shower, his gaze all intense for me, the strain of him.

He presses me down. I pull him close. And he sucks on my nipple rings in turn. I moan like something else possesses my voice, his slick fingers working me, teasing my arse till I'm ready for him. And he spreads me, admiring.

Shuddering at being so vulnerable before him, I press my hips closer.

"You want this?"

And my face is on fire, compromised for him. Anything.

"I want *you*," I manage.

Blake rubs himself against my arse, seeping and hot.

He shifts to kiss me lingeringly, our hands linked as I wrap my legs around him. And he eases himself inside, my back arching with the thrill of him as I gasp. The weight of his body on mine is intoxicating. In his arms is safety, comfort. Feeling wanted and cared for, even in our urgency.

My body is more than ready, pressing to meet him. After tonight, the stress of the party—of Eli, specifically—and the drama of the burst pipe, everything has more meaning.

He shifts to grip my arse and rolls to sit up. And I straddle him, stroking my cock, wild for him. It's hard to think with him like this, the burn of his mouth tonight, the extra intensity to seeing him so undone and desperate.

For me.

Impossible to imagine. Instead, I give over to raw emotion.

Wanting. Needing. Feeling.

Blake works me with relentless fingers and I ride him, panting and shuddering, till we abruptly roll over and I'm belly-down on the bed, face pressed into the duvet. Goose bumps cover my body.

And then, holy fuck.

He slaps my arse and rides me like the apocalypse is at our door and the last thing he wants to do is have me. And I'm his, all his, desperately his. His urgency only makes me more wild for him.

"*Fuck*," I sob out. "Blake."

And when he comes, thrusting intensely, his mouth burning at the nape of my neck, his arms heavy over mine, he sobs out my name, over and over, smothered in my hair.

When he finally collapses on me, the length of him still inside me, I shudder hard as I come against myself and the bed, not even needing to touch myself to get off. Because there's the thrill of him, so close, so wanting. His fingers are tight against my hips.

"Aubrey, Aubrey..." He's whispering in my ear, ragged.

"I'm right here..." I gasp, turning my head slightly as he nibbles on my ear.

"I want you so much."

"I'm here. I want you too."

And then he slides off and flips me over, taking stock of the mess I've made of myself and the bed. He gives a low, throaty chuckle that thrills me. Then, he bends his head to lick me clean. It's hard to imagine there was a time in my life before Blake. Our bodies are caught in a call and answer that feels too raw, too instinctive for us to have known each other for only a couple of weeks. As his tongue runs along my belly, I shudder, raking my fingers through his damp hair, cool against my skin.

When he takes my cock into his mouth, so sensitive after coming, I buck slightly. He holds me down, working me gently. And I sob out, writhing between pleasure and pain.

And honestly? It's so hot.

"Oh God— Blake—"

I can't think. Not for any sum of money. Or anything else.

Instead, I moan and sob like a wild thing. Everything's raw.

He continues until I'm stiff enough and then, before long, my body jerks as I come powerfully, flowing over his tongue. Blake's fingers are tight on my wrists, holding me down.

Finally, he sits up, kneeling.

God, he's a vision, dark hair sweeping over his brow, taut muscles in the light. And then he wraps me up tight in his arms and the duvet, kissing me reverently, like I mean everything to him. And him to me. Our fingers trace each other's skin, our bodies imprinted on each other.

Eventually, we return to ourselves, wrapped in each other in bed. Blake nuzzles me and I shiver, highly tuned to his touch. "I need to tell you something," he says softly, giving me a kiss.

I gaze at him, smiling. "You own a bean emporium?"

He grins. "You'd be the first to know if I did. No. My agent called again..."

"Oh?" I shift to see his face better, propped on an elbow. All the better to admire him, his soft expression, see his hesitation. "News about L.A.?"

Blake shakes his head. "Not quite. News about New

York."

"New York?"

He swallows, searching my eyes. I'm getting nervous as he draws this out.

"You can say anything to me, you know," I murmur, tracing his chest and taking his hand. We intertwine our fingers.

"It's another audition. A really important audition. It's for a lead role in a major film that's booked to start shooting. The actor they had just backed out last minute, so they're casting again. I'm just waiting on confirmation on a date, but it's probably very soon."

"'Kay." I kiss his fingers, then gaze at him. "Then you should do it."

Blake makes some small unhappy noise. "The honest truth is that I'd rather stay here with you. Or in your flat. Or get back out to the countryside together, you know? New York's the opposite of where I want to be."

Some part of me thrills to hear this, to know Blake wants me so badly. And the realization that I want him just as much. "Lovely, I don't want to stand in the way of your dreams. And...one thing at a time, I suppose. An audition's one thing, landing the part is another."

"Why're you so sensible?" Blake groans, scooping me close and showering me with kisses. I couldn't speak then if I wanted to, but having Blake greedily to myself right now is a thrill.

And we spend the night like this, drifting off to sleep at last quite some time later, me holding tightly onto Blake like he might disappear in my sleep if we happen to make the mistake of letting go. Wanting him like this is terrifying, but the thought of him absent from my life is devastating.

There's a sharp rapping at the door at some unholy hour.

I can tell that much as I squint at my watch, head resting against Blake's shoulder. The bedside lamp is still on, casting a small glow in the room. Beside me, Blake stirs with a groan, a silhouette.

I shift closer to him. Must be some drunk trying to get home. It's so early that the sun's not up, though I can see the first streaks of pink toward dawn through the small gap between the curtains.

A loud rapid-fire knock again.

"Blake," someone calls. A man's voice.

Ugh.

Definitely a voice. I'm definitely not at home. I kiss his shoulder sleepily, lifting my head to peer at him. "S'mebody's here. Should I hide?"

He groans again and rolls onto his back.

"It's Andrew," says the voice through the door. "I need to talk to you."

"Shit," says Blake, sitting up so abruptly that I collapse on the pillow beside him. He springs out of bed, finding a robe in record time. My immediate instinct is to pull the duvet over my head and hide, because I'm brave like that.

Who's Andrew?

Another lover? Who else would come knocking at this time, wanting to talk? Though his film project does seem to keep stupid hours, late and early both, to be fair. The film industry apparently has hours well outside of my shop hours, that's for certain.

A moment later, I hear the door open.

"Hey," Blake says. He's still perfectly audible from where I'm hiding beneath the down duvet.

"Hey, sorry to disturb you so early, but I thought you'd want to see what the local press is reporting," mystery Andrew says, all apologetic in tone. "I've got a couple of papers. There's more online. Check your phone. I'll let you have a chance to look at these too. Then call me and we'll figure out a strategy. Don't say anything online to anyone, for any reason."

There's a rustling of paper.

Mystery Andrew must be some sort of filming person.

"Okay. Uh, thanks. I think. For the heads up." Blake's voice, curt. "It's early."

"Don't mention it. Thought you'd want a chance to see before we start the day. Oh, and it's hit the US news too."

The door clicks shut.

I peek out from under the duvet. Blake stands with a paper tucked neatly under his arm, the *Daily Mail* open in his hands.

"Don't read that," I groan sleepily at him. "It's a pack of lies, whatever it says. Speaking of tabloid fodder."

He's still as a statue. Unmoving.

"Blake?"

Nothing.

Reluctantly, I get out of the warmth of the bed and retrieve my boxers from where they were flung in the heat of the moment at the foot of the bed. I go over to Blake and slide my arms around his waist from behind, resting my head against his shoulder. I skim the text before going to the photo essay across the top half of the two-page spread.

> *Filming for* Hollywood Ending, *the American feature rom-com being shot in London, heats up between Lars Madden and Faith Rivers. Romance strikes the cast. Lars and Faith caught in an exclusive, kissing at a cast party.*
>
> *Co-star Kelly Greaves spotted yesterday night locking lips with magnate William Locking outside of Severn's. Meanwhile, up-and-coming Blake Sinclair's all caught up in a whirlwind romance with*

local bookseller Aubrey Barnes of Barnes Books in Soho, as spotted in Cumbria and London…

The article goes on but I stop reading and gawp at the photos.

Me and Blake, in an intimate kiss in Cumbria, in our waterproofs outside in the woods on one of our walks. Then I see:

Lovers holed up in posh London hotel.

My eyebrows shoot up, while my stomach lurches at the violation of our privacy. How did they know? Did the holiday cottage manager give us up? Or other holidaymakers? How could this happen without us noticing? I give Blake a sidelong glance.

He's staring, pale. I kiss his cheek but he doesn't respond. Distractedly, he disentangles from me, goes to his phone on the bedside table, and starts scrolling.

"I don't think any good will come of looking yourself up online," I say. "If I know anything about the media."

"Fuck," he says at last, on the verge of tears as he looks at me. "It's made a couple of the gossip sites. Like TMZ."

"Well, gossip sites are just that, gossip. And the others?"

"E! News, for starters. Access Hollywood. As if our relationship's entertainment." He snorts, sounding uncharacteristically bitter.

I make a face, trying to find the positive in this situation. Struggling, I chew my thumbnail. "At least we're not doing anything worse than kissing?"

He shoots me a dark look and I fall quiet.

"Sorry," I say, chastised. "It's an epic invasion of privacy for both of us, I know."

"It's a whole fucking nightmare. They've gone through half the cast, I swear," he says with dismay.

"People think the lives of celebrities are extra entertainment. Whether on-screen or off. Somehow, they feel entitled—"

"Thanks for explaining how it works, Aubrey. I didn't realize," Blake says, irritated.

I blush and shut up, sitting on the edge of the bed. "Look, I wish I could undo this. And it's crap that they give no fucks about your privacy or mine or that of your castmates, but… thing is, that's all out there. And—it's not so terribly bad, is it? You know the saying, there's no such thing as bad publicity?"

He stares at me and promptly bursts into tears. I feel horrible for having said very much the wrong thing at the worst moment. I get up and go to him, to draw him into my arms, yet he backs away like he's been burned.

"What's going on?" I ask, searching his eyes. Obviously, he's upset, but I don't get why he's mad at me. "I haven't said anything other than to my friends last night. And Lily before that, but Lily wouldn't say a word. Obviously, some paps have an agenda—"

"You don't get it!"

I gawp at him, not used to Blake being out of sorts like this. "Tell me so I *do* get it," I urge him.

He throws the newspaper down on the desk, rubbing his eyes furiously with the heels of his hands. "People will read that."

Heat stings my cheeks. "Yeah, and anybody with half a brain knows the *Mail* is a rag and who knows about the rest of them to be taking tabloid photos and calling themselves journos. Fuck them. It's not real, is it? You're real. I'm real."

Blake stares at me. Almost through me, haunted. "People who matter will read this too. Casting directors for films. And…" His voice breaks. "My family."

I just stare at him. "Are you…*embarrassed* by me?" I ask at last, my voice barely audible as the room spins.

"I'm— People don't know I'm attracted to men." Blake just stares at me. "Well, I'm attracted to women too, for the record. I guess that makes me bisexual."

"Or pansexual, if you're attracted to all genders. Or just plain old queer." Tears prick my eyes. I grip the edges of the bed to steady me, struggling to make sense of what Blake's telling me. "So you *are* embarrassed by me, then. Like, I'm not good enough for you."

"It's not that. I just…I just can't be gay."

I gawp at him. What sort of internalized homophobia is this? "Blake, you're not gay. You've just said yourself that you're bi. Which is totally, absolutely fine. I don't get why you're losing your shit like this and making this out to be my fault somehow—"

"It's not your fault!" Blake snaps as he scrubs at his face again.

"Then?" I demand.

"Then…Hollywood's traditional. People might do what they like, but there's not much space for people being queer and out if they want major parts. Especially not for men."

"Toxic masculinity much?" I say through clenched teeth.

He just stares. "But it's even worse than that."

"How?"

"My dad will find out I'm…I'm some kind of queer."

"And?"

"I'm not out to him."

Quiet and slump-shouldered, I sit on the bed, watching him go to pieces. "Fuck, Blake."

"He won't understand," he says in a brittle voice. "Even if I try to explain. He's hopeless."

It's such a foreign concept to me, being closeted in some way, in whole or in part. My parents were always supportive of my sexuality and never questioned it. I can see now I was lucky.

"Does anyone know in your family?" I try gently, holding

my breath. Is this wrong of me to ask? Am I violating his privacy too?

"My sisters."

"And what do they think?"

"They think it's fine."

My expression softens. "Because they love you. And people who love you will find a way through, I'm sure of it."

He eyes me warily as I get up and approach. Again, he backs away. "Don't," he says sharply. "You'll just make this worse."

I throw my hands in the air. "So you're punishing me for this? All I want is you, Blake."

God, what just came out of my mouth?

"Fuck, I'm sorry," I say immediately, guilt rising. "I'm acting like an arse. I'm just upset. For us. For you especially. I mean, God, your family—"

"I—we—can't do this. Not anymore. I—I shouldn't have fallen for you in the first place. It was a mistake." He just stares at me for a long moment, his expression hard and distant.

"What? What do you mean?"

Wait—he fell for me?

And then all the air goes out of me. White-knuckled, I ball my hands into fists, stuck in place. Nauseous, I'm trying and failing to keep it together as I shake. Having Blake and having lost him in an instant is too much to take. I'm not cut out for this.

Blake's crying. He can't look at me. "I think…I think you should go."

"But—"

"*Please*, Aubrey. If you care about me even a little bit, you'll do this for me."

"I—" I choke on my words, not sure what to say.

But his expression's hard and unyielding when he at last stares through me, eyes full of tears, face red with emotion.

And with unsteady, shaking hands, I dress, barely able to manage socks and jeans and a black T-shirt, and stuff my feet into battered trainers. Packing my bag in some surreal unreality, Blake remains frozen in place, watching me. And I can't think, just going through the motions of packing up my few possessions, trying to act calm when I'm anything but. My stomach lurches.

Then, I stand in front of him, pack slung over my shoulder. I hesitate, my mouth opening and shutting. There are so many things I want to say to him—how important he is to me, how in two weeks he's come and turned my world upside down.

Turned my heart upside down.

And now everything's over, just like that. In a flash of a photographer's camera, something private and sacred is now media fodder, some clickbait online for someone's idle scrolling on their phone for a second before the next thing catches their attention.

But for me, my world's gone, with the most important person in it in front of me.

And I can't have him. Because he doesn't want me.

All because of perceptions, some stupid paparazzi nightmare.

"Blake—" I choke out.

He shakes his head abruptly, turning away. His shoulders shake. "Please go."

I'm a wreck, gawping at him. I can't believe this. "Just promise me you'll do your audition. Fuck the media. It's your dream."

"I don't know. Aubrey. Please. I need you to leave." His voice breaks, his face covered with his hands.

And, with the last scrap of strength I have, I do as he asks, attempting to dry my tears on the cuff of my lightweight jacket. How could I lose everything that mattered so quickly?

Dizzy, I go out into the dazzling sun, lost.

Chapter Twenty

I'd like to say that I handled the next couple of days in an upstanding sort of way, the model of calm and grace. Which would be a pack and a half of lies. What happened instead was that I showed up outside of Lily's work, texting her in a flood of words till she had to leave work early and take me to hers. Plus, I had no working water at home.

Lily's flat is bright, gallery-white with art from her travels hung on her walls, fresh cut flowers on the coffee and dining tables. We're in her sitting room. After having slept like a bear headed into winter, I helped her today with editing exhibition text for her upcoming show. Now we sit with a pint of ice cream between us on her sunny sofa. I'm calmer. But my eyes still have that raw feeling.

She's gone through the *Daily Mail*, the online gossip sites. Blake's Instagram hasn't been updated. There're no texts from him either. I don't dare text.

I've spilled my guts out to Lily, sobbed on her shoulder till I had no tears left. Now, I just feel wrung out.

I'm scrolling aimlessly on my phone when I search Blake's

name for filming news.

Hollywood Ending Wraps in London, says the headline.

Reading that feels so final. Points for accuracy, extra points for the visceral wound.

"That's it, then. He's gone home for good."

I show Lily my phone. She frowns and scrolls.

All I can hope is that if he's back in America, he's going to that audition. And then hopefully to try to sort things out with his family.

"I'm so sorry." She squeezes my hand. Generously, she gives me the last of the ice cream.

Miserable, I just stare at her, at a loss for words. How could Blake have come to mean so much so fast? It doesn't make sense.

"Tell you what. I'll order takeaway. We'll eat far too much and stay up too late watching dreadful films, drinking wine. I promise not a single romance."

"Good, because I can't bear it." I sigh, eating the last of the chocolate ice cream.

• • •

After a couple of days at Lily's and a plumbing repair later, I'm back at Barnes Books. While I was away, the lorry came with the rest of my boxed-up stock. With Gemma's help, we work to put the shop back together again. Being so busy at least keeps me from dwelling every waking moment on Blake.

I take a break to go through the post that Gemma's brought in. Bills, junk mail...and a seemingly innocent letter till I open it up. The letterhead is from one of my competitors, a mega bookshop chain.

Dear Mr. Barnes,

We admire the work that you and your family have

put into Barnes Books for over fifty years, a fixture in Soho. Your bookshop is a well-recognized brand.

To that end, we are pleased to offer you a bid for the shop, with financial details enclosed. We would like to operate this shop as a satellite location to our franchise, and hope that you would be willing to stay on as the branch manager for continuity.

Please respond at your earliest convenience.

Kind regards,
Percy Green

My eyes widen, chest too tight. Indignant and relieved, I stare at the stupid letter for a long time before shoving it in my ledger and slamming the drawer shut.

It could be an out, selling this place and walking away from the constant financial stress.

Except, I'd be letting my parents down. And letting myself down too, after everything I've worked for. And sacrificed.

It'd be failure.

But, if I take their offer, it'll take care of the bills. I'd no longer have to worry about the next thing to break, because how on earth is an indie shop supposed to survive when there's a major chain with every book known to humankind?

• • •

Aside from the new floors, the only new thing in the bookshop is the rich aubergine paint. The street's restored back to its usual self, without sign of any filming-related inconveniences or hassle. It's back to the usual hum of traffic and flocks of tourists during midday in the summer.

And my phone stays silent. No messages from Blake.

Alice Rutherford confirms that the filming's wrapped

when she sends me payment for using the shop as a film location and makes sure that the repairs are done to my satisfaction. Everything has a sense of finality to it.

As with the filming chaos, the heatwave's also gone from the height of summer. Along with the heat sparked inside me that Blake brought into my life.

Sensing my dark mood, even Gemma doesn't give me a hard time like usual as we work. And when I work on the poetry section, alone, kneeling on the floor, I find the book of poetry Blake returned that first day, complaining about the poet's bad Twitter behavior. I flip it open and a piece of paper falls out.

> *It's tough to get your attention, but a man's gotta do what he must. Even if it that means putting* Brideshead Revisited *in the Comedy section and* The Song of Achilles *in Romance.*
>
> *Call me sometime?*

Followed by his initials and number.

Fuck.

And thank God it's lunchtime and that Gemma's gone out, so nobody sees me crumple alone in my shuttered shop. I slip the note into my pocket. Something I should have the good sense to throw away.

However, because I'm daft and a sentimental fool committed to self-torture, I keep not only the note but also the book of poetry safe up in my flat.

The sun is shining but it doesn't reach me in August, the first stirrings of autumn in the air.

Later that afternoon, calmer and restored after some tea, my pocket buzzes. Checking my phone, there's a text from Lily.

Don't forget the private view tonight. Please come. You can bring a plus-one if you want. Or not. I'll leave a couple of tickets at the box office under your name. Lxx

I would much rather run full tilt toward the typical introvert response, which is the opposite direction of a private view for Lily's exhibition. I'm in no sort of mood for people, especially upbeat people. If the private view was guaranteed to be full of sullen, moody goths, I might be in for a round of emo and The Cure. If only they had cocktails tailored to that niche, something over the top like the Velvet Tear.

This is why I'm destined to be single forever from this point on.

No more men. No more heartache. No more putting myself on the line like that, opening myself up to more raw vulnerability, because it doesn't pay off. I'm not cut out for this.

Gemma gives me side-eye. "Aubs? You've been staring at the Romance section for five minutes."

I side-eye her right back. She's right—I have been rooted in place, staring dejectedly at the wall of books I'm arranging. Foolishly I started another romance novel last night. This time, I found one with a man falling for another man, the poor arsehole. And yet I stayed up far too late reading.

"Not you too. That's Mr. Barnes. Remember?"

"Chill." Gemma shakes her head, her dark ponytail swinging. "I mean, you should be happy, right? The shop's been fixed up. It's gonna be ready to reopen in, like, a day or two." She gazes at me. "And...I heard you were in the papers kissing Blake Sinclair."

My face warms at the mention of his name. "Never mind Blake Sinclair."

"That's juicy, Aubs. Well done." She looks pleased. "Why're you upset?"

"Because tabloids. Because invasion of privacy?" I say immediately, getting worked up. Never mind the ache of missing Blake terribly.

She considers me. "I guess now that the filming's done you won't see him, huh."

I scowl. "Let's focus on the shop."

There's also still the not so trifling matter of the whopping council tax bill. It'll be a bit better with the payout from filming. That's for future Aubrey, not today's Aubrey, who has an explosion of book boxes everywhere to deal with. Gemma's hip-deep in sci-fi and fantasy.

"Reopening's good at least?" she tries.

I chew my lip. "Yeah."

"Yeah." Gemma smiles at me. "So, good news. Cheer up."

If only it was so easy to cheer up on command. Everything just seems duller. I stare down at my cuff watch, absently rubbing at it, and the hidden heart tattooed inside my wrist. At least I was clever about that: hearts were meant to be hidden.

"Any chance you want to go to a private view tonight?" I ask her. "I'm really not up for it."

"Why, Aubrey, I didn't think you felt that way about me," she laughs, clutching at her heart in a faux swoon, an obvious effort to try to make me laugh. "I might need to tell my girlfriend you're making a play for me."

"What happened to the boyfriend? I'm not going to use the ticket, so you can take a plus one."

"Oh, I still have him too, but he's not my primary right now," Gemma assures me easily, shelving a tome on dragons with a satisfying *thump* on the shelf. "Don't worry. I'm hardly exclusive. Polyamory is where it's at."

My eyebrows climb. Imagine the heartache involved there for someone like me. "I think you're made of stronger stuff than me. Power to you."

"You should try it. You might even like it."

My lips twitch. "Well. Do you and your partner or partners happen to want to go to a private view?"

She considers, rubbing the small of her back. "Well, Neil's working. Jackie's... I don't know. I'll text her. What's the show, anyway?"

"Um." Frowning, I shrug. "I don't know the name of the exhibition, but it's some edgy fashion thing with street art and punks?"

Gemma beams. "Brilliant. I'll go if Jackie can make it."

"Great," I say, relieved. People successfully avoided. I'll apologize to Lily. She'll understand, won't she?

"What will you do instead? Hot date?" She peers at me.

I snort, nodding at the mess around us. "No. I'll just keep working. There's loads to do."

"That's not very fun."

"I'm Aubrey 'No Fun' Barnes, remember? Just keeping my reputation in check."

Resigned, I sigh and reach for another armful of romance books. A cheerful, bright cover of a light-hearted romance is at the top of the stack. Hurriedly, I shelve it, safely out of view. Happy things remind me of Blake, and thinking of Blake's just going to lead to more moping. I've spent the afternoon successfully avoiding thinking of him after the earlier poetry book debacle.

She tuts, hands on hips. "You seem even more out of sorts than normal."

"Yeah. Speaking of reasons why," I say, frowning at her, "by the way, there's that whole issue about you signing the consent form for filming. That was terrible, Gemma. Like, the sort of thing people would get fired for."

Gemma shrugs easily. "Look, I know it's beyond what I'd normally do, but I knew that you really needed the money for the shop. And you won't fire me—you need my help too much and can't be arsed to train someone else."

I sigh. "Fair enough. I guess that's all true."

"See?" She looks triumphant, holding an armful of books too.

"Just...don't do that again? Please. I really can't bear it."

"I solemnly vow that if anyone comes in here wanting to turn the shop into a film set, I'll send them straight to you."

"Thank you."

We work in silence, or near silence. The radio's on, playing some rock tunes by Halfpenny Rise. The front door is open for fresh air but I have a rope across the door with a TEMPORARILY CLOSED FOR BUSINESS sign hanging from it in Gemma's best block printing.

As the afternoon passes, sultry with heat, Gemma leaves at 5:00 p.m. to go home to round up Jackie and get ready for the evening's private view. I pop out for a quick kebab since I skipped lunch and get back to work right after, steadily working on the rare and collectible books section by the front counter. Slowly, the stacks of boxes everywhere are starting to thin, and the stack of flattened boxes is starting to grow to a respectable height in the middle of everything, where my entry table with featured books would ordinarily go. Bits of cardboard litter the floor, but they'll be hoovered up soon enough.

"Knock knock," calls an all too familiar male voice after 6:00 p.m. at the front door, wide open again for the evening breeze. "Can I come in? I hear the safe word's Noble."

Chapter Twenty-One

Of course. Nothing like the universe kicking sand in my eyes when I'm already down. That'll teach me to make like an ostrich and try to hide in plain sight. Why not a little more torture?

"Come in," I call over my shoulder as I finish alphabetizing the section.

Eli can wait.

There's the sound of footsteps across the wooden floor, the rugs not down yet. Eli comes to stand beside me, admiring the wall.

"Looking good," he says lightly.

I glance at him, unimpressed. "You need to try harder if that's some sort of come-on."

Eli holds his hands up, eyes wide, sandy hair falling over his brow. "I come in peace. Honest."

Scowling, I'm not so sure.

"Have you eaten?" He looks at me with concern.

"Yes. I actually paused for a meal not long ago."

Finally, I face him. He's polished in a light linen suit,

summer personified. His hair's groomed into stylish waves, his tan leather briefcase slung across his shoulder. The arsehole's at his most appealing. And he knows it.

"Headed home?" I ask unnecessarily.

"Maybe. I was thinking about seeing if you needed some dinner and seeing if I could lure you out to Lily's private view like a good Samaritan. She said you were 99% going to ditch it."

I open my mouth to protest in half-hearted outrage. She knows me too well. "Well."

"Caught out, I'm afraid." Eli gives me a wry look. "It's not healthy to work all the time. And Lily really wants you to go. You don't need to go for long, but I think it's not right to bail on her."

Guilt twists my stomach. She's been such a good friend to me, again and again, especially lately in the throes of my heartbreak. Plus, I've eaten a shocking amount of her ice cream which she faithfully replenished the few days I stayed with her, never mind all of the constant tea and sympathy she's provided.

A heavy sigh escapes me.

"Fine. You're right." It pains me to say it, because I hate Eli being right. Some part of me wants to be spiteful just to be contrary, but the more mature part of me takes over for Lily's sake.

"Do you think there'll be enough canapés to make a meal?" Eli asks with a smile. "Or do you mind joining me for a quick bite before the opening?"

My lips twist. Of course. "You'd tell me that canapés aren't an appropriate meal."

He chuckles. "I just don't want to take up more of your time. I know you're busy."

"How about you help me a little and then we can go?" I try. "I'm on the G section here. You want to start with Z on this shelf?" I gesture.

"All right." He slides out of his jacket, revealing a hint of biceps in his short-sleeved shirt. Which reminds me a bit of Blake. God, with Blake I would say that would have reminded me of Eli. I never knew I had a type, but apparently I should pay more attention to men doing the sports ball and working out.

Eli gets to work, and we continue for longer than I meant to, shelving books in a familiar if not comfortable silence. Once, he used to help me regularly in the shop like this, the occasional evening spent together after he had come home from a day of lawyering, only to moonlight as a bookseller like me.

"Sorry," I say at last, startled when I look at my watch. Apparently we were caught up in a shelving frenzy. "I lost track of time. Let me get changed quickly."

"We're going to have to go straight there."

Canapés and wine for dinner it is.

• • •

A change of clothes and a taxi ride later, I'm with Eli at the private view of the fashion exhibition Lily's been working around the clock on for the last few days. The large gallery has several floors, and the exhibition is on the first floor, a prime location for major shows. The private event is sold out, people filling the gallery and lingering in front with wine and nibbles. A DJ plays music.

And it's more than fine, it's brilliant. Mannequins stand on podiums through the gallery hall, showcasing bespoke fashion. A series of dolls shows samples of various punk fashions before they were made to full-size production scale.

Walls have displays of impressive clothing, framed fashion drawings. In display cases are sketchbooks and notes and tools of London's historic and up-and-coming designers.

In the distance, through the crowd, I thought I glimpsed Gemma and her latest girlfriend, but they soon disappeared out of sight. The place is jammed full of people, a great sign.

I'd get to Lily to congratulate her, but she's flitting from her director to guest designers, media people and donors of note. Smiling, I'm happy for her that the night's gone so well.

As for us, Eli's winning the fashion prize, cutting a striking figure in his suit. I'm in a black shirt and dark jeans, going for smart-casual with the shiniest Docs I could find in my closet. Vintage cherry red eight-hole, so at least I might have street cred. Plus, I've put on a touch of eyeliner for the occasion, a scrunch of styling product in my hair.

A hipster gives me an approving nod at one point. Relieved, I get another round of wine for me and Eli from the bar. Eventually, Lily finds us, giving us each air kisses. She looks beautifully dramatic in her black dress with a full skirt, bare arms, a touch of cleavage, and devastatingly red lipstick. Her hair's up in a twist and she has on her most chic glasses.

"You look amazing," I tell her over the din of the crowd and the upbeat music that the DJ is playing. I guess they can't go full-bore punk quite yet, but I have hopes that they might as the evening wears on. "And this is brilliant."

"Very well done," Eli agrees.

Lily beams. "Cheers, lovelies. I'm sooo relieved. The curator from MOMA managed to get on the red-eye last night and hand-delivered the last exhibit this morning, and I'm so happy about that I could fall over."

"Don't fall over. Here." I give her my wine and shift into the queue for the barman to get another glass of red wine for myself. "I think this is the best show you've done yet." I smile at Lily, who's rightfully glowing with the success of the night. "People seem really impressed."

"Oh, I hope so. It's been so much work, but it's been great

fun, visiting ateliers and studios and interviewing designers in their homes," Lily enthuses.

It's her first big break as a curator and I'm so glad for her that it's going well. She's been an assistant curator here for the last four years since she graduated from uni. She received the promotion six months ago. If I thought she was busy before, she's found a whole new level.

I can see someone trying to get her attention, so we exchange another round of kisses and congratulations before she hurries off. We do a slow lap of the gallery, admiring the art and the effort in putting the whole show together.

Eli patiently waits for me as I insist on reading all of the exhibit labels, nearly as fixated as Lily making sure they all are correct. I don't spot any shocking typos, so that's a relief at least.

By now, we're well canapéd and wined, somewhat loose-limbed and arguably more loose-tongued.

"What happened to your man?" Eli asks as we stand looking at a ripped taffeta dress in mint green and massive boots on a podium.

I give him a sharp sidelong glance. I've been carefully not thinking of Blake tonight, because losing him is too raw.

Back in my ordinary life again without Blake, everything is flatter. The only sign that Blake was even here to begin with are the handful of London photos on his Instagram, and my photos from the sunset and our Cumbria trip together. If it wasn't for that, I could be convinced I may have conjured him up out of loneliness from the depths of my imagination in the height of summer. His Instagram has been suspiciously quiet, with a couple of city shots of New York, all skyscrapers and gray skies. Very atmospheric.

Every rare shot lacks for people. And there hasn't been a single selfie in ages.

"Aubrey?"

I shake myself out of it and down some wine. "Sorry. He's back home in America. And he's not my man. He's his own man."

You're acting weird. Don't be weird.

"Where's Ryan?" I ask just as pointedly, though with more edge than he asked after Blake.

Eli sighs. "I don't know. Wherever Ryan is on a Thursday night."

"You know what I mean."

"I do."

He gives me a long, appraising look. The sort of look that misses nothing, scrutinizing every detail, like a dressing down. It's also the sort of look that undoes my composure, and in the past, made me wild for him.

"Want to get out of here?" Eli asks suddenly.

By this point, the music's gone up, some people are dancing, and it's too warm for my liking. I'm not about to hit the dance floor myself and Eli definitely doesn't have that party vibe tonight. He's all intensity.

Finishing our wine, we put our glasses down on a side table, and we head out. The evening's cooled down, and the air is a bit on the chill side instead of sweltering, hinting toward the change in seasons around the corner.

We walk briskly to the tube, headed back to Soho. Like so many nights we had shared in years gone by, nights out, returning home to our flat after an evening together, visiting with friends or dining out. Eli's flat.

"I thought everything was brilliant with you and Ryan." I tap my Oyster card through the gates and we disappear into the hot underground world of the tube network.

"We have had our ups and downs."

"His health's okay?" I ask tentatively.

"Physically," Eli agrees. "I think he's having a hard time too. Obviously. Between the accident and us breaking up."

"Did he find a flat of his own?"

"He's staying with his parents in Balham."

I just nod. We cram onto the next tube, full of late commuters and evening travelers. Standing shoulder to shoulder, I feel the heat of his body as we're pressed against each other, too close for comfort. It wasn't that long ago I would have been desperate for this time with him, this closeness.

Now, I just feel heavy-hearted. Sad for Eli, sad for Blake, sad for myself. No one's winning right now.

We emerge to the regular world before long and walk through Soho. Hesitating as we wait to cross the street, I glance at him. We've been mostly traveling in silence. Not quite one of those comfortable silences, but one of those acutely aware silences where every fiber of my body is highly sensitized to him.

We're outside another pub at the corner while we wait for the light. We're halfway between my place and his. "Want to go for a drink?"

"Didn't we just have one?"

And yet we go to the traditional-looking pub, with hanging baskets that overflow with a cascade of flowers. Pubgoers gather on the patio and pavement, drinking. Others are sat at the picnic tables.

Inside, at least it's warm, and we grab pints at the bar before finding a corner to stand together.

"I miss you, Aubs," Eli murmurs.

I splutter my ale mid-sip, coughing.

He winces. "Sorry. Maybe I'm just doing the whole grass is always greener thing, like Ryan said. Idealizing the past."

"Probably," I agree, recovering quickly. He ought to warn someone before trying something like that. "I mean, I wouldn't go with my judgment on this one, 'cause I didn't know you were unhappy till you told me you were leaving."

Finding some strange strength, I dare meet his gaze, all silvery blue in this light. I hold my breath.

Eli's mouth jerks down slightly, and he looks crestfallen. "I know. I'm so sorry. I wish… God, Aubrey, I was such an idiot. I mean, I realize now I should have brought things up well before getting to that point. It's one of my biggest regrets, doing that."

"Really?" I say wryly. "It wasn't even a month later after we broke up before you were with Ryan. If you weren't already."

He's quiet, looking sad. "I was faithful to you, Aubs."

"Maybe physically, but in spirit?" I retort.

God, the wine and ale combo is making me sassy tonight. Also, I'm a man who really has no fucks left to give. And, frankly, I didn't grill him enough back then, too heartbroken at first, then upset after he was with Ryan so soon, I kept away for a while. Till the shocking newness of my singledom and their relationship wore off, the sting of being so easily replaced.

At least Eli has the decency to redden like a tomato.

Weirdly at that moment, unbidden, I think of Blake. Does he still think of me at all? Or was I just someone he could pass the time with in London?

"You were always special to me. You still are." Eli's gaze doesn't waver.

"Maybe you're just jealous."

"Maybe I am."

"Wanting what you couldn't have."

"Possibly."

We consider each other. And drink. I set my glass down on the small bar in the corner where we stand, between dark-stained oak panels topped with stained-glass partitions for privacy. The roar of laughter from the next group of pub patrons spills over, light-hearted and easy.

"All right. So I *was* jealous when I saw you with Blake."

Satisfied for that one victory, I nod. "How'd that feel?"

"Rather shit, if I'm honest."

"Imagine how it would feel if it was your best friend."

Eli reddens again. He touches my arm lightly. Goose bumps rise immediately as I glower at him. Stupid body and its betrayal.

"It would be worse," he admits.

"Exactly."

"Aubrey... I'm really sorry for hurting you the way I did. I handled things poorly. I hurt you and Ryan and I feel terrible."

"I believe you that you feel terrible, but are you just trying to backpedal now that you're on your own? You weren't saying these things to me six months ago."

"I wasn't ready."

I sigh and drink. I've had several drinks by this point. Enough to feel a bit distant from everything, more careless with words, but certainly in possession of the majority of my judgment and all of my thoughts.

"I'm saying them now, aren't I?" Eli asks archly, looking at me intensely. "Hurting you was one of the biggest regrets of my life."

"Good," I snap. "It should hurt when you do that to someone. I mean, for fuck's sake, you could have given me some warning. A chance. Anything."

Eli rests his hand on my forearm. I don't move away as we stare intently at each other. Vibrating with emotion, I'm caught and claustrophobic in the corner, not sure what I want, conflicted. There's the part of me that will always be for Eli. But my heart wants Blake.

When Eli moves in to kiss me, I put my hand on his chest to stop him. He searches my eyes, standing too close.

I shake my head. "I'm sorry. I can't. I can't be that

anymore for you. I'm—well, the truth is—I'm in love with someone else."

Eli looks about as startled as I am to say it. But in my heart, I know it's true. I miss Blake so much, it's visceral. He's who I long for. Not Eli.

My guts twist at the realization.

The din of the pub continues around us. Then, it's a shuffle of awkwardness, quickly finishing our pints and leaving. I stand on the pavement, watching him walk toward his flat. I take a moment to draw in a breath, to steal a peek at Blake's Instagram, something I should know better than to do.

There's a brilliant sunrise in Cumbria, all gold and pink and orange. Clouds scatter at dawn. He must have gotten up early while I slept, after the call from Eli at an unholy hour. The caption reads:

Sometimes the most beautiful things are the most fleeting, but what I wouldn't give to go back to that moment.

For a moment, my lungs empty of oxygen and I reel, longing for that moment too.

Chapter Twenty-Two

The next day mercifully brings more work to occupy me in the shop with getting ready to reopen. There are more books on shelves than not. Everything's starting to look very promising, even better than pre-filming. I suppose the fresh paint and new floors were worth it. We stand by the broad front window, having just put the curtain rod back up again. I climb down the ladder. Hanging curtain rods is about the extent of my DIY expertise.

DIY makes me think of Blake, and I sigh.

Meanwhile, Gemma thinks I'm sighing over decor, which is probably for the best. Less explanations that way.

"I can even sew new curtains for the window, if you want," Gemma muses, holding the old fabric curtains over her arm.

"You can sew?"

"I'm a woman of many talents," Gemma informs me breezily. She grins.

"It might be time for a new look, I suppose." I consider the old curtains in her arms. They've been up for at least ten years. At the very least, they could use a wash.

"Let's take some measurements. I can go get some fabric samples and we can pick something out. Or look at fabric online."

"'Kay."

Gemma looks dead impressed. "Wow."

"Don't go wild with ruffles. Just promise me."

"No ruffles, no valances, no blinds," she promises, counting them off on her fingers.

"Do you mind putting the curtains in the kitchen so I can do the wash later?"

"No problem." She goes off.

Relieved, I go back to shelving in the J section. There's comfort in the familiar routine as I lose myself again in Blake-related thoughts. Rash thoughts, if I'm honest. My furtive peeks at his Instagram have only escalated from that lapse after leaving the pub. I've had several looks today at that sunrise and Blake's words.

What if I went to America to find him? To tell him how I feel?

I can't decide if that's terribly romantic or terribly creepy. Probably terribly creepy. Let the poor man put his life back in order with his family. Obviously, they're the most important people in his life. He has to put them first. And audition for his breakout role.

Plus, going after Blake means taking a very long flight and I nearly died from nerves on the plane last year going to Berlin from London. Shit, I barely made it onto the plane. Going to New York or wherever Blake might be would be the end of me.

His life's in America, Aubrey. Sometimes you just have to learn to let go.

As the afternoon stretches on, I continue shelving books in the Classics and Collectibles section. Gemma's tackling Young Adult two bookcases over. The curtains whir away in the washer in the kitchen. I continue to torture myself over Blake. If only I had a magic bean to bring him back.

The things you do to yourself.

"Knock knock," calls yet another familiar male voice from the cordoned doorway, once more open to the bright day outside for a breeze.

It's not Eli or Blake, but Ryan.

Ryan?

It's been a while since my friend's been by the shop on his own. My stomach tightens as I think back on the awkwardness in the pub with Eli last night. It feels like a lifetime ago.

As I turn, it's definitely Ryan in his wheelchair at the door. He's all dark hair and friendly smile. His arms are well-muscled, as evidenced by that form-fitting white T-shirt, from wheeling himself around London, which he says is a good workout and that he's still getting around on wheels like he did before.

"Hey!" I say with surprise.

He peers curiously into the shop. "I was hoping to buy a book but I see you're still closed."

"For you, anything. Though I still have plenty of inventory in boxes and I can't guarantee that I'll have what you're after right away. But I'll find it," I assure him with a grin, opening the cordon and waving him in. "Sorry for the treachery of boxes and books everywhere. I wasn't thinking about making this shop accessible while we put everything back on the shelves from the filming."

"Heard about that," Ryan says. "Things are coming together well?"

"Yeah." I nod. "Maybe."

He chuckles. "Don't worry if you can't find the book

right away, either."

"What're you after?"

"Something hopeful."

"Hopeful... What sort of hopeful?"

"Something to restore my faith in humanity." Ryan grins, a familiar and warm sight. "Surprise me."

I purse my lips, looking at him thoughtfully. "How do you feel about queer romance? I've been reading some interesting stuff lately."

"Go on." Ryan perks up. "That's outside my usual. Exactly what I need. And they're good?"

"They're fab," I assure Ryan, with a smile that comes from I don't know where. "How about *Red, White & Royal Blue* and *Boyfriend Material*? A couple of recent queer romances."

Out of the corner of my eye, I see Gemma's broad grin as she pretends not to listen to our exchange, while I likewise pretend not to notice her. I go to the shelf and retrieve a copy of each. I pass them to Ryan.

"How much do I owe you?" he asks.

I wave him off. "Nothing. Honestly. Consider it part of your birthday gift."

"Aubrey, how can you run a business like this?" Ryan chastises me good-naturedly.

"Ugh. Let's not even go there." He's got a point and it stings.

I think of Blake then. Of his talk of sales strategies and the nonsense I've never thought of. Which leads me straight into other memories. Is he missing the bean of the day? Missing me?

A sigh escapes me. I focus back on Ryan as Gemma returns to shelving books. "Thanks for stopping in, by the way."

"Well, I was in the neighborhood. Thought to check in.

I'm going later to meet up with Eli," Ryan explains.

"Yeah?" I give him a curious look. Now that's interesting.

"I need a couple of things from the flat. And to talk."

I redden. "I'm, er, very sorry if I've come between you at all."

Ryan gazes at me. "I think it's less the real you than the fantasy version of you that Eli had in his head. He was never a hundred percent in, you know? Kind of like he was holding out some hope you'd come back."

That I'd come back? He left me.

I shake my head. "That's not going to happen." I'm certain of it, part of my realization after drinks with Eli. At long last, I'm letting go. There'll be a part of me that'll always love Eli, pain in the arse that he is, because he was my first love, my first long-term boyfriend as an adult. "He'll always be important to me, but I don't see a future together. Just history, I guess. And history sometimes makes people foolishly nostalgic, remembering only the good bits and glossing over the bad."

Ryan chuckles at that. "Sorry, I didn't mean to intrude."

"Not at all. Honestly, you can ask me anything at this point," I say.

"What happened to the man you brought to my birthday?"

My shoulders sag. "He's gone home. To America."

Thousands of miles away, and part of me was still hoping that it was him who turned up earlier on my doorstep unannounced.

"And…are you still seeing each other?"

I shake my head as loss washes over me, too close and uncomfortable. What to say? "I don't think he was ready."

Ryan gives me a curious look. "I saw the way he looked at you, though."

I blink. "The way he looked at me?"

"Like you were the only person there." Ryan considers me

thoughtfully. "Like you were the only person that mattered."

I gulp. "Well, I'm sure you saw the papers."

"I did."

"That complicated things. Made things more real, and harder for various reasons. Mainly for him. I don't really care what the media says about me. I'm terribly boring and won't hold their interest for long. But Blake's a different story. He has a lot more riding on his public image."

Ryan nods as he listens. "As an actor, right?"

"Apparently he's a hit on Instagram too."

"Like an influencer?"

I give a helpless shrug. "That's well beyond me, I'm afraid. I just know that he wanted to be the one to control what was being put out there about him, rather than it being done on his behalf."

"Can I ask you something?"

"Of course."

Ryan gazes at me. "What do *you* want?"

"Want?" Normally, I'm a reasonably literate person and words are up my street. A simple word like "want" shouldn't be such a shock to my system, like he's speaking another language. It's like ice water to the face. The idea of "want" is an unthinkable shock.

He nods. "Want."

I open my mouth and redden. God. The thought of Blake is dizzying, something much greater than want. That feeling of something more.

And I need him. As much as any person can need another.

He gives me a smile. "You know it's all right to pursue what you want?"

I blink again.

"Truly," says Ryan.

"I suppose...I haven't thought of things like that before." And it's well past time that I did, to be fair. Like I've been hiding out in my own head to try to keep from living with my heart. From getting hurt again. I've been trying to protect myself from feeling too much, expecting things not to work out. Despite my best efforts, I feel everything for Blake, regardless of things working out. Or not. Apparently, heart wins out.

"Maybe," he offers, "you should."

Ryan's right. Since I feel everything already, I should tell Blake. Maybe he feels the same and maybe he doesn't. Maybe it'll be worth him fighting to keep his career alive and maybe it's not. And what about Blake's family back home, and coming out to his dad? There's so much on the line, but I couldn't imagine trying to keep a huge part of my life secret. What will Blake do? Will he dare? But I'm already in so deep, I need to take the risk of telling him how I feel about him, about how much I want him, about how important he is to me. Because if there's a chance that he feels the same way, there might be hope for a future together. If I don't take that chance, there's no hope.

My stomach does flips in response. Flips of longing and need and desire. Things that I might have written off a month ago.

"Gemma?" I call out.

"Right here." She emerges from between the oak stacks where she's been working—the occasional thump of books as testament—but she's obviously also listening to our conversation. Which would be difficult to avoid overhearing in the front room of the shop. Her hair's knotted up in a bun and she's wearing a Kelly-green blouse that flows over her jeans.

Gemma grins at us. "You should totally listen to Ryan."

Ryan laughs, pleased. "Thanks. I've done my part here."

I look intently at her. "I might need you to mind the shop for a couple of days at least. There's something important that I need to do."

"Of course," Gemma agrees and salutes. "Reporting for duty."

"Promise me you won't rearrange any furniture while I'm away or sign any more agreements?"

"Scout's honor."

My shoulders relax, tension ebbing. "I'll hold you to that." Relieved, I nod. "Brilliant. I'll need you both to excuse me." I need to call Lily and come up with a plan.

"Good luck." Ryan winks, then turns his chair to go. "And thanks for the books."

"Of course."

"Let us know how you get on?" he calls over his shoulder.

"I will."

What I want is so clear: Blake. Because, against all odds, I've fallen in love. And God help me, I'm going to America to find Blake and tell him that.

Chapter Twenty-Three

The problem with madcap plans is that...well, they're madcap. So much for the comfort and routine of the shop, and the fact that it's ready to open again tomorrow. Instead, I'm upstairs packing a small suitcase for America while Lily sits on my sofa bed, drinking wine like she was born to it.

"You know the road to hell is paved with good intentions," I inform her, rolling another T-shirt and wedging it into my suitcase. "God, I don't even know what I'm packing."

"Let me help, being the jet-setter that I am."

"How long am I going for?"

"However long it takes to find Blake and deliver your message. Clearly." She gives me a knowing look, as though that was achingly obvious and I'm regrettably a day late to the party.

"New York is big," I point out.

She ignores me. "Pack a week's worth of underwear. A couple of T-shirts, a couple of nice shirts, a jacket, a pullover. One pair of *nice* jeans. Toiletries. Anything else you can buy if you need it. And just take one good pair of shoes in your suitcase, the other one is whatever's on your feet."

I glance down at my well-loved brown leather boots. "Passport?"

"Now you're getting into the spirit of this," she enthuses. "Make sure you have your bank cards too."

"God, I'm going to regret this."

"Have faith." Lily's grin outshines that of the Cheshire Cat. Clearly, she loves seeing me out of sorts, flailing in the shallow end of the pool.

She goes through my suitcase to make sure I'm equipped to her liking. I round up Lily-authenticated toiletries and give her a wry look. "I think that's me sorted, then."

"Abso-fucking-lutely." She gives me a hug and a kiss on the cheek. "This will be brilliant, you'll see."

It's a long train ride out to Heathrow, plenty of time for second thoughts and even more abundant fear to settle in. Fear of flying. Fear of actually finding Blake and having to see him—and talk about feelings. Lily won't hear of any of these second thoughts, shaking it off as we walk into the terminal, which bustles with summer holiday travelers, sunburnt and festive.

"Get water once you're through security." She pats my arm. "Just like a proper jet-setter."

"I think I'm going to be sick," I inform her as we look at the oversize departure board for my terminal and gate. It's a digital cascade of flight information.

"You aren't." She eyes me with no small amount of concern.

"Don't worry, I'll warn you if I actually puke."

Meanwhile, I'm eyeing the person who takes the sniffer dogs around the gathered travelers. The dog gives my bags a thorough snuffle while I watch, perturbed. Finding nothing, dog and handler move on.

"Seriously. I'm so not cut out for this."

Lily pats my face and wraps a blue scarf around my throat over my black T-shirt. "There. Chic but also practical when the air-conditioning goes overtime on the plane. You packed sunglasses?"

"Yes..."

"A book?"

I give her a look.

"All right, all right," she laughs, entirely undaunted. After all, she's not the one flying to New York. "I'll walk you to security after, but then you're on your own. Time to fly the nest."

"Are you sure this is a good idea?"

"It's a brilliant idea. You'll see."

At takeoff, my eyes are squeezed shut as I tremble. It's terribly unbecoming, but I really do hate flying. It's a sharp takeoff, precise. My stomach lurches somewhere behind us over London.

It's a full minute before I dare peek out the window at late evening summer sky, still bright.

The only thing keeping me from full-bore panic is thinking of Blake. Thinking of how upset he was after the paparazzi photos hit the press. And, importantly, our time together before that.

God, the heat of his mouth and the weight of his body and the things the man can do with that tongue...

I barely look at my book during the flight to New York, lost in daydreams to distract myself and the occasional restless nap. Except they're fake naps, because I can't stop thinking about Blake.

I don't want to stop thinking about Blake.

In a daze, I deplane in New York. Despite hours of flying, albeit west across time zones, it's still evening local time. Adrenaline's kicked in to keep me going.

By some miracle, I've arrived intact, with my things. And I didn't puke, not even once, though my stomach's in knots. It's not any better now that I'm on the ground again. Even with my dread of planes and flying, I have half a mind to turn around and get back on that same plane home. Forget about this harebrained idea. But I'm here, and I want Blake.

After checking into my hotel, I study his Instagram for any clues. Still no selfies. But there's another New York photo. It's all silvery skyscrapers.

How many people did Blake say lived in this city? Twice the size of London, at least. And how to find him through all of this?

If I was Blake, where would I be? Where do actors hang out?

I refresh his Instagram, then sit bolt upright.

It's a bloody miracle. Have the social media deities been paying attention to my suffering?

He's at the New York Public Library, the big one with the lions under the evening sky. At last, a photo with landmarks. And it's just been posted.

Time to read some of my favorite poets, says Blake's caption.

I gulp.

I needed to catch a taxi ten minutes ago.

Chapter Twenty-Four

I race to the taxi queue outside of the hotel, barely remembering to take my wallet and key cards as I head out. The evening's warm and close. I slide into the next available taxi.

"To the library on Forty-Second Street in Manhattan, please." I'm breathing hard from my sprint as I attempt to settle into the back seat. It's exciting—till we're caught in a traffic crawl.

Unfortunately for us, New York traffic is as dreadful as London's no matter the time of day. Eventually I give up on the taxi in favor of my chances on the subway. I'm blindly relying on the map app on my phone. It's not far on the subway, but this is the most off-script thing I've ever done in my life. There's fares and gates and far too many people—people who clearly know where they're going.

Before long, I rush up from the subway to the library. Looking wildly around, I scan the scatter of people for Blake, but of course he's not there. Granted, his photo updated at least an hour ago, and he probably didn't linger outside in the very unlikely event I appeared out of the blue, unannounced, to pounce on him.

After a lap of the imposing library building and even a peek inside, I'm Blakeless.

Glum, I sit on a bench.

Idly, I scroll through the phone again. I need a new idea. Maybe casting calls? There's a website that's got loads of casting calls, but it's hard to figure out where they actually are without signing up and getting screened in. Hopeless. I don't think I could convince anyone, least of all myself, that I'm an actor. I might be able to fake being a musician for about five minutes, but that's about where my performance skills end.

The madcap adventure was all madcap and for nothing.

Do I stay to keep looking or do I leave? Is there any point to holding on to the unlikely hope that I'll find Blake in a city of millions?

I have no idea where he lives, aside from his family being back in Georgia. I don't know the name of the town, even if I drove the fourteen hours down south to make a grand spectacle. If he was there. But that seems like a more unlikely scenario than the current one, so I stay here.

How could I have such strong feelings about a man I know so little about?

In the hotel that night, I toss and turn, not just from the jet lag, but because my brain won't stop. Where exactly did my feelings start to change? Was it the first date dare? The dancing that night? His challenges to me? Like he could see some part of me that slumbered for ages like a hibernating animal.

I don't know what to do. I don't know how to give up.

I don't *want* to give up.

• • •

Early the next morning, I shower and go for breakfast at a little café not far from the hotel. The night passed one restless hour after another while I tried to figure out how to find Blake. Even the impressively comfortable mattress, an entirely different universe than my old sofa bed, couldn't lull me into sleep. By morning, I have a plan. Better yet, I have a growing constellation of plans, because I'm determined.

I look over the detailed list of casting calls, agents, and local studios I put together over a pot of tea. I've made five calls so far without any luck, but I'm going to call every last place an actor might be connected with if I have to. I don't care how many people I have to call. I'll even try Alice Rutherford, the set designer from the last film, if I need to. Or media Andrew, who brought the news to us back in London that dreadful day about the paparazzi photos.

Last night, I also tried to sort out what to tell him when I find him. In my head, I replayed my speech a hundred times. Every time it sounded daft. But I need to tell him in person how I feel, no matter who's there. Obviously, I won't burst onto a film set mid-scene, but if I can find his location, and with a little luck on my side, I might get to talk to him.

I miss Blake so much. His energy, kindness, fun. The bean jokes. The drawl of his voice. The taste of his kisses. I miss his ease, the fun we have together, his attentiveness. His kind heart and living with such openness.

The way it feels to lie in each other's arms, in turns debauched and reverent.

In two short weeks, he made a permanent mark. Indelible. Not that I want Blake to be delible—not even close.

To that end, I've got loads of work ahead of me today.

I only have...forty-seven more calls to make this morning, according to my list. That's totally doable. I've got *purpose*. It's not just any random sort of call. These are calls that *matter*. Forget I'm an introvert and that I hate making even one call. It's only forty-seven more pleading, shameless calls for a very important Blake-shaped cause. I don't care how desperate I sound, or how much groveling is in my future, or how unlikely any of this is to turn up Blake.

I can't think like that.

After all, I've literally just crossed an ocean for him.

If none of my calls pan out, I'll go to a couple of casting events that I've seen advertised on social media. It doesn't matter if I'm shit at auditions. I'm willing to go through that and embarrass myself like I haven't ever embarrassed myself in my life if it gets me in the door.

It's a long shot, but I figure if Blakes's not there, maybe I can find out where actors usually hang out in New York. Maybe I'll get lucky and someone will say, *"Hey, he's always at this bar or that coffee shop,"* and I can pretend to run into him by accident.

Or, you know, I could go the simplest route—figure out who his agent is, and come up with a watertight, compelling story that only someone truly coal-hearted could deny. Like, say, Blake forgot something very important in my shop while he was filming, something that's irreplaceable. Maybe a watch from his family. Or, say, a lucky figurine that he always has to have on set. But it'd have to be really outrageous, like a Barbie Ken doll or a baby Yoda or even a My Little Pony. Something so silly that it'll be bound to get his attention, that his agent will think is so ridiculous it has to be true.

Worst case, I'll very predictably send him a book if I can't find him. But not just any book—that damn poetry book he returned on the day we met in my shop. It'll be my turn to put a note inside and I don't care who reads it. Because I'm in love and I want him and, God, we just need a chance, a proper chance, to try to make this work.

Please, universe. I don't ask for much.

We've just had a handful of days together. Enough to tease of a promise of a future together. Enough that he's impossible to forget, to see a million possibilities of a future together, of what things might be like. I'll learn every bean on the planet to impress him, learn fluent vegan and ethical zero waste, and be an all-around better human.

Okay, let's try to keep this a little real.

So, I *might* lapse and have the occasional guilty kebab like I did on our first date, but he'll totally understand, because he's Blake and he's cool like that. Way, way cooler than I am, that's for sure. And that's only one of a million reasons why I fell in love with him.

Which is what makes coming to America and risking making a fool of myself so worthwhile. Because I couldn't live with myself if I didn't go all out in search of him.

My heart couldn't bear not taking the risk.

Out of habit, I open up Instagram as I have the last of my tea. And I'm rewarded, because the algorithm knows what I want. Right away, there's a dramatic black and white shot of Blake. He's glorious, his bare chest peeking out from an unbuttoned black shirt in the obvious heat, that navy cap.

I'm starting to sweat just looking at him.

God. He's gorgeous, all svelte muscle and serious smolder. Top shelf selfie. A++ would recommend. I shake my head, flustered. Even here, by myself.

And then I notice something important about that Blake photo. Forget the summertime swelter and Blake raising the heat by at least a hundred degrees in one selfie. Or that it's fine material for a consolation wank later on. Forget all of that.

I groan. "Mother*fucker*."

He's standing in what clearly is Trafalgar Square, a broad expanse of space by the fountains in front of the National Gallery in London. It takes a fraction of a second to register the scene, the accompanying caption.

Back enjoying the sights because I can't stay away.

Blake's back in London.

God help me—I'm in the wrong damn country.

Chapter Twenty-Five

In shock, I just stare at Blake, as if I haven't memorized his face, or the scent of his skin. My fingers trace the screen, seeking the feel of him again, but instead there's cool glass.

This is obsessive, Aubrey. There's nothing attractive about this. Lily shouldn't have encouraged this dumb idea in the first place.

And yet here I sit, getting all nostalgic over a man who doesn't even have the decency to be in his country of origin when I make the unlikely grand gesture to come here and find him.

Unable to stand it any longer, I text Blake. There's no further dignity left to make the pretext of saving it any longer.

You never gave me that answer to the black and white bean trivia. x

There's no response. I check the time. In London, it's getting on late afternoon. A reasonable time for him to be up and awake.

Maybe he's filming? It's got to be filming, right? What else would it be?

But what if, in the very unlikely chance Blake missed me, he's come back to London to find me? Not just to find me—*for* me. And I'm not there? What if we actually have a chance and I miss it, because I'm in the wrong damn city? What a disaster.

I need to get back home. Right now.

My credit card is smoking, between the taxi direct to the airport and the last-minute flight to London, but luckily I find some last-minute deal that makes the fare only moderately terrible instead of catastrophic.

Another flight alone. I buy a pack of gum and try to channel my inner jet-setter Lily. Sunglasses, check. Passport, check. Wallet, check. I tie the scarf like she showed me.

And, fuck it. I buy some soft pink lipstick and eyeliner and detour to the toilets to do myself up. If I'm going to be petrified, I may as well look as good as I can while doing so.

My phone remains dark. I shut it off for the flight.

As predicted, the flight's excruciating. My fists are balled beside me, eyes shut for most of the way, feigning sleep. More like trying to pull a Dorothy and click my heels to arrive back home, but I'm definitely no longer in Kansas, whether that's New York or London. When my eyes are open, I attempt to write poetry about Blake to distract myself. Nothing sounds right, but that's okay. Somehow, I feel different for having tried being vulnerable with this trip. For putting myself out there to seek out Blake, to reveal my heart. That's got to count for something, at least a compensatory pint and a consolation wank when I get back home to the comfort of the flat, if I still can't find him.

But I can't think like that. I *have* to find him.

When I land in the late evening and get through passport control, I could—almost—kiss the ground at Heathrow in gratitude. God help me, I'm not taking a flight anytime soon if I can help it. I turn my phone on, and it comes alive with notifications. I texted everyone when I landed in New York, but I was so focused on finding Blake that I hadn't given an update in my haste to return to London.

Gemma: *You are coming back at some point right? Or Barnes Books is mine bwahaha. Also: really, come back. I'm gonna have a sale if you don't.*

Lily: *Status report! All hands on deck! I'm dying of curiosity on how Day 2 is going? I won't sleep till I hear back.*

And then I stop breathing.

Blake: *That's the rare orca bean. Hard to get in America, tends to be found elsewhere. You need to go looking. B.*

My hands shake as I stare at my phone. Now he's just messing me about. He can't possibly know what I've been up to. Can he?

With a breath, I exit out to the concourse. The tube rattles me back home, straight into central London, living a surrealist experience. Down here, it's too warm, the air stuffy. People jam together in the overcrowded carriage. The Piccadilly line's deep underground and has me out of phone reception for approximately one eternity till I reach the surface again in central London the better part of an hour later. It's late by the time I'm outside again checking my phone.

And I send a text.

Where are you? x

Soon, there's a one-word answer from Blake:

London

That's it? As if this isn't an important development? I stare at my phone before tapping back a one-word response. Touché. I can play this game too.

Why?

Lingering outside of the station before continuing the rest of my journey home, it takes about ten minutes for a response to come.

We need to talk

Shit.
The "we need to talk" line is never a good omen.

Do you want to talk now? x

A moment later—

Yes

Chapter Twenty-Six

My heart thuds in double time as I finally arrive on my street, having texted Blake back that I was about fifteen minutes away from home. The August night has a chill to it, my black jacket zipped up. I'm still wearing Lily's scarf.

As I wheel down the dark street, quietish at this late hour, there's a familiar silhouette waiting for me down the street. Cars are parked half on the pavements. Streetlamps cast a soft glow. Overhead, clouds reflect the city's lights.

Getting closer, I see Blake leaning casually against the entry of Barnes Books, shuttered for the night. After everything I've been through the last few days—the flights, the angst of searching, begging strangers for info—I can't believe I find him right where we started: at Barnes Books.

Home.

I stop to stand an arm's length away from him. He doesn't move, his pose languid and easy. He owns the street in his leather jacket, dark hair soft without product to keep it in place. My heart clenches. He's so devastatingly handsome. The streetlamps cast strong shadows over his face, highlighting the striking planes of his cheekbones and his jawline.

He gazes at me, not moving. His expression's unreadable.

"You're in London," I say unnecessarily. I pull up my suitcase beside me as we flank the entry to the bookshop in our nighttime tableau.

"I am."

I take in the sight of him again. Still damnably hot. Still like he has my heart in his pocket, the thing I've been missing since that horrible night we fought in the hotel after the paparazzi's photos hit the press.

The abrupt ending to something that could have been fantastic.

"I've been trying to find you," I say as neutrally as I can. Luckily, my voice doesn't waver, but it's not quite the carefree and confident delivery I was hoping for.

I can't read his expression in the dark. "I know."

He knows? How does he know? Did someone tell him? Maybe one of the people I called in my frantic pleas that a desperate Englishman was roving New York looking for him?

Keep it together, Aubrey.

Keeping it together is not quite my forte.

"Look–" Blake begins, but I don't let him go on.

"No. Listen to me." This time, it comes out curt and urgent. Not quite detached, but confident. Despite how I'm burning up inside, despite the part of me that's ready to unravel to feel all the feels.

His eyebrows lift. I don't think either one of us was expecting that to come out of me.

"I went to America. I went to find you–"

Blake smiles at that.

"–and, for the record, I *hate* flying and I'm not a good air traveler but I went, because it was important. Because… I couldn't live with myself leaving things how we did. Leaving them like that because of some stupid paparazzi bollocks."

Everything is riding on this. Because it is. My future, his future. The potential of us, together. And it doesn't look like I'm winning, given his frown.

He opens his mouth to say something but nothing comes out.

Not good.

"I know," I rush on. "It's mad and desperate and pathetic and all of those things. You were clear that things had gone too far, that you weren't comfortable with us in the media and because of your family. I can only imagine what you faced back home. And I'm sorry if it makes me sound like a creeper, because I'm really not, and if you never want to talk to me after this again, I get it. I'll respect that. I didn't text you because I needed to see you in person. To talk to you."

Blake's gaze stays fixed on me. He barely moves.

Out here, the street is empty and dark. A taxi drives by. Someone walks past us on the opposite side of the street, paying no heed. Overhead, the overcast London night reflects the soft glow of city lights. But down here, it's only Blake and me and an ocean vaster than the Atlantic of awkward between us.

"And," I continue, "I figured out that you were in New York auditioning for a film. *Serial Kisser*, I think."

His lips twist. "Yes. That's right. I was."

"And I saw your Instagram—which has mostly been dark, by the way—at the New York Public Library in Manhattan. You had to be there. Obviously."

This time, it's my gaze that's unrelenting, taking in the sight of him. He's slump-shouldered as he looks at me, his expression contorting slightly, shifting from something unreadable into another version of unreadable.

Not helpful. Damn actors.

"I…I can't believe you tried to find me."

I gulp, unable to read him. Is he happy? Unhappy? Oh

God.

"I went to the audition," he confirms. "No news yet."

"Good." I'm holding my breath, fists tight while I wait for any hint of how he's taking the news of my impulsive search to find him. I can't believe I did that. Stupid, really. I mean, what was I thinking? Obviously, he's going to be upset.

"Tell me something," he says, shifting. "Why would you do all of this? Go to New York? Looking for me?"

"Because..." My voice drops into something low and unsteady, but I'm channeling every last bit of resolve I have, the sort of confidence Blake usually has by the bucketful, where I'm usually flailing about, far from being in control of my emotions.

Deep breath in. Deep one out.

"Because I had to tell you something in person."

"You said that before," he acknowledges.

"I did."

We contemplate each other, the tension hanging between us like a veil between worlds, heavy and thick. Like there's glimpses of our shapes behind the curtains, but we're caught in them, struggling to break free from their confines.

"I'm in love with you," I say softly, at last letting the emotion out in my voice, because I can't keep that in. I've gone this far. May as well say it all. There's nothing to lose, and if I'm lucky—very lucky—there might be everything to gain. "And, well, I couldn't live with myself without telling you. I know that the strong odds are you don't want me, but I need to tell you anyway. Rather than stuffing it away and never saying it. Even if you don't feel that way about me—"

Blake comes close, so close I can hear the softness of his breath. His eyes are bright with tears. Hesitating only for a moment, he slides his arms around me and draws me into a kiss that I can only describe as heated, leaving me reeling, and thank God his arms are around me, because I could fall over, and if this is the last kiss I get, it's going to count for something—

Finally, he breaks away, expression raw. Vulnerable. "I love you too, Aubrey. More than words can say."

"Oh God," I choke out, my hands covering my mouth.

Words I never actually expected him to say. A feeling I couldn't believe I let myself feel, then give voice to it—and have it reciprocated? Is this a dream?

I grab him tight for another kiss, and he presses me against the door of Barnes Books, against the glass front with the sign flipped to CLOSED. We kiss like nothing we've done before, leaving me hot and shivering and overwhelmed.

"I missed you," he breathes against my ear, holding me tight, leaning his head against mine. "So much."

"I missed you too."

I laugh and cry a little, and he does the same as we consider each other, both with eyes too wet and emotions too raw.

"But," I whisper. "Feelings…feelings are brilliant. But reality's quite another thing altogether. I hate to mention that. Like, you being from America. Me being from here. The paparazzi. Your career. My damn shop."

A million reasons why this is impossible. We're so different. How on earth did this even happen? Of all the very unlikely things.

Finally, Blake straightens. "You made me feel things that I didn't think I was capable of. And made me question everything, to figure out what matters."

"Blake, I don't want to cause problems for you with your family—"

His face is mostly in shadow. Hard to read, but he holds up a hand. "And yes, I love my family. But my sisters are right. I can…well, I can love you and love them. Even if Dad doesn't understand. Call me an optimist, but maybe…one day he will."

"You talked with him?" I dare ask, my gut in knots. "I was thinking of you and wondering if you spoke."

"I did." He takes a shuddering breath. I slip his hand into mine.

"I'm sorry it's difficult with your father," I say softly, searching his eyes. "I know your family means the world to you. More than."

"It's been hard," he acknowledges, "pursuing a career in something he doesn't approve of. And not approving of… well, who I love. It just felt like loss after loss, you know? That I always admired him and wanted him to be proud of me. And I had to let go of that approval." Blake gulps. "The girls were right. I'm an adult and I make my own decisions. And, by the way, they're very happy. About you. When I told them."

I smile, squeezing his fingers. "You told them about me?"

"I did. I saw them before going back to New York. To see them, and Dad." He sighs. "Dad… Well, he didn't want to hear about London. Or you." He looks unhappy. "But the girls wanted to know all about it. About you."

I lean into him, resting my forehead against his shoulder. His hand smooths my hair, fingers tracing the nape of my neck. Unable to keep from shivering, I burrow closer to him.

"That means a lot to hear it," I confess. "I told my mum I fell for a man and I was devastated it didn't work out."

Blake tilts my head up gently with his fingers. His voice is uneven, raw. "I want things to work out between us. You mean everything to me."

God, such dizzying words. Words that I'm desperate for, wild for. Wild for Blake. And yet I can't let myself enjoy even that, because guilt strikes over the cost to him of falling in love with me.

"You mean everything to me too," I murmur. "After you

left, I realized I had to face myself. To let go of the past. To let go of what was, the life I once had with Eli, that held me back. That kept me from living now. But with you, I feel free. Like there's a future ahead."

Blake holds me tight. "That's all you," he whispers. "But I'm glad to hear it. Eli sounds like a tough one to follow."

I chuckle softly. "He has good bits and bad bits, like anyone. I had to let him go. I have to live now." I gulp. "Blake?"

"Yes, gorgeous?"

"You never said what you're doing back in London."

His laugh is low, intoxicating. "I needed to see you. 'Cause if I was away from you any longer I might burst."

"And you knew I was away?"

"I didn't know till tonight. I caught Gemma as she was closing up shop," Blake explains. "And she reamed me out for not being in America because you were there looking for me. I thought she was joking, couldn't be serious. She was *so* annoyed."

I start laughing as tears stream down my face. I press the heels of my hands against my eyes to wipe them away, trembling.

"Classic," I gasp.

He holds me then, and we stand together like that for ages in the street, letting ourselves feel all sorts of things we didn't dare feel before. We start kissing again, desperate and sweet and God, how I've missed him.

"We"—I manage between increasingly urgent kisses—"ought to go in."

I blindly feel for my keys in my jacket pocket, having checked three times on the tube from Heathrow that I hadn't lost them in my mad dash to America, which would lead me to either calling Gemma at a terrible time to let me into the shop or, more likely, crashing at Lily's in North London.

We go inside, and upstairs. And there, we're well away from any prying eyes, up in my tiny bedsit, exactly as I left it. In a secret world meant for two. Books still cascade, the space is too small for one person, never mind two. In the corner, my sofa bed is made up neatly as a bed.

Standing by the bed, our kisses grow urgent. Seeking something we've both craved, our emotions too near the surface to suppress after everything we've said, and everything we've done.

Blake slides my jacket off my shoulders. It drops to the ground. I return the favor with his biker jacket, helping him out of it and tossing it with more care onto my desk.

"You look so beautiful," Blake offers against my skin, his hands roaming. Along my chest, my hips, my arse. His fingers trace the scarf still tied at my neck. "Love this."

"Mmm." Leaning into him, I'm all searching kisses, too raw to speak. I'm working on unbuttoning the many stupid buttons on his shirt. My fingers fumble in the low light.

"You're shaking."

"Guess so." It's been a lot, and I'm exhausted, and beyond overwhelmed.

And so very fucking happy.

His shirt eventually drops to the floor too. The light from the hall is enough to see the glory of his built torso, the hint of a V-cut, the washboard abs. My fingers trace his skin reverently. A homecoming, really.

Blake's much more efficient at getting me undressed. Down to my boxers, I laugh, gazing at him, feeling unsteady. "You know what you want, hmm?"

"I always wanted you," Blake breathes against my ear, pulling me down to the bed. "I never doubted that."

"When there's so many men out there, you picked a London bookseller." I start to laugh and he kisses me something fierce, taking my breath away in a gasp. I dig my fingers into his back as he's on me.

"The hottest fucking bookseller I've ever met," he growls, kissing and nipping at me.

And I can't stop laughing, overwhelmed with emotion. Till his hands are inside my boxers, teasing me. Then I shudder and sober, gasping out. My cock's more than ready for his attention.

Kissing him roughly, I unfasten his belt and jeans, enough to release the pull of his cock that reaches for his belly. So damn hot.

Kneeling, I go down on him, the taste of Blake on my tongue making me reel. His hands run through my hair. And it's all I can do to keep going, listening to his soft gasps, clutching his hips as he starts to rock with me. His fingers caress my face. It's not long before he's groaning with pleasure.

I can't imagine how many miles I've traveled over the last three days to find this man on my doorstep. I can't clock the miles in my heart, the ocean between us that we're navigating in this moment. This yearning for someone I so desperately want, and he wants me too.

In his arms, I'm cherished. Special. His.

When he comes, fingers taut in my hair, the sear of him in my mouth, I'm desperate with desire. And soon, he's working me with his hand and mouth. Everything's all shivers and gasps.

"Blake— God— Blake—"

"Mmmhmm?" He glances up, kissing my belly as I shudder hard.

"Don't stop, for the love of—"

He laughs with delight at how indignant I am. Then, he's ruthless. I writhe, lost in the burn of him, the heat of the night between us, sparking our own heatwave.

"That's it," he murmurs when I'm on the edge, "come for me."

"Fuck—"

And I do and I can't think and I can't breathe and his mouth, God his mouth— I can't stop shaking with the release, spasming till he gathers me tight in his arms, kissing me like his life depends on it. Like our lives depend on it.

"I want you so much." I grip his biceps, staring desperately at him.

"You have me, gorgeous. You have me," he breathes against my skin, caressing me.

It's impossible to remember a time before Blake. Before this incredible feeling. We spend the night making up for every night we've missed, every day apart.

Together, there's no him and no me—there's just us.

Chapter Twenty-Seven

Late the next morning, I awaken in a tangle of limbs, plastered against Blake's chest. God, what a fabulous way to wake up. His chest rises and falls. I keep my eyes closed, not wanting to spoil this moment if I'm still dreaming. But as the day starts to drift more fully into my consciousness, it turns out to be true when I open my eyes.

I really did find Blake.

I can't help but smile thinking about last night. The strange twilight with Blake appearing outside of my shop. Feeling like my heart might break or burst at any moment. The euphoria at realizing he wanted me as much as I wanted him.

Our insatiable night.

And now, he's here. Gently, I nip at his jaw and he stirs awake, sleepy-eyed and beautiful—and mine.

The smile he gives me when he wakes is brilliant, filling some gap within me at the thrill of him beside me.

"Best morning ever," he whispers drowsily, holding me close.

I kiss him thoroughly in response. He's delicious against my tongue.

My limbs are heavy with our exertion last night. Well worth it, every ache this morning. This is probably where athletes have the advantage at marathon sex, but I'll do my best to keep up.

"So," Blake says, tracing my shoulder, "what're we going to do today?"

Sleepily, I rub my eyes. Between the night of sex, the jet lag, and the stress, I'm still thoroughly wrecked. But reality encroaches, even so.

"I need to see what Gemma's done to the shop," I blurt instantly, sitting up.

Blake laughs, grinning up at me. He traces my spine, giving me shivers.

"Probably a shower first," I concede.

"Probably for the best." Blake kisses me and it's so tempting to go back to bed with him and pretend everything else doesn't exist.

"You're really here? You won't disappear?"

"I promise I won't disappear." His mouth yields against mine.

Contented, I sigh. "'Kay."

With reluctance, I get up and go to the shower and start the familiar rituals of getting ready for the day. Blake takes his turn and I'll never tire of the sight of him clad only in a towel, the thrill of his fine physique.

When I come back upstairs with two cups of tea—made the proper way—I see Blake browsing the poetry book that he returned those weeks ago in the height of summer. He gives me a bemused look, glancing up.

"I see you found my note. Secret's out." Blake's smile spreads like a thrill across his lips.

"You're a rotten man, messing up my system like that,"

I chastise Blake affectionately, setting the mugs down on the desk beside him. "Misfiling books. Putting them face down to crack their spines. You probably fold over corners and roll softcovers too."

He grins shamelessly and pulls me onto his lap. I shift to straddle him, my arms around his neck. Blake leans his forehead against mine, then kisses me thoroughly.

I forget my complaints. Forget everything as he draws me down to the bed, and we start over again.

It's some time later when we drink cold tea.

• • •

Eventually, we get downstairs, a bit too giddy and happy. The shop's warm. Something smells of cinnamon, and I spot Gemma's tea on the counter. There's a couple of customers browsing in the shop, which still looks amazing after our hard work restoring it after the filming.

Gemma grins at us.

"So, you found each other, then?" she teases.

We gaze at each other. Our smiles are too broad to hide. What is this light-hearted feeling that's taken over me? Unthinkable.

"We did," I say when I come back to my senses. Blake squeezes my hand. "How's the shop?"

"Still standing, as you can see." Gemma waves a hand around. It looks as it did when I left, all the boxes gone, the shelves full and in order. It looks better than ever, to be honest.

"Are you fine to stay on today and help? We were just going to go out for brunch." It's late in the day for breakfast, practically lunchtime. My stomach rumbles a bitter complaint.

"Yes. Now shoo."

Laughing, we head out and down to Charlie's café for

some brioches and coffee. If we stay long enough, we could hit up their lunch special too.

"Welcome to our new reality," I say softly to Blake once we're seated by the windows of the café, bustling with customers. Crockery clatters behind us, the shriek of the steamer. I'm holding a flat white. Blake got us a buffet of pastries to work through.

"A fantastic reality," he says affectionately. It's surreal, seeing him here. Together with me. His blue eyes are warm, his hair still slightly damp from the shower.

Blake gazes at me, expression soft. What's he thinking? Feeling? "I can't believe I'm here with you," he murmurs. "It's like a dream."

"I can't believe it either." A thrill runs down the length of my spine. I'm afraid I'll never be able to stop smiling, but that's a tiny price to pay compared to the idea of life without Blake.

"I'll keep you, of course," I say.

Blake laughs delightedly. "I'd be lucky to be a kept man," he teases. "I can at least be useful with making dinners till I hear back on my auditions. Whatever I end up getting—or not—I can do based from London."

"Brilliant." I'm so happy it's embarrassing.

"And there's films for auditioning here too. I'll be okay," Blake assures me. "Something will work out."

"I think for you, it will. You work very hard. And...you've got Instagram."

"I have a few sponsorships and things, but it won't keep me fed. Or pay the rent," Blake concedes. "I mean, I'm happy to wait tables in the meantime like any good struggling creative if I need to, though. I also have some savings to carry me for a little while." He frowns slightly at me. "What about you?"

"What about me?"

"The shop." He lifts his eyebrows meaningfully at me, pausing to take a bite of his croissant. "How are things?"

"Well." I redden slightly. "Obviously I've been away and I don't have the latest. I have massive bills because of some recalculations and I need to pay them. But I don't think I can afford it and probably will need to sell...which means disappointing my mum. More than that, I won't be able to help her." I give Blake an unhappy look.

"Is there any other option?"

I hesitate. Confession time. I have to face the simple reality that I have no clue how to run a successful shop on my own without help. "I saw an ad for some business courses. I might take those and learn a few things so I don't make a right cock-up of the whole thing like I've been doing."

"Well, if you want, I can help." Blake's gaze is steady. "Starting with a marketing plan. I think you can turn things around, to be honest. I mean, if you want to, that is."

I frown. "How?"

Everything with the shop feels so daunting. I want to save the shop. Badly. For my family, for me. But, honestly, on my own it's exhausting. And I don't have the business head for things like my dad did, plus bookselling is a lot different now than even ten years ago.

"You just need to find your niche," Blake explains. "People still go to indie bookshops. Why not Barnes Books? You just need to sell what it is that you offer versus the big chains. Like—a totally different experience, customer service, that sort of thing. And then when the shop's doing better, then you'll be free to do more of what you want."

I blink. There are no plans to sell to Percy Green, or any megashops, his letter tossed away. With the income from filming, and Blake's ideas, there's a strong chance Barnes Books might make it after all. "I want the shop to do well."

"Course. But you told me that you write poetry?"

A furious blush comes. I glance away. Oh shit. In some moment of weakness, I did say that. It's true. But I've never told anyone before. Only Blake, now. "Well, I'm far from a proper writer."

"Do you like it, though?"

"I love it," I admit.

"Then, at the very least, you should explore that. And I can help with the shop. Not just plans. But you've got Gemma and you can teach me. And things will be okay."

I gaze at him, overwhelmed. Setting my coffee down, my chest is tight. Something like gratitude washes over me. "You really would stay in London? And do all of this? For me?"

Blake's expression is soft. Open.

"I love you, Aubrey."

God. This man.

"I love you too."

"And I want a future with you. If you'll have me. After everything."

"I...yes." I swallow hard, searching his eyes. "I very much want that—a future with you."

The din of the café fades, just us in here despite the clatter and crowd. Together, we're at a beginning, a fresh start. I don't know what that future is, but that's all right, because Blake's in it.

When we return after brunch, Gemma's running a duster over the shelves.

We all pause to have a break around the front counter with the coffees we brought. Behind us, shoppers are browsing. Even better, we've already had sales. If the closure sparked renewed interest in Barnes Books, so much the better.

Blake leans over to kiss my cheek and I laugh, chiding

him good-naturedly. "You'll make me spill my coffee. Again."

"Oh, that's not the only thing I'll make you spill..."

"My ears!" Gemma clamps her hands over her ears, shuddering. "God."

Blake pulls me into another kiss. I wrap my arms around him in response.

"'Kay, but you two are *adorable*. Somebody give me their phone for a photo," Gemma demands. Blake offers his phone up, then pounces to kiss me thoroughly, my lips, my face, even my ear. Laughing, I fall into him, his arms around me. Somewhere in the chaos Gemma snaps a couple of photos.

"I wanna buy a green book..." Blake drawls between kisses.

I can't stop laughing. What's he done to me? I never thought I could feel so light and free again. A glorious reality.

"Adorable," Gemma confirms, handing the phone over.

We look, and there we are, Blake's arms around me, both of us laughing. And we look happy and carefree. More important, I *feel* happy. And so does he. We've a new start before us. There'll be days again when things are difficult, while we navigate life together, but today we'll enjoy the simple joy of being together. This is a happiness that we've fought for.

"Do you mind if I post this on Insta?" Blake asks after we gaze at the photos, nuzzling me. His arm's still around me as he expertly navigates his phone with one hand.

I smile, looking at him. His dark hair's slightly messed up, sunglasses on his head, striking in a trim blue T-shirt that leaves little to the imagination and matches his eyes. "Go for it."

Blake kisses me and posts our photo to an immediate cascade of hearts. Which is no match to the rhythm of our own hearts as we begin a new life together in London.

Epilogue

The day crawls. Each minute is a year.

By the time late afternoon rolls around, I've cleaned our new flat top to bottom, made a vegetarian lasagna, and bought sparkling wine to celebrate. A couple of hours ago, Blake texted to say he landed at Heathrow. He'd be home as soon as he could get through the crush of commuters.

And when the lock at last turns in the door, despite said commuters, and the usual snarls at getting around London at peak hours, my heart pounds. I jump up from where I've been sitting perched on the arm of the sofa, fidgeting with a book in a failed attempt at reading.

When Blake walks through the door, he's gorgeous as ever. He's tanned from generous California sun and his dark hair's slightly tousled from travel. Next thing, I'm kissing Blake and he's kissing me, and we've just kissed away almost two months of him being away. His mouth is soft, seeking mine. And he kisses me with reverence.

"I missed you," I breathe against his skin when we finally straighten. He slides his arms around my waist. One of us somehow nudged the door shut.

"I missed you too, so much. Couldn't wait to get home to you," he murmurs.

I shiver at that, our new London home. Together.

Since the end of November, we've been living in a compact but perfectly formed red brick maisonette in Soho, not far from the shop. After all, two people can navigate around each other in a pocket-sized bedsit and sleep on a sofa bed for only so long. It's Blake's film money that makes this possible, and certainly not my bookseller's income, though at last I now have one again.

Our new flat has a loft level that leads to one of two bedrooms. Throughout, we've hung framed film and band posters, plus a few photos taken of us together, including from Cumbria. There's a kitchen with reliable plumbing. We even have a little dining table.

The second bedroom is part home office, part guest room, so Blake's sisters can come visit from America. My dad's guitar sits in the corner alongside Blake's. Predictably, there're books everywhere, with plenty of shelving.

"I can't believe you're back." It could be that I've just conjured Blake from my imagination, but the kisses he's given me provide assurances that he's real. And I'm real. And that, in fact, this is all very real.

"I like what you've done with the place," Blake says affectionately, nipping at my ear, his arm around me as he at last takes in the flat. Fresh flowers, the table set, even a couple of candles in jars. London shifts to twilight beyond the window, deepening blues with broken cloud.

"I'm glad. Want some water? Wine? You must be exhausted."

"Water first, then wine. I was exhausted, but being back, I'm a new man," Blake teases.

"Hardly recognize you," I quip without missing a beat.

"Some strange man's in my flat."

"Hey!" Laughing, he pretends to growl and sweeps me up for more kisses, and then we're carrying on like people who've been apart for an eternity, which, to be fair, it's been at least one, if not two.

"Mm." I'm unable to stop smiling. "Though I *might* recognize those kisses."

"Might!" Blake shakes his head affectionately at me.

"Might," I affirm, as we go into the sleek kitchen with gray glossy cabinets and wood countertops. I pour water for us, and then open the wine as Blake downs his water.

We clink wineglasses. "Welcome back," I say.

"Good to be back."

"How was California and the celeb life?"

He laughs, shaking his head. "All right. No comparison to being back with you. How are you? How's the shop?"

"It's getting busier every day. And hopefully with the lead into Christmas, it'll get busier yet."

"It will," Blake affirms. "I've got a plan to get some of that Christmas traffic."

"Can't wait to hear about it."

Earlier today, I worked with Gemma. With Blake's long-distance help over video chats and emails during the last couple of months, we've come up with a business plan to turn the shop around. We're working to update our website for online sales of new and used books. I've put out ads. We're starting to book events, like having authors come read. The shop's gotten busier and if this keeps up, Gemma will need to be full-time, and I'll need to hire more help. The bills are settled with the payout for filming. The shop is starting to build a reserve already, thanks to Blake's help.

"Gifts now or later?" Blake says affectionately as we go sit on the sofa. Blake splurged and bought us a vegan-friendly oversize sofa that fits two snuggling together very comfortably. And I'm definitely pro-snuggling when Blake's home.

I pretend to consider. A small gift sits wrapped and waiting on the coffee table. "Who said anything about gifts?"

"You fool no one, Mr. Barnes." Blake grins at me, warming me to my core. It's so good to have him back.

"Who says that's for you?" I can't stop smiling.

"What, you're wrapping gifts for yourself now?"

"Well," I say matter-of-factly. "With you away, I need to pass the time somehow."

"Pfft." Blake reaches into his pocket and pulls out a tissue-wrapped gift. It's a long tube, and for a moment I reflect back to Gemma's threat months ago about a cross-merchandising campaign of dildos and books and wonder if she somehow got to Blake while I was away. I'm all for inappropriate gifts, even if that might not be the first thought about gifts from America.

He puts the gift into my hand, and it's definitely…dense? "What…?"

"Go on and open it," Blake encourages, grinning broadly, dimples showing. Because of course he has them. "Your face." He kisses me.

"Mm, keep that up and there'll be no gift opening at all. There's dinner warming in the oven. Don't let me forget." I give the gift an experimental squeeze. Still firm. "Huh."

At last, I unravel tissue and tape, and I'm stunned to discover that, in fact, it's no kind of sex toy. Instead, it's a cellophane tube of…black and white orca beans?

And, silly me, all of a sudden I have something caught in my throat.

Blake rubs my back lightly. I'm getting emotional over beans, something I didn't know about myself before now. I just look at him. "Oh…"

Blake gives me another kiss for good measure, and it's

bliss. God, I could get used to this. "I know it's a strange gift, but sometimes you need to find the rare ones, you know?"

"Did I ever tell you I love you?"

"You've never given me love confessions over beans before."

"There's always a first time," I assure Blake. I inspect the tube, complete with a cellophane twist at the top secured with twine that holds a card with a soup recipe. "This is really cool. Cheers."

"Course."

I give him the small gift on the table. It's actually two gifts in one. I watch Blake unwrap the package with care, loosening the ribbon, peeling back the paper. Inside, he finds a small framed photo of us that Gemma took of us laughing together in the shop, as Blake covered my face in kisses. And a small handmade booklet of a few poems I'd written while he was away.

And when I look at him, it's his turn to be suspiciously tearful.

"You wrote these?" Blake marvels at the small hand-bound booklet. "And made this?"

"For you, lovely. I did." Nights while Blake was away, after the shop work was done for the day, I started working on my poetry in earnest again, finding freedom in writing.

"Nobody's ever done anything like this for me before."

"Aww. Well, there you are."

And then we kiss and I curl into his arm. We settle together on the sofa as he reads aloud a couple of the poems I wrote. And he reads brilliantly, his voice smooth and deep, practiced from his acting life.

Comforted like this, we have cozy winter nights together ahead of us, before the days lengthen once more to summer. Together, we'll forge our own kind of heat, of heart and home.

Acknowledgments

There are so many people along the way who have encouraged and supported me in my writing journey. I hope you've all enjoyed reading this story as much as I have enjoyed writing it.

Special thanks to my editor, Heather Howland, for believing in my work and making these stories so much stronger. Many thanks to the amazing Entangled team for bringing this novel to life, from all of the different departments.

Several critique partners have read versions of this story along the way, providing great feedback and encouragement: Ambrose Hall, C.N. Steinhour, T.M. Delligatti. Chandra Fisher, Anita Kelly, Charlotte Kinzie, and Jen Tarr. Special thanks to Gwynne Jackson and Andy Palanzuelo for believing in me as a writer and in my writing.

Last but not least, for my loved ones.

About the Author

More animal than mineral, Hayden Stone is a writer of fun queer fiction, especially with kissing. He currently lives in Victoria, Canada, and has previously lived in Vancouver, Canada and London, UK. He likes strong coffee and is owned by two cats. You can find out his latest news on Twitter or Instagram, or at his website: haydenstonebooks.com

Discover more New Adult titles from Entangled Embrace...

The Breath Beneath the Waves

a Titanic love story by Charlotte Anne Hamilton

Forced to travel to America for her father's new job and abandoned by her girlfriend, Penelope isn't looking forward to journey on the RMS *Titanic*. Until she meets Ruby. Her new adventurous roommate makes her yearn for a future of her own choosing. But just as their whirlwind romance turns into something more serious – the ship crashes into an iceberg, and it's no longer about expectations – but pure survival.

Rough and Tumble

a novel by Shae Connor

My name's Grant Clark, and I managed to screw up my entire life. In triplicate. I fell in love with my best friend, I thought he was straight, and because of number two, I didn't make a move until it was too late. Or is it? When I accidentally interrupt him with another guy—and he turns out to be the worst—well, I think it's time I finally make a move. Don't you?

Falling for the Player

a novel by Jessica Lee

Bad boy and former NFL running back Patrick Guinness is tired of meaningless sex. Ever since his scorching hot one-night stand three years ago, no one has interested him. So when Max Segreti wanders into his mechanic shop—and his life again—Patrick can't stop thinking about the totally-out-of-his-league law student and the possibility of getting him out of his system once and for all...

Made in the USA
Middletown, DE
04 October 2021

49607991R00169